CW00468707

This novel is entir
The names, chara
are the work of th
Any resemblance or act relating to any
persons, living or dead, locations or
events involving them, is entirely alleged
or coincidental.

Proof read/editing by Zeldos
Cover art by Orphan Print

BEN NEVIS AND THE GOLD DIGGER SERIES

London private detective, ex SAS/MI5 and his ex Mossad lady partner get mixed up in international crime and politics. No holds barred.

All the books are available as e-books and paperbacks.

OTHER BOOKS

LONDON CRIME 1930s-present day. A factual in-depth look at the geezers, the gangs and their heists by one whose family was involved in quite a few! Includes the Brinks Mat Robbery, Great Train Robbery, Baker Street Bank and Princess Margaret Photos robbery, Hatton Garden, the Krays, Richardsons, Billy King, Jack Spot and much, much more. ebook & paperback.

'It is all true but reads like a crime fiction book, a tremendous read!!'

UK SERIAL KILLERS 1930-2021. 44 UK Serial killers, their lives, crimes and punishments. Many you won't have heard of as well as the Wests, Brady, Shipman, Christie etc. with much new information.

FRED KARNO a short biography of the man who gave the world Charlie Chaplin, Stan Laurel and a host of other greatr entertainers and who died in poverty. A real rags to riches and back again life story. ebook only

All available from Amazon, bookshops or the author's website
www.barry-faulkner.com

THE PALMER CASES BACKGROUND

Justin Palmer started off on the beat as a London policeman in the late 1980s and is now Detective Chief Superintendent Palmer running the Serial Murder Squad from New Scotland Yard.   Not one to pull punches, or give a hoot for political correctness if it hinders his enquiries Palmer has gone as far as he will go in the Met. and he knows it. Master of the one line put down and slave to his sciatica he can be as nasty or as nice as he likes. The early 2000's was a time of re-awakening for Palmer as the Information Technology revolution turned forensic science, communication and information gathering skills upside down. In 2012 realising the value of this revolution to solving crime Palmer co-opted Detective Sergeant Gheeta Singh, a British Asian, working in the Met's Cyber Crime Unit onto his team. DS Singh has a degree in IT and was given the go ahead to update Palmer's department with all the computer hard and software she wanted, most of which she wrote herself, and some of which is, shall we say, of a grey area when it comes to privacy laws and accessing certain databases! Together with their civilian computer clerk called Claire, nicknamed 'JCB' by the team because she keeps on digging, they take on the serial killers of the UK. If more help is needed in a case Gheeta calls on a select number of officers in other departments who have worked with Palmer before and can't wait to do so again.

On the personal front Palmer has been married to his 'princess', or Mrs P. as she is known to everybody, for nearly thirty years. The romance blossomed after the young DC Palmer arrested most of her family who were a bunch of South London petty villains in the 90's. They have a nice house in Dulwich Village and a faithful dog called Daisy. His one nemesis is his next door neighbour Benji, real name Benjamin Courtney-Smith, a portly, single, ex-advertising executive in his late fifties who has taken early retirement and now has, in Palmer's estimation, too much time on his hands and too much money in his pocket. A new car every year plus at least two cruise holidays to exotic parts; Benji wears designer label clothes befitting a much younger man, a fake tan, enough gold jewellery to interest the Hatton Garden Safe Deposit Heist gang and all topped off with his thinning hair scooped into a ponytail also befitting a much younger man. Benji has a habit of bringing calamities into Palmer's settled home life.

Palmer is also unsure about Benji's sexuality, as his mincing walk and the very female way of flapping his hands to illustrate every word cast doubts in Palmer's mind. Not that that worries Palmer, who is quite at ease in the multi-gender world of today. Of course, he will never admit it, but the main grudge he holds against Benji is that before his arrival in the quiet suburb of Dulwich village, Palmer had been the favourite amongst the ladies of the Women's Institute, the Bridge Club, the Church Flower Arrangers and the various other clubs catering for ladies of a certain age; but now Benji has usurped Palmer's fan base, and when he stood for and was elected to the local council on a mandate to reopen the library and bring back the free bus pass for pensioners Benji's popularity soared and their fluttering eyelashes had turned away from Palmer and settled in his direction. Gheeta Singh, Palmer's DS and number two is twenty six and lives in a fourth floor Barbican apartment in London. Her parents arrived on these shores as refugees fleeing from Idi Amin's

Uganda in the 1970's. Her father and brothers have built up a large computer parts supply company in which it was assumed Gheeta would take an active role on graduating from University with her IT degrees. However she had other ideas on her career path, and also on the arranged marriage her mother and aunt still try to coerce her into. Gheeta has two loves, police work and technology, and thanks to Palmer she has her dream job.

SUCCESSION
DCS Palmer case 11.

Chapter 1. MONDAY

Eight o'clock in the morning, and the drizzling rain made the wet streets of West London in January shine in the early light. At the base of the two towers that form the front of Her Majesty's Prison Wormwood Scrubs the judas door swung open, and after a short time a figure emerged hunched against the rain. He stood and took a deep breath, relishing the moment; it was, after all, Harry Jones's first breath of air as a free man for three years. Across the yard on the public road two men got out of the back of a shiny Range Rover Vogue, and hunching their shoulders against the rain waited beside it as Harry, clutching his small bag of belongings, made his way over to them.

'Couldn't he come himself?' Harry's words had a sarcastic tone.

'He's busy,' was the brief response from one of the men as the other held a rear door open for Harry to get into the car. He settled back in the warm seat, enjoying the soft luxury after three years of metal chairs and hard wooden benches.

'Where are we going then, big party at the Dorchester, eh?' Harry knew that wouldn't be the case, and he knew he wouldn't get much out of his minders who sat either side of him in silence. His memory recognised them as being members of the Dawn crime firm, and he began to get a little worried as the car moved smoothly off. He had expected his release to be a happier affair, maybe a bottle of champagne and some backslapping by one of the crime bosses; but this had an air of menace hanging over it.

****

Heathrow was looking busy as the motor made its way off the M4 towards the terminals. Harry was getting a little more worried as the driver dropped him and the minders off at Terminal Three car park and drove off to park and wait for instructions.

They walked three abreast along the concourse towards the check-in desks. On the other side opposite the desks, a Costa coffee shop was doing good business. It was busy, very busy, but two tables in a far corner at the back were not busy; one had a 'reserved sign' preventing customers from using it, and the other had two men sitting at it with half-drunk coffees in front of them.

The younger one was in his mid-forties, smart and well-groomed; the other older, mid-sixties with a receding hairline badly disguised by an obvious comb over. They had no luggage and looked out of place in smart suits under thick loose overcoats. Their expressions were not those associated with happy people going on holiday; more ones associated with two men who had business to do, and wanted to get it done and move on.

The younger one, James Dawn, tapped his fingers on the table and nudged his uncle Stan sitting beside him when he saw Harry Jones being ushered towards them through the Costa crowd by the minders.

'He's here.'

Stan Dawn raised a hand and gave his comb over a stroke. 'One bullet in the head at the Scrubs door would have been easier than all this.'

'We talked about that, we made a decision. This way we have control.'

'I hope you're right, James. I hope you are right.'

'Dad said no. If he got it wrong then you can put a bullet in Jones's head at a later date, all right?.'

'I'm looking forward to it.'

They didn't bother to stand as Harry Jones reached their table.

'Hello Harry, welcome to freedom,' James ignored Harry's outstretched hand. 'Sit down.'

Harry nodded as he took a seat opposite them. 'James, you've got bigger.'

'It's been three years, Harry. I'm older and wiser too.'

Harry looked at Stan. 'You look the same, Stan. Still got a comb over, eh? I bet most of it's false by now.'

Stan didn't reply. He had never liked Harry Jones. Stan was a man of few words, most of them expletives.

The minders sat at the reserved table alongside.

'So, what's happening? What's all this about, and why isn't Dad here?'

James's father, Alfred Dawn, was known to all and sundry in the London criminal fraternity as 'Dad', and was the head of the South London Dawn crime family business; a business he'd built up from market stalls in the fifties, with fruit and veg for sale on top of the stall and stolen watches and smuggled cigarettes for sale from underneath. The cigarette trade had developed with the burgeoning club scene in the sixties and seventies into ecstasy tablets, and from there into the family's current business of providing South London's addicts with enough cocaine and crystal meth to keep them happy and coming back for more, and the Dawns in the luxury lifestyle they had become accustomed to.

'Dad's got pneumonia,' said James. 'He's tucked up in bed at the Royal Marsden, so he's taken a back role in the family business lately, Harry. Not in good health, Sends his best wishes.'

'I would have sent a kid on a scooter,' said Stan.

Harry understood what Stan meant.

'Okay, what's all this about then? Why am I here, am I catching a flight?

'That's exactly what you are going to do, Harry.' James pulled Harry's passport out of his overcoat pocket and slid it across the table. 'You're going on a long holiday – a very long holiday. In fact, you aren't coming back.'

'I'm not?'

'No, you're not.'

'How comes you've got my passport?'

'Let me explain, Harry. You were good at your job, very good; a bloody good solicitor and a bloody good fence. You took the money you washed it, took a commission, and gave it back all clean and legal. When you got pulled and sent down for laundering, you kept quiet. The family appreciate that too.'

Stan butted in. 'If you hadn't kept quiet you wouldn't be here now – you'd be dead, strung up in your cell. Tut-tut, nasty business, that poor Harry Jones, they'd say, couldn't take the time so he topped himself, sad fucking loss.'

James waved a hand to silence Stan. 'So there you were, Harry, banged up inside, and that gave us a problem – what happens with the business we do with you? Where do we go, eh? Well, as you know I like to keep everything in order, and didn't want any records or paperwork that referred to our business dealings that might be detrimental to my family's business if they got into the wrong hands hanging about in your office.'

'So we hoisted everything out, all the ledgers, and then torched the fucking place.' Stan gave Harry a wide grin. 'Whoooosh! Shame you weren't inside.'

Harry nodded. 'Yes, I know. My wife told me there had been a fire the day after I was arrested. I guessed it would be one of the clients getting worried about what the police might find. I was quite relieved – being arrested and denied bail didn't give me any time to clear things out. At least any evidence was gone up in smoke.'

James raised a finger. 'I don't think you heard Stan right, Harry. He said we hoisted everything out and *then* torched the place.'

Harry was getting uncomfortable; he had a feeling he knew what was coming next.

'We bunged it all in a lock-up, Harry,' said James. 'Your other half said the money was all safe offshore, and we knew where you were so we weren't worried. And then,' continued James, 'a month ago, seeing that you were getting towards the end of your sentence, we had the bookkeeper that does the books for my wife's nail parlours take a look at the paperwork to see what you owed us. Oh dear, Harry. Oh dear, oh dear. Do you know what she found? Of course you do, Harry, of course you do.'

He leant forward nearer to Jones's face. 'You disappoint me Harry, you really do. I thought we had a deal? I thought we had a deal that you took fifteen percent of the washed amount, Harry. Fifteen percent. Wasn't that the deal, Harry?' He sat back waiting for an answer. None came, so he continued. 'Seems that fifteen percent wasn't enough for you, Harry. So you skimmed it up a bit – quite a big bit too. Very naughty.'

'And very dishonest,' said Stan.

'Yes,' agreed James. 'As Stan says, very dishonest too. You took advantage, Harry. You knew that we trusted you to just take your cut from whatever came back from the laundry. We trusted you to get the best deal you could for our money and take your agreed cut off the top.'

He reached inside his coat and pulled out a sheet of folded paper from his inside pocket, flattened it out, and laid it on the table in front of Jones. 'Recognise it, do you Harry? It's a page from one of your ledgers, the one you listed your dealings with my family in. Always silly to write things down when the deal is not kosher, Harry. But you kept a ledger of all our dealings, and that ledger told our lady from the nail bars the amount we gave to you, the amount you got back washed, and the amount you gave back to us. And the difference between the amount you got back washed and the amount you gave back to us didn't tie in with the fifteen percent we agreed. In fact, sometimes you skimmed off double that.'

Stan shook his head in mock disbelief. 'I could hardly believe it. I was so upset, Harry. I'd have had you topped in prison if Dad hadn't stopped me.'

Harry Jones was beginning to sweat, and was thinking he'd been brought to Heathrow to be put onto a private jet and thrown out of it a few miles out to sea.

'I'll give it back. Whatever it is, I'll give it back.'

'No need, Harry, we took it back last week. You see, I paid a visit to your wife as soon as our lady from the nail bars showed me the figures, showed your wife the ledger, and she was very upset as well, Harry, very upset. But, not as upset as I was when our lady from the nail bars pointed out that the extra you skimmed off us went straight to

Jack Dooley's account. Jack fucking Dooley, Harry. Want to explain that to me, Harry? Want to explain why a firm that runs the West End gets a slice of the laundered money made by our firm that runs South London?'

Harry's voice was getting a bit shaky, 'He got it as a commission for bringing your business to me. I had to do it, or he'd have cut up rough – he threatened my wife, said he'd slash her face.'

'You could have given it to him out of your cut, Harry.'

'Dooley insisted it came out of yours, said it was like you were working for him. He said he'd laugh at you every time he got the money.'

'Well, he can't slash your wife's face now she's in Panama.'

Harry was getting lost. 'In Panama? Why?'

'She was very accommodating, Harry. She reimbursed us with the two and a quarter million the ledger told us you skimmed over the years – she transferred it from that little Mossack Fonseca account in Panama in your name that nobody knows about. I told her that as long as she did that and didn't tell you what she'd done until you got out there then there would be nothing to worry about; you wouldn't be touched and I'd look after you when you came out, which is what I'm doing now. Don't worry, Harry, there's still a few million left in Panama to set the pair of you up for life. But if word gets out about how you cheated on us with Jack Dooley, it would make us look very silly – and wouldn't be very good for you or your wife's health, you understand me?'

'Yes.'

'And maybe those other businesspeople you dealt with might want to look at their ledgers and do some sums, eh? And I might feel obliged to let them have them.'

'For a price,' said Stan.

'Of course for a price. And then maybe after looking at their ledgers they'd want to have a word with you, Harry. I expect they would, don't you? Except for Jack Dooley of course, who I'll take care of all in good time. So here's the deal.' James folded the ledger page and put it back in his pocket and pulled out a flight ticket which he slid across the table and slipped inside Harry's passport. 'You're going to Panama, Harry. There's your ticket and passport – it's a one way ticket, the plane leaves in twenty minutes, and it's boarding now. Your wife flew out yesterday, Harry, all part of the deal I made with her; we booked her into a hotel last night and she will meet your flight when it arrives. And then, Harry, you are on your own.'

Harry felt relieved – it wasn't a trip to the bottom of the sea. 'Is that it?'

'That is it – and Harry, don't ever come back, or my uncle Stan here will get his wish to end this episode his way. You understand?'

'Yes.'

'Good. Your plane boards from gate eight, and these gentlemen who brought you here will make sure you get on it.' James stood up and buttoned his coat, his face hardened, the smile gone. 'I'm going to visit Dad now, Harry, and I'll tell him how grateful you were that he vetoed Stan's wish to eliminate you, at least for the time being.' He motioned the two minders to escort Harry to the check in, 'Now piss off.'

****

'How did he take it?'

James was sitting beside his dad's bed in a private room at the Royal Marsden.

'He wasn't happy, but it was that or over to Stan.'

'Yes, I blame myself – I should have checked him out better at the beginning. Should have known anybody Dooley recommended was not kosher.'

'I didn't know Jack Dooley had recommended him?'

Dad shifted himself to a better sitting position. 'Yes, said he'd been using him as a laundry for years. I should have guessed Dooley would have some kind of angle on it, cheeky bastard, getting a cut of our money. We'll deal with him later.'

'We've got a list of Dooley's dealings with him in one of the ledgers we took out of his office before we torched it – could always slip it into an envelope and deliver it to the Yard.'

Dad laughed. 'Be interesting wouldn't it, eh? Dooley never was more than a pavement artist – likes to think he is, but we could move on him anytime.'

A pavement artist was a bank, post office or security van robber, most of whom moved into drug dealing when the advent of CCTV and DNA profiling put paid to their previous business model.

Dad coughed a couple of times and took a breath from an inhaler.

'You want a nurse?' James was concerned.

'Nah, nothing they can do except pump these antibiotics in and feed me oxygen. I'll be okay in a few days.'

Dad's pneumonia was a regular occurrence; attacks usually lasted a week or so, one of those things that once they get hold of you they flare up now and again.

He took a sip of water from the bedside tray. 'Talking of Jack Dooley, is he behaving himself?'

'So far yes, he's keeping off our manor. A couple of his street kids strayed in, but Stan's men soon put them right.'

Dad laughed. 'Your uncle Stan only knows one way to make a point: go in hard and come out with less bruises than the other guy. He's always been the same and he won't ever change. Keep an eye on him though, James – he doesn't rate Dooley and this little episode won't help. He'd love to take him out and take that West End manor.'

'That's not a bad idea. Dooley must be shifting half a dozen kilos a week that would make a nice addition to our business – organic growth they call it in city business circles.'

'Yeah, they might do – I call it suicidal. If we whack Dooley and take over his West End patch, it'll be like tossing a match in a box of fireworks. We aren't the only firm that would like his manor. Johnny Robinson would be in like a shot if he thought he had a chance.'

'Johnny's got enough with North London he struggles to keep the Romanians out of that turf as it is. He's got no power, not enough muscle – small potatoes.'

'Don't you believe it, I've known Johnny for donkey's years and he's old school; knows the right people. He could pull in a mob from up north to help him kick Dooley out if he wanted to; the Roonans in Manchester for starters would love to get a foothold in London, and I know he does a lot of business with them.' He took another sip of water. 'No, leave Dooley alone for now – we know where he is and what he's doing. So, how's the street doing, what are the figures like?'

'Good, we're pulling down a million and a quarter overall every week – with a net margin of eighty percent and a growth chart showing fifteen percent annual compound turnover.'

'See, that private education your mother insisted on paid off in the end.' They both laughed. 'Is the supply line good?'

'I'm changing it as often as I can, Dad – can't be too careful. We had a boat come in to the Royal Docks last week with fifty kilos in the cargo; got an air drop being made on an old wartime runway in Lincolnshire tomorrow by a plane from Belgium, and my man in Europe is keeping the body mules coming in. They keep Customs busy; we lose one in seven of them, which isn't bad.'

'No, that's a good return. Do you ever feel sorry for the ones who get caught? Going down for a stretch – six, seven years?

'No. They know the risks, and if they get through it's more money in their pocket than they'd earn in a lifetime in their own countries.'

'Yes, I suppose so. Right, good to see you – I'm a bit tired now James, so need a kip. Off you go. What you up to now?'

'I'm going to confession.'

Dad laughed; the laughing brought on the coughs, and a sip of water soothed his throat. 'God moves in mysterious ways, eh?'

****

St George's Cathedral on the Westminster Bridge Road in Southwark is an imposing building in size and architecture. It was late afternoon when the car parked on the front courtyard, and James walked through the massive doors and away from the noise of the rush hour traffic outside into a place of peace and tranquillity. He wasn't there for confession or to pray; in fact he was an atheist, which was just as well considering all the bad things he'd done in life. No way would the Pearly Gates swing open for him.

The confessional booth was in use and there was one middle-aged lady waiting in a nearby pew for her turn. He gave her a nod as he walked past and sat two pews back from her to wait his turn. It wasn't long before another lady, much older, came out of the booth and gave them both a smile as she passed by. James couldn't imagine what ghastly sin she could have done at her age that she needed to come and confess to it.

The second lady couldn't have had much of an exciting week as she was in and out in a couple of minutes. James took a furtive look around before entering the box; nobody else was in the cathedral, it was empty.

The seat in the booth was uncomfortable; the slim cushion on it had been pressed flat and almost solid over the years by the penitent bums of a myriad of sinners. His eyes met those of the clergyman through the wooden grill and they nodded a greeting; no words, just a nod of recognition. The grill was removed and two boxes, each the size of a shoebox, were passed through to James, who took a hefty sealed envelope from his inside coat pocket and passed it back through to the clergyman's waiting hand, that quickly slipped it under his surplice. The grill was replaced, and James left the booth and the cathedral.

Outside, his two minders and the driver sat in the car waiting, the driver nodding his head in time to the beat of rap music playing through his headphones. James took a free copy of the Evening Standard newspaper from a youngster handing them out to passers-by, got into the back of the car and relaxed, putting the two boxes beside him on the bench seat

'Where to, boss?' the driver asked, removing his headphones and stuffing them into the glove box.

James had never really got used to being called 'boss'. It was the term of deference used to address Dad, before illness had forced Dad's stepping back and James taking the reins; but it still didn't seem right.

'Drop me off at the club and then you lads can go home. Pay day tomorrow, so don't be late.'

The hub of the Dawn operation was a snooker club at the back of an industrial estate in Camberwell. Pay day was the day of the week the gang masters who were in charge of the numerous street dealers that sold the cocaine and crystal meth that James imported came in to make their weekly payments of the take. It was all done under the cover of the club. One snooker table at the back of the club was kept for the gang masters to play on; each had a set time to come in and hand their week's takings over at the toughened glass ticket booth inside the entrance. They would then go and play at the table as the money was checked and counted, and if the money matched the weight they'd been given to sell on their last visit the previous week less their twenty percent skim, they got more 'product' to sell; if it came up short they got asked to step inside the back office at the rear of the hall, and if they couldn't explain the shortfall they were slapped about by two rather large chaps who enjoyed inflicting pain. The gang masters very rarely came up short.

James's car pulled off the cathedral forecourt into Westminster Bridge Road. The rush hour traffic was heavy; they made slow progress to the Elephant and Castle, round the roundabout and into the Walworth Road. Two hundred yards further on and they came to a standstill in the traffic. James buried himself in the Standard sports pages as the driver and his minders engaged themselves in a heated conversation about the benefits of Tottenham Hotspur bringing Mourinho in as coach.

None of them noticed the two scooters drawing up one on either side of the car until the gunfire from the pillion riders' pistols smashed through the car windows into their heads and bodies. When the shooting finished the pillion rider from the kerbside scooter leapt off, opened the rear door, took the two boxes from beside a very dead James Dawn, put a last shot into his head from close range just to make sure and got back on the scooter, which was off down the narrow side road, East Street, with the second scooter following behind.

****

Afternoon visiting was over at the Royal Marsden, and the medicine round was under way as the senior nurse pushed her trolley of pills and medicines from room to room, dispensing each patient his or her prescription.

'Wakey wakey Mr Dawn, medicine time,' she said cheerily as she pushed her trolley into his room and pulled up beside the bed. 'No good pretending you're asleep. Doctor's orders – you've got to take these and if you don't I'm in trouble, so sit up a bit and I'll get a pillow.'

She gathered a firm pillow from a cupboard to put behind him to make it easier for him to take the pills. Dad hadn't moved when she came back to the bed, pillow in hand. It was then she noticed the red blood seeping through the blanket from the two bullet holes in his chest and the one in his forehead.

****

DCS Justin Palmer was sprawled on the sofa in his lounge that evening, trying not to doze off as one of Mrs P.'s favourite television programmes was thankfully ending. *The Great Pottery Throw Down* wasn't one of the most exciting programmes on TV in his book.

'Thank God for that,' he said, pulling himself up into a sitting position as the end credits rolled.

'Well, *you* couldn't make a teapot from a lump of clay,' said Mrs P., defending the potter's skills.

'Why would I want to, thousands of them on Amazon for a couple of quid each?'

'You know very well what I mean, their skill and creativeness.'

'Skill? Two of the teapots collapsed in the kiln.'

'These people *are* amateurs, Justin!'

'Yes, you can tell that.'

'Switch over if you want the news.'

Palmer picked up the remote and switched over. The Dawn shootings were all over the news, of course: gangland killing, father and son shot dead in London drugs gang feud, pictures of body bags lying beside the bullet hole-ridden car, an excited correspondent in a throng of reporters and paparazzi at the front of the Royal Marsden, and archive pictures of James and Dad. The newscaster gave as much as they had from the police, which wasn't much, and a resume of the Dawn family, a well-known London organised crime family.

'Well, at least that one won't fall onto your desk,' said Mrs P.

'It might – five bodies is a serial killing.'

'Yes, but it's organised crime, different department.'

'We work together sometimes.'

Secretly, Palmer was hoping it would fall on his desk. Chasing down organised crime killers was far more exciting than chasing down a relative who murders

two siblings for the family jewels, or a similar
domestic serial killing.

Chapter 2 TUESDAY

It did fall onto his desk.

He was in the Team Room on the second floor of New Scotland Yard with DS Gheeta Singh, his number two, and Claire, the civilian computer clerk, tidying up the remaining paperwork from his last case, the one the press had named ' The Bodybuilder', when Assistant Commissioner Bateman came in with a file tucked under his arm. Bateman was all smiles, so Palmer knew immediately that he wanted something. The file was probably one of Palmer's case reports that hadn't adhered to the strict Bateman guidelines and would have to be done again. One thing Palmer hated was writing reports, but in these days of defence legal eagles looking for any slight mistake in law procedure by the officers conducting the case, it was necessary for the Yard's legal team to check that everything in the case had been done within the strict confines of the law.

AC Bateman was forty-eight years old, slightly built and the epitome of a social climber in society, but the ladder he was intent on climbing was in the police force; he sucked up to anybody in authority that he thought might assist in his career path towards his ultimate goal of being Commissioner. He was always immaculately turned out in a uniform with ironed creases so sharp they could cut bread.

His nemesis was his head, in that it was bald, totally bald. It didn't worry anybody except AC Bateman, who had tried every remedy advertised to re-thatch his dome; potions, creams, massages and all sorts of oils had failed to deliver on their promised results. It was hereditary; his father had been bald, his brother was bald, and he wasn't sure but he had a suspicion that his elder sister had started to weave false hair pieces into her receding locks at an early age. He had once tried wearing a wig, but the silence from everybody in the Yard on the day he wore it, and the number of staff who kept their hand in front of their faces to cover broad smiles as he walked past put paid to that idea.

There had always been a distrustful undercurrent to Palmer and Bateman's relationship; nothing you could pin down, but Palmer didn't like or agree with fast-tracking of university graduates to management positions in the force. He'd have them do two years on the beat first, see how they handled a seventeen-stone drug dealer waving a ten-inch knife who just did not want to be arrested. Bateman, on the other hand, would like to be surrounded with graduates with '*firsts*' in various '*ologies*', and was very pleased when the government brought in the minimum recruitment requirement of having to have a degree in order to even apply to join the force. He believed the old school coppers like Palmer were outdated dinosaurs, and that crime could be solved by elimination and computer programmes, which is why he had tried unsuccessfully to transfer DS Singh away from Palmer and back into the Cyber Crime Unit from where Palmer had originally poached her. Bateman had no time for an experienced detective's accumulated knowledge being an asset in the war against crime, and the sooner he could shut down the Serial Murder Squad and combine it with the Organised Crime Unit, CID and Cyber Crime the better. Cutting costs was paramount in Bateman's personal mission statement.

The trouble was that Palmer's team, the Organised Crime Unit, CID and Cyber Crime were producing good case solved figures, which the political masters at the Home Office liked, and they therefore insisted the units carried on working as they were. But what really irked Bateman most of all was that they really liked Palmer too; the press also liked Palmer, and the rank and file loved him. So Bateman managed to keep the false smile on his face as he looked across the Team Room to Palmer.

'Good morning all,' he said with a little nod of the head.

They returned the greeting, wondering why he was here.

'I take it you saw the reports of the shootings last night, the Dawn organised crime family?'

Palmer was getting excited, 'Couldn't miss it sir, all over the news last night and this morning. OC have their hands full with that one.'

'Yes, well…' Bateman moved his head as though his starched collar was chafing. 'They already have their hands full, so I'm going to have to drop this one onto you, Palmer.'

He shifted the file from under his arm and passed it over. 'Witness statements, photos and initial reports from first responders and the attending officers – not much to go on, but it's a start.'

'What about this paperwork you want for the CPS, the Bodybuilder case paperwork?' asked Palmer. 'You said it was of the utmost urgency – those were your very words.'

'Yes, well, that's been overtaken by events – have to wait. This one is to get major priority – can't have gang shootings on the streets of London and inside hospitals. Keep me up to date on it, daily reports, and let me know if you need more men.' And with that he nodded again and left.

'He's been hit on by the politicians, guv,' said Gheeta after waiting long enough to make sure Bateman had gone. 'Somebody has said get it solved and get it off the news. When have we ever been offered *more men* without pleading for them? He's getting hassled from on high.'

Palmer nodded. 'Home Office, they would have come under pressure from the PM's Office and pushed the pressure down the line to Bateman. I can see Boris now…' He went into a very poor Boris Johnson impersonation. *'Can't damn well have this, Home Secretary. We are the party of law and order – yes, law and order. Damn shootings in the street, not on – no, not on, I'll be roasted at PMQs if we don't sort it! Get that twerp Bateman to put his best man on it, that Palmer chap he's the man for the job.'*

Gheeta was looking right past Palmer to behind him towards where the door was. 'Was there something else, Mr Bateman?' she said.

Palmer stood for a second as his heart missed a beat and then he slowly turned. The doorway was empty. He turned back to find both Gheeta and Claire making figure ones in the air with their index fingers and holding back laughter. He'd fallen into the trap.

'One day Sergeant, I *will* put you back on the Brick Lane night beat, so help me if I don't.' He smiled and made his way to the door. 'Right then, you two raise a file or whatever it is you raise on the computer, and input everything you can find out about this Dawn family: what they do, where they do it, and who with. Cross reference everything and let's see if we can't find a few enemies with enough anger to shoot them all. Get onto the hospital for any CCTV they have of the killer, and ask Traffic to do an ANPR trace on James Dawn's car, I want to know where it had been during the day before it was attacked. I'm going into my office to read this report.'

'Hang on guv,' said Gheeta. 'Let me make a copy of it as there's going to be quite a bit in it to upload as well.'

She took the report and made a print copy and gave it back to Palmer, who retired to his office across the corridor to read it. The adrenalin that hit him every time a new case fell on his desk was beginning to flow. Every case was a step into the unknown, a jigsaw that needed completing. He closed his office door behind him and sat behind his desk, resting his feet on top and tipping back his regulation government issue metal chair into the ever widening groove he'd made in the wall plaster over years of tipping it back.

****

Later that day Palmer walked through the Organised Crime Department Team Room on the first floor of the Yard to the glass-fronted office at the back. He gave a tap on the door.

Commander Peter Long looked up from the paperwork he was reading and smiled.

'Come in, Justin. Take a pew.'

Palmer did just that and sat opposite Long, who put his paperwork on a side shelf and sat back. 'So you got the Dawn family murders, eh? Bateman told me he'd given them to you. Good luck, mate.'

'Yes, your neck of the woods really Peter – Organised Crime – so I need some information, and a little help. Why didn't you get it? Bateman said you hadn't the men.'

'Blame the cuts, Justin – I really don't have a team I can put on it unless I shelve another case we are working on and I told Bateman I wasn't going to do that. You got nothing on at the moment then? Serial killers on strike, are they?'

'That would be nice – no catching up on reports, tying up that Bodybuilder case paperwork. A bit gruesome, that one, I don't want another one of those'

'Well, at least you found the bodies. With the OC gangs we almost never find the bodies; might find a couple of bones at the bottom of a lime-filled pit in the middle of a forest somewhere, or a tooth in the bottom of a barrel of acid, but that's about all.'

'Well, I've got five bodies for starters in this one, two of them being from the Dawn family. Clue me in on them.'

'Third generation criminals, very clever; so bloody clever that none of the actual family have ever been arrested and had the charge stick. They're well into drugs with control of South London, estimated to be pushing out five kilos of cocaine and a similar amount of crystal meth and other amphetamines each week. The family make so much that they don't mind losing a couple of million a year in accountant's fees to find loopholes to keep them straight with the tax people. Top of the tree was Alfred Dawn, the one shot in the hospital, known affectionately as 'Dad' in the underworld; very shrewd operator, invested the family's money in London office blocks and offshore trusts in the Channel Islands, Caymans and Panama; all legally done, and through a blind trust in the Channel Islands. Suffered with pneumonia for the last few years and son James gradually took over the reins. Big business, Justin – the money gets laundered through various schemes, including a chain of nail bars and beauty salons run by his wife, Eve. Only other family member is Stanley, known as 'Stan';

he's Dad's brother, acts as the enforcer, has a tyre and exhaust business based in Stockwell, with ten branches around the south; also got a so-called 'security' company that provides ninety-nine percent of the door staff to the clubs and pubs in London. Always a bit in the background is Stan; we had him about eight years ago on a murder charge, but the witnesses decided to retract their statements the day before we went to court. Judge threw it out. So it would seem that with James and Dad gone Stan will now be running the business. He could go one of two ways; if he knows who put the contracts out on James and Dad he'll stamp all over them and we will have a bloodbath. If that happens he could lose – not very likely if it's just a local firm trying to take over, as the Dawns have a lot of soldiers and muscle power, but if whoever planned this has got a few of the northern and Midlands teams as backup it could go either way. But if they take out Stan next then the way would be open to control South London, so I would think he's holed up somewhere planning his next move.'

'I see,' Palmer nodded. 'So he's on a sticky wicket isn't he, eh? If he goes to war, he could lose; if he doesn't and others

41

see it as a weakness and whack him, he loses too. Either way the Dawn family is rubbed out of the London drugs scene. Who are the likely suspects to have made the hits?'

'Well, to be honest only two spring to mind, Justin, but both of those would lose in a one-on-one war with the Dawns. That's Jack Dooley and Johnny Robinson – Dooley has the West End sewn up, and Robinson's turf is North London.'

'So if it's one of those two they've lowered the odds now, haven't they; but still have Stan Dawn to deal with.'

'Correct.

'What about this Eve Dawn and the nail bars, James's wife – is she likely to take over, sounds like she is a pretty tough lady?'

'She is a very tough lady; ten years younger than James, attractive, late thirties, not one to mess about with. Known to have thrown awkward customers out of her bars personally and finish them off with a good kicking.'

'I think I'll be needing more officers on this one.'

'You won't be getting any of mine.'

'No, don't worry – we've got a list of those we've used in the past. I'll get DS Singh to ring round and see if any are on leave and want the overtime. Bateman said let him know if I needed extra hands – seeing as he usually resists any request from me for extra officers he must be getting hassled big time to get this case cleared up quickly.'

****

Bateman authorised two additions to Palmer's team and Gheeta started ringing round the officers that they had used before. She wasn't far down her list when two who were on leave jumped at the chance to work with Palmer again. Palmer was old school, got off his backside and was out with the team, not like most of the DCS's these days who sat in an office sending emails, writing reports, choosing between custard creams and ginger snaps and letting their DS's and DC's do the legwork, and then take the plaudits for a successful case.

'Who have we got then?' asked Palmer.

'DS Simms and DS Johnson,' answered Gheeta. 'They worked with us in the Royal Mint Robbery case.'

Palmer remembered. 'Oh yes, good men. Well done.'

'They'll be in tomorrow morning.'

Chapter 3
WEDNESDAY

Gheeta brought Simms and Johnson up to date with the case in the Team Room the next morning and issued them with high frequency radios from the communications department. She also got one for herself and Palmer and linked them all through Claire's computer which acted as a base; being HF meant that they would be assigned a bespoke frequency for the duration of the case, making communication between the members of the team immediate rather than having to go through the usual communications network.

'Good to see you two again,' said Palmer, greeting Johnson and Simms. 'Right, let's get a plan going and see if we can't rattle a few cages and tie up this case in double quick time.'

They all sat down at a table and Palmer continued. 'Claire gave me the visitor list for Alfred Dawn at the hospital; nobody visited him who you wouldn't expect to, all family. Did we get the CCTV?' he asked Gheeta.

'Yes guv, but nobody we can identify. This killer knew exactly what he was doing.'

They turned to look at the big screen as Claire put up the hospital CCTV footage and Gheeta talked them through it. 'This is the main entrance. Our killer can be seen entering; he's done his homework and is aware of the camera, because as you can see he has a baseball cap with a large front peak that covers his face from the camera's angle.'

The screen flicked to a new shot. 'This is him coming along the corridor to Alfred Dawn's room and entering it. I've timed it as nine seconds before he's back out and leaves the hospital. Identification is impossible, he's a pro – he kept his face out of camera shot at all times.'

The screen flicked off.

Palmer's voice showed his disappointment. 'Bit of a dead end there then, pardon the pun. I hope we get more from the ANPR cameras tracking Dawn's car.'

'I've asked for all the recordings of the car on the day of the killings to be sent through to us from Traffic, guv. Once I get it Claire and I will be able to put a journey together on a map, should have it in a day or so.'

'Good, that could prove very interesting. Tomorrow is the Dawns' funeral. I thought it might be one of those big events with horse-drawn carriages and the whole works, but apparently Peter Long tells me the information he has is that it will be very low-key, family and friends only. I think we should put in an appearance, in the background – give us a chance to get to know a few faces. I've asked for a snapper to go as well, so we'll have some pictures afterwards.'

'Do we stay out of sight, sir?' asked Simms.

'No, stay in the background but be seen. Let them know we are interested.' He stood up. 'Right, Sergeant Singh and I have an appointment with James Dawn's wife Eve in half an hour at the Dawns' luxury apartment by London Bridge. Simms, you follow us in a plain car and keep an eye on the apartment block after we leave – see who turns up, or if she rushes off somewhere. Johnson, take a stroll down the Walworth Road and see if any of the shops near where the shooting happened have CCTV. All meet back here at four.'

****

Palmer paid a visit to the Murder Morgue with DS Singh on his way to Eve Dawn's; both were south of the river so it seemed a good idea to pop in and see what Professor Latin, the chief Pathologist, had made of the bodies. Neither Palmer nor Singh enjoyed visiting the morgue; the mixed smells of dead flesh and disinfectant weren't very nice, and seemed to attach themselves to your clothes and linger. Professor Latin was well-known for his use of expletives so Palmer preferred not to have DS Singh with him, but she had insisted on coming inside rather than wait in squad car.

They both donned the plastic pathology gowns, head caps and rubber boots before entering the main lab, which was like a small hangar with steel tables in lines, each with a body or body part on it with the pathology staff working on them. Latin saw them and came over.

'Justin my friend, how are you?' He waved a hand towards the tables. 'Got yourself a right fucking game with this lot haven't you?' He acknowledged Gheeta. 'DS

Singh, how are you? Still putting up with this old fart then?'

Gheeta smiled. 'Hello Professor, good to see you again.'

Palmer didn't want to stay longer than necessary in the morgue. 'What have you got anything interesting?'

Latin shrugged. 'Well, the most interesting bit was that the Dawn bodies were collected yesterday.'

'Really, bit quick wasn't it?'

'Yes, I thought that too. Couldn't do anything about it; the funeral director had a magistrate's order granting him custody, so my hands were tied – so to speak.'

'Why would the magistrate do that?'

'Apparently the Dawns were Muslim and had to be buried within a certain time span.'

'Muslim my arse, what's Eve Dawn playing at?'

'I've no idea – anyway, it didn't make much difference; by law the time span can be stretched if the person is killed in war or if foul play is expected – definitely foul play in this case – so I managed an extra twenty-four hours which was time to do all the measurements, take photos and pull out the bullets. I sent them over to Reg Frome. I'll send copies of the photos over to you. They're a bit gruesome – bullets to the head generally make a bit of a mess.'

'What about the other three bodies, have they been nabbed too?'

'No, we have them here. Police have identified them as known felons but we need a family member to confirm their identities, we're waiting for that. We've put them off for a couple of days whilst we clean them up – half a dozen bullets can make a bit of a fucking mess of your face, not very nice for the widow or children to see that. I'll get all the details and bullets over to Frome as soon as I can.'

'Okay, well done. Let us have a copy of your reports when they're done.'

'Of course,' Latin got serious. 'Justin, you take care – looking at the injuries to this lot you're in the middle of something very nasty. Just take care.'

Palmer smiled and they left.

****

'You are not being very helpful, Mrs Dawn.' Palmer gave Eve Dawn a withering look. It didn't have any effect.

Palmer and Singh were seated on the large leather sofa in the Dawn apartment lounge. Eve Dawn stood by reinforced tinted glass that formed one wall of the lounge and gave panoramic views over London Bridge and the Thames.

'I don't know how I can be helpful, Mr Palmer. My husband has been murdered in a gang killing. I don't have any knowledge of his business with these people, or why somebody should do this.'

'Mrs Dawn, I know exactly what kind of business your husband was in, and so do you.'

'Property mister Palmer property, investment and development.'

'I see. Building a mosque somewhere, was he?'

'Pardon?'

'Well, rich Muslims like him and his dad usually bequeath money to a mosque. I always thought that magistrates are the weakest link in the judiciary process, and now I'm sure. How much did you pay him?'

'I don't know what you mean. Pay who?'

'How much did you pay the magistrate for the false Muslim death certificates for James and Alfred? And more to the point, why? Why do you want the bodies in the ground so fast?'

Eve Dawn laughed loudly. 'I could say that they were both converting to Islam, or I could tell you the truth, Mr Palmer.'

'The truth would make a nice change.'

'All right, the families of the driver of James's car and the men with him have been offered twenty thousand pounds cash by the tabloids to take a photo of James or Alfred with holes in their heads when they go and identify their own relatives in the morgue. I couldn't have that happen.'

Palmer looked her straight in the eye. 'That I do believe.' He rubbed his chin and thought for a few moments. 'I have to send in a report on this meeting, Mrs Dawn, and I will state in my report that you were a very unhelpful person and should be treated as an obstructive witness. But be assured, this investigation will not go away. The

Metropolitan Police will not allow gang-type killings to happen in London. Whoever instigated this will be caught and will be sentenced, and may I remind you that withholding evidence is a crime, and in some cases carries a prison sentence.' He stood and put his trilby on. 'Goodbye, Mrs Dawn.'

Gheeta packed away her laptop which had been quietly filming and recording the interview and followed Palmer out.

'She didn't seem to be the grieving widow, guv.'

'No, tough as old boots if you ask me, Peter Long said she was, and he was right. You can bet she's got feelers out though; she wants to know who did it, 'course she does. She's not just going to fade into the background and let a multi-million pound drugs empire slip into somebody else's hands without a fight, not that woman – no way.'

'Twenty thousand pounds for a picture, guv – what does that make the photos Professor Latin's sending to us worth?'

'Don't even think it.'

'Top up the pension pot nicely guv,' she smiled.

They gave Simms a quick nod as they passed his parked car outside the block and made their way back to the Yard.

****

The Team meeting at four o'clock didn't add anything of use to the case. The shop owners in the Walworth Road valued their windows and businesses, and so, 'No, I haven't got CCTV, didn't see anything' was the stock answer DS Johnson got from all of them with premises near the murder scene. Palmer had half expected that.

DS Simms couldn't match any of the people going into Eve Dawn's apartment block to any of the mug shots on the list, and Eve Dawn stayed put.

Chapter 4 THURSDAY

The funeral at the South London Crematorium in Streatham was low-key judged against the usual major criminal funeral, but that still meant a hundred or so mourners turned up to pay their respects; mainly an assortment of heavy-looking men in dark glasses with wives and girlfriends whose annual Botox bill would pay off the national debt.

Palmer stood fifty metres away in full view as they gathered in the car park; some faces he knew, the majority he didn't. The snapper was clicking away, as were several media photographers and paparazzi. It was Palmer's intention to be seen, and to that end he had DS Singh stand with him in her uniform. There could be no mistake left in the mourners' minds; the police were very interested in them and in this case.

Once the horde had gone inside for the service, Palmer and Singh made their exit and went back to the Yard where they were joined in the Team Room by Simms and Johnson.

****

They all sat looking up at the large plasma screen on the wall above Gheeta's bank of computers and servers. Traffic department had pieced together the Dawn car's journey on the fateful day using ANPR camera records. The screen showed a street map of London with a red line following the route that James Dawn's car had taken. Claire was sitting working at her keyboard as Gheeta stood and took them through the fateful journey, referring to her page of notes from Traffic who had listed the timeframe.

'The car was parked somewhere in West Norwood overnight, probably at a chap called David Ramsay's house; OC say he was Dawn's regular driver, and the driver who lost his life in the shooting in the Walworth Road. He lived in Windsor Close, West Norwood, just off the High Street, where the first ANPR camera clocked the car at 6.30 that morning and tracked it to Brixton, where the other two men joined it. OC says they are a couple of known Dawn firm faces. Ramsay picked them up somewhere near the tube station as the camera before the station shows only the driver in the car, but the next one shows all three. Then, and this is interesting, the next stop is Wormwood Scrubs at about 7.45am.'

'Really?' Palmer was surprised. 'No visiting at the hour of the morning?'

'No, but prisoner releases are made at 8am.'

'So, they were picking up somebody who was being released that day?'

Gheeta nodded to Claire, who pulled up a police mugshot picture of Harry Jones and flashed it onto the screen in the bottom right corner. 'Harry Jones was the only release that morning, guv. Claire checked with the Home Office.' She looked to Claire to continue the narrative.

'Harry Jones was inside for major money laundering; he was a solicitor who specialised in representing the criminal classes and washing their drug money, using his client money account to hold it in. He was sentenced to six years – good behaviour, so out in three. The Scrubs's CCTV shows him leaving and getting into the car.'

'So do we assume he was part of the Dawn set-up?' suggested Palmer.

'Well, 'said Claire. 'If he was this was the first physical contact he had with them since he went inside. I checked his visitor log and he only had visits from his wife Lilian, until the final month of his sentence when Jack Dooley saw him a couple of times, both times with Jones's wife.'

'Interesting,' commented Palmer. 'Carry on with the journey.'

Claire cancelled the mugshot and posted up a video of Harry Jones as he left the prison and walked to the car, where he spoke for a moment to the two minders before getting inside and being driven off.

Gheeta took over. 'Next stop for the car, as far as we know, is Heathrow Airport. Traffic picked it up on seventeen cameras on the way there, and one at Terminal Three car park as it entered. Four occupants, so we don't think it stopped on the way to pick anybody else up.'

Palmer knew better than to interrupt Gheeta's flow, as one thing was as sure as night follows day: in the world of IT she would have dotted all the i's and crossed all the t's, and left nothing to chance.

She continued. 'Three occupants are picked up leaving the car park and walking into the terminal building – they are Jones and the two minders, so the driver stayed with the car.' The CCTV on the wall screen showed them doing just that and entering the terminal. 'The inside cameras at the terminal caught them entering and walking down the crowded main concourse. They made for the departure lounge and into the Costa coffee shop.'

'Tasteless dishwater,' Palmer couldn't resist commenting as the Costa logo came into view. He loved his coffee, preferably French strength 5, and could just not understand the hordes of people on the London streets every morning in the rush hour with their mobile in one hand and a takeaway coffee in the other. For a few pounds you could buy a kettle and a filter jar and have the real thing!

Gheeta took no notice of his remarks and continued. 'Costa CCTV shows them meeting two other men who are already there and having a conversation. Not a very clear image as the place is rammed, but when we looked back through the in-house Costa CCTV and at the later images from the car park when they left, we identified James Dawn and Stanley Dawn as the ones in the coffee shop that Harry Jones met. It wasn't a long meeting as the departure lounge camera shows Harry Jones passing through Passport

Control fifteen minutes later, on his own with no luggage to board a flight to Panama.'

'The offshore money launderer's Heaven no surprise there, but no luggage?' Palmer looked closely at the images. 'You sure?'

Claire answered, 'Positive sir, I checked. No luggage booked onto the flight in Jones's name, and the ticket was bought just the afternoon before for cash at a travel agent's in Hampstead.'

'So I get the feeling that having no luggage could mean that Mr Jones was not aware that he was about to take a holiday.'

'One-way ticket, sir,could be more than a holiday.'

'Yes, we had better take a good look at his Solicitor business and see if the Dawns were amongst his clients and if there was any contact with them whilst Jones was in the Scrubs. Also find out if the travel agent who sold the ticket has CCTV; be interesting to see who actually bought it. But that's for later – carry on.'

Gheeta checked back to her notes. 'Okay, so after Jones has left the Dawns and the two minders, they leave and go back to the Terminal Three car park.

Stanley Dawn leaves the others and presumably goes back to the car that brought him and James Dawn to the airport earlier before the others arrived, and James and the two minders take the car that brought them and Jones and they all leave. We don't know which car Stanley was driving so can't track it, but the car James takes, which is the one he is later killed in, leaves the airport and comes back into London.' She pointed to the red-outlined route on the wall screen. 'It makes its way to the Fulham Road and stops there for thirty-five minutes in the Royal Marsden Hospital car park.'

'Visiting his dad Alfred,' Palmer said. 'Did he shoot his own dad?'

'No, the time is wrong. Alfred had two nurse visits between the time James left and he was shot; on both those visits he was obviously alive and talking. This visit by James was two hours before Alfred was shot. I had a look at the footage and it just shows James Dawn going into his dad's room and leaving ten minutes later, nothing of interest.'

Palmer was very much aware that such was Gheeta Singh's expertise in the world of IT and cyber that she would be able to hack into the hospital CCTV records without much problem and extract any information they wanted on Alfred Dawn's visitors. Many of the algorithms and programmes on the Team's computers were bespoke built by Gheeta, or '*borrowed*' from other law enforcement organisations worldwide; many '*borrowed*' without permission and without the source even being aware. Palmer turned a blind eye to this; if it helped him run down serial killers, it was okay in his book.

The unspoken deal was that Gheeta could run his IT systems as she thought fit, but he was to be kept out of the loop of anything she added that might be termed as 'dodgy', just in case something hit the fan later. Bateman would love to have an illegal action to pin on Palmer to underline his case for the DCS's retirement, and then at least one department could be integrated with CID. So Palmer kept all Gheeta's downloads and uploads strictly off the record.

'I take it that's CCTV footage supplied by the hospital.' Palmer didn't expect an answer, and Gheeta's innocent eyes didn't fool him either.

'Anyway,' she continued without answering. 'After the hospital stop Dawn's car travelled on to Southwark and made a stop at Southwark Cathedral, where their CCTV camera outside the main door shows Dawn going inside. I had the recording picked up by the local branch and sent over.' Claire played it on the big screen.

'Why is he going in there?' asked Palmer. 'He doesn't come across as a religious type.'

She shrugged her shoulders at Palmer's enquiring look. 'No idea guv, unfortunately they don't have CCTV inside. I did ask, and was told the privacy of the worshipper is paramount.'

'Until some lowlife nicks the silver?' Simms made the point.

Gheeta continued. 'They have priests on a confessional rota all day inside guv, and the whole place is shut at night and alarmed.'

Palmer perked up. 'That's good, so we need to have a word with the priest on duty when Dawn went in. Carry on.'

'Not much else now, guv. We've Dawn coming out and walking back to the car...'

'Hang on! Stop the video.' Palmer moved closer to the big screen as

Claire stopped it. 'Move it back slowly'. The video was taken by a camera high above the cathedral main door looking down at an angle at worshippers entering and leaving. Claire took it back frame by frame. 'Hold it there. That's Dawn leaving, isn't it?'

'Yes.'

'And that's him getting a paper off a kid, yes?' It was a pretty grainy picture as the young newspaper vendor was a good way away from the door and was just about shown in the top left corner of the picture frame.

'Yes.'

'Can we get a better image, a bigger one?'

'Hang on.' Claire worked on her keyboard and brought the image of Dawn holding out his hand for a paper into the centre of the screen and enlarged it.

Palmer pointed. 'He's getting a paper with his right hand, but look at his left arm. It's not very distinct, but he's got a couple of boxes tucked under it hasn't he?'

Gheeta nodded. 'I think you're right, guv – definitely something there. Take it back to the doorway Claire, just as he leaves.'

It wasn't a very good picture; it didn't show any boxes as the camera angle was looking from the right-hand side and from above.

'He's not moving his left arm, is he,' Palmer stated. 'He's moving his right arm as he walks, but not his left one.'

'No boxes found in the car at the murder scene, guv.'

'So perhaps they were killed for those boxes then? Dawn could have met somebody inside that Church...'

'Cathedral,' corrected Gheeta.

'Inside that *cathedral* and picked up two boxes that four people were killed for. Five if we count Alfred.'

'Drugs.'

'More than likely – can't see a hit like that for two boxes of prayer books can you? I think we might take a pilgrimage there tomorrow'

****

'What the Hell is happening, Stan?' Eve Dawn was dressed in black, having just returned from the funeral and sat on the large leather sofa in the Dawns' large fifth-floor executive apartment on the south side of London Bridge overlooking the Thames. 'Who is doing this?'

Stan shrugged his shoulders. 'Could be quite a few in the frame, Eve. More than one firm would like our turf.'

'Our options then, what do we do now? Can't just do nothing.'

'Wait until word comes through from whoever it was with a deal, which is the way these things usually go. Or we might get a grass give us the name, then we'll know who we are dealing with. I've put out a hefty reward.'

'And once we know?'

'Hit them harder than they hit us.'

'Start a war?' The doubt at this response showed in Eve's voice.

'No, just one big – and I mean *very* big – hit. Whichever firm it is, we totally wipe them out.'

Eve shook her head in disbelief. 'I sometimes think you are living in the seventies, Stan.'

'At least you knew who did what in them days. Lines were drawn, and you kept within them.'

'Okay, so what are *you* doing now – are you keeping low? You're the obvious next target.'

'No, I've got enough protection around me. We carry on as normal, Eve. We missed one payday because it was the day after the killings, but we're back on schedule now.'

'What about the gang masters, have they been approached by anybody to swap supplier?'

'Haven't told me if they have, and they all turned up to the cemetery this morning. Money talks, Eve, and they like taking money.'

'Yes, I was hoping for a more low-key turnout this morning.'

'More plain-clothes police than mourners if you ask me.'

'Which means the police aren't any closer to knowing who did it than we are. Now, to business – do we have everything under control? Have you had a word with the suppliers that everything carries on as normal?'

'I have, I put their minds at rest. The drop at the old Second World War airfield in Lincolnshire went ahead as planned, no problems, so we've plenty of product for our dealers I've moved a few of the trusted boys up a notch in the pecking order – it's all under control, business as usual.'

'And the families of the men killed?'

'They'll be looked after.'

'Big time, Stan – look after them big time. Anything they want, they let you know, and you give it to them.'

'Okay.' He reached into his inside jacket pocket and pulled out a bulging envelope. 'Four hundred grand from the payday we missed last week. I sent some of our people round to collect it. This week's payday is tomorrow.'

Eve took it and moving to a picture of *The Hay Wain* by Constable on the wall, she pulled it at one end and it opened like a small door to reveal a wall safe behind, which she opened, put the envelope inside and closed again, pushing the picture back into position. 'Good week. I'll have to open a couple more nail bars soon to shift these amounts.'

Stan nodded towards the picture. 'Is that the original?' He wouldn't have been surprised; lots of major stolen art had passed through the Dawns' hands over the years as collateral for large loans. Insurance companies would offer a 'no questions asked' amount for the return, which was well below the payout they would have to make to the insured owner if the work disappeared for good. So a thief with a picture that had a million pound insurance return offer on it and who wanted to finance a big heist could raise half that from a major player with money like the Dawns at fifty percent interest. Borrow £500,000 on the picture against the insurance money offer, pay back £750,000 and get the picture back. Other than that, he could sell the picture to another villain who needed to raise money at a price that would leave him room to borrow against its insurance value.

Eve smiled. 'It might be original, Stan. Then again, it might be a Tom Keating.'

'Right.' Stan stood to leave. 'If you want me I'll be at the tyre place at Stockwell; if anybody's going to grass, they'll come there.'

Eve looked him straight in the eye. 'Stan, you don't make a move before asking me. Okay?'

Stan Dawn felt a little anger rise within him. 'You're not the boss, Eve. If anyone takes over it should be me.'

'Nobody is *taking over*, Stan – not until we get through this, and then we'll come to an agreement. So I suggest we keep the ship on an even keel and play it by ear for now. Agreed?'

Stan gave a slight nod and left.

Eve Dawn watched him leave the building and be driven away from her tinted window. She opened her mobile and speed-dialled a number. The answer was terse.

'I thought we agreed no contact for a fortnight.' Jack Dooley sounded annoyed.

'I don't trust Stan.'

'What do you mean?'

'I think he's likely to upset the apple cart and start a war.'

'With me?'

'You are the obvious choice if he was trying to make it look like a revenge killing.'

'Crafty bugger. I told you he came to me with the idea in the first place: get rid of James and Dad and split the manor between him and me.'

'Perhaps he has no intention of splitting it with you, never has had – get you out of the way now and it's all his.'

'What about you, Eve? James's men would be loyal to you, not him.'

'Yes, so if he thought it through I'd probably be next. He'd take me out first, blame you, and then hit you. That would make sense to the men and they'd rally round him, and he'd have South London and the West End to himself – no sharing it with you.'

'Does he know about you and me?'

'Nobody knows about you and me.'

There was a few moments of silence.

'Okay, leave it to me.'

****

Lucy Price walked into the Team Room and gave Palmer one of her 'you know why I'm here' smiles. 'Good afternoon, Justin.'

'It was, until you walked in. Don't tell me, Bateman has chickened out of doing the press briefing?'

Lucy Price was in charge of Press and Media. She was a brilliant PR lady who had the unenviable task of keeping journalists in line and controlling just how much information on a case was made public and when; in her late fifties and with a reputation for no nonsense, and a tongue that could turn a wayward journalist who had overstepped the parameters into jelly in front of their peers in the Press Room, that was her domain and that was where Lucy Price ruled.

She laughed at Palmer's assumption that Bateman had 'chickened out', which basically he had; Bateman, like most ACs, didn't like to take questions from the press when a case was active because he didn't know enough about it. Bateman liked to present himself – preferably beside the Commissioner on the main steps of the Yard – when a case was solved and take the plaudits. Until then, he would rather sit at his desk and push paperclips around.

'Assistant Commissioner Bateman is tied up in very important meetings Justin, and has asked that you take the press briefing. It's set for an hour's time so we catch the six o'clock news. Come down to the Press Room twenty minutes before and let me know what you want to say and what you don't want questions on. It'll be a short one, I just want to get something out for the public; too many rumours about gang warfare on the streets, the Minister's been on the phone asking that we squash that with the press. Okay with you?'

Palmer nodded. 'Yes, I'll tell them the Mafia's moving in and because of the cuts we haven't a hope in Hell of controlling them and to expect ongoing street murders. How's that?'

'Lovely, just what the Minister ordered. See you in a while.' Lucy was used to Palmer's cynicism.

****

The press briefing went well. The crime correspondents were mostly well-versed in Palmer's way of handling things; he would tell them what he wanted them to know, and wouldn't tell them anything he thought might prejudice the ongoing case. He told it like it was: an organised crime family, well-known to the police, seemed to be having *a bit of a spat*, as he put it, with somebody else. Nobody in the frame as yet, and all options open. Mafia? No, the Mob? No, just a local spat that seems to have got a bit out of hand. His low-key handling of their questions, giving the impression it was just another ordinary day at the office for him, meant there would not be any 'shock horror' headlines in the papers the next day, and the Home Office would be happy.

****

'What's all this?' Palmer stood in his front hall at home, having nearly tripped over a row of full bin bags stood just inside the door.

Mrs P. shouted from the kitchen at the end of the hall. 'They're going to the council's charity appeal for funds for books for the library, they'll collect them tomorrow. Leave them alone.'

Palmer removed his Crombie and trilby and hooked them onto the hallstand, before wandering into the kitchen where the lovely aroma of a Mrs P. steak and kidney pie met his olfactory senses.

'Smells nice.' Other than catching serial killers, one of Palmer's greatest 'likes' was Mrs P.'s cooking; he would kill for her toad-in-the-hole. Gheeta knew that quite a few times in the past, when Palmer had checked his watch around five in the afternoon and said 'Must go, got a DCS meeting', what he really meant was that Mrs P. was dishing up her famed burnt cheese-topped lasagne, toad-in-the-hole, or steak and kidney pie that evening, and no way was he going to miss it!

He sat at the kitchen table in anticipation. Daisy, his faithful English Springer, moved from her basket in the hall to beneath the table, in the hope he might pass down a morsel or two; strictly forbidden by Mrs P., but often Palmer would manage a sleight of hand when she was not looking.

'No good you sitting there waiting. Dinner is going to be about fifteen minutes, so go and sort through the charity bags and see if there's anything you want to keep.'

'What's in them?'

'Half your wardrobe.'

'What do you mean, *half my wardrobe*?'

'I saw your press thing on TV earlier and I thought I was in a time warp back to the sixties. When did you last buy any new clothes?'

'No need to, the ones I've got are all right.'

'Men's trousers don't have turn-ups anymore – not for the last thirty years they don't – but they do have creases! It was embarrassing watching you. And did you have to wear that damned Prince of Wales check jacket?' He was still wearing it, she pointed at it. 'Everybody could see the ink stain on the lapel, it's big enough – and I've lost count of the times I've sewn the elbow patches up. Take it off, empty the pockets, and put it in one of the bags. And as for that buttoned cardigan you were wearing, the button halfway down doesn't match.'

'*You* sewed it on.'

'I sewed it on because I was going to throw it away ages ago and you said you would use it for gardening, not standing in front of the whole country on television – and anyway, nobody wears cardigans these days, except old men in care homes. Look at you – a museum piece! No, Justin Palmer, enough is enough. I felt so embarrassed I went straight online this afternoon and ordered you some new clothes.'

Palmer hurried to the bin bags and rummaged through them, pulling out some old favourites.

'I like this cardigan, it's warm in the winter.'

'Which one?' Mrs P. shouted from the kitchen.

'The blue stripe.'

'Twenty years old, and horizontal stripes make you look fat. Put it back.'

Palmer reluctantly put it back in the bag. 'My suede shoes!'

'Nobody wears suede shoes anymore, Justin.'

'That MP chap does.'

'You mean Kenneth Clarke? He's about a hundred and twenty years old, same age as the fashion for wearing suede shoes – and anyway, he's retired now.'

'I don't see any of your stuff in the bags.'

'No, because I regularly send my old clothes to the charity shop and buy new ones; they're cheap enough nowdays. You should take a leaf out of Benji's book, he's always smart and modern.'

Benji was Palmer's next-door neighbour, and his nemesis. Real name Benjamin Courtney-Smith, he was a portly, single, ex-advertising executive in his late fifties who had taken early retirement, and now had, in Palmer's estimation, too much time on his hands and too much money in his pocket. A new car every year, plus at least two cruise holidays a year to exotic parts; he wore designer label clothes befitting a much younger man, a fake tan, enough gold jewellery to interest the Hatton Garden Safe Deposit Heist detectives, and all topped off with his thinning hair scooped into a ponytail, also befitting a much younger man.

Palmer was also unsure about Benji's sexuality, as his mincing walk and the very female way of flapping his hands to illustrate every word cast doubts in Palmer's mind. Not that that worried Palmer, who was quite at ease in the multi-gender world of today. Of course, he would never admit it, but the main grudge he held against Benji was that before his arrival in the quiet suburb of Dulwich village, Palmer had been the favourite amongst the ladies of the Women's Institute, the bridge club, and the various other clubs catering for ladies of a certain age; but now

Benji had usurped Palmer's fan base, and when he stood for and was elected to the local council on a mandate to reopen the library and bring back the free bus pass for pensioners, his popularity soared and their fluttering eyelashes had turned in his direction.

Palmer grunted at the mention of Benji. 'I don't think the Commissioner would appreciate me doing a press briefing on the front steps of the Yard in a tie-dyed rainbow tee shirt looking like Picasso's pallet.'

'Well, you're going to get some new clothes for three weeks' time; there's a cheese-and-wine at the library to celebrate the council voting to keep it open and fund it. And that, Justin Palmer, is because Benji took the cause to heart and bashed the rest of the useless councillors into line. If you think I'm going with you on my arm looking like an advert for a vintage clothing shop, you are mistaken.' She walked out of the kitchen and joined him. 'Off.'

'What?'

'The Prince of Wales check jacket, take it off and clear the pockets out.'

'Can I go to appeal?' Palmer knew it was pointless arguing with Mrs P. once she had made up her mind. He reluctantly did as ordered, and watched as she stuffed his pride and joy into a bag and tied the cord.

'Your pie is getting cold.'

Chapter 5 FRIDAY

Inside the foyer to the cathedral Palmer and Gheeta shook the raindrops off their coats.

'Been lovely all day so far, and as soon as we leave the office it pelts down. Typical.' Palmer shook his trilby and brushed his coat.

'Could be Him upstairs sending us a message,' said Gheeta, taking her laptop from its shoulder bag and wiping a few drops off it. 'Could be a sign.'

'Yes, a sign that I should have brought my umbrella to work today.'

'Detective Palmer?' a voice enquired from amongst the rows of pews. A young clergyman in robes approached and offered his hand. He was slim verging on thin and although in his thirties looked about twelve, with a mop of black hair that clashed with his very pale skin. Probably spent too much time inside the cathedral and not enough outside in the sun, thought Palmer as the clergyman introduced himself. 'Arbuthnot Perryman, the Bishop's assistant. I spoke to a lady on the phone earlier.'

'You spoke to Detective Sergeant Singh earlier, sir.' Palmer indicated Gheeta. They all shook hands.

'Was the CCTV disc I gave your officer the day before any use? I do hope it was,' said Perryman excitedly. 'It's all very intriguing for us to have a visit from the police. You hinted that it might have something to do with that terrible shooting in the Walworth Road. Awful affair, truly awful.'

Gheeta pulled up a picture of James Dawn on her screen and showed it to Perryman.

'Ring any bells?' She hadn't thought of the significance of that remark being in a cathedral until she saw Palmer roll his eyes.

Perryman looked at the photo. 'No. No, can't say it does. Should it?'

'He came in here about thirty minutes before he was killed,' said Palmer bluntly.

Perryman was visibly taken aback. 'Oh, dear God – he was one of those killed?'

'Yes he was,' said Palmer. 'Can you throw any light on why one of the capital's organised crime bosses should come in here?'

'Well, sinners do repent – he could have been coming to confession. We operate the confessional from 10am to 5pm daily. Mind you, I was on duty that day taking confessions and I don't recall that face. Perhaps he just came in to pray.'

'I doubt it.'

'I could show the picture to the other clergy?'

'No, no that's not necessary just yet,' If one of the clergy was involved with Dawn, Palmer certainly didn't want to send out alarm signals and frighten them into hiding. 'No, not yet. But I may want to have a chat with them later though. Could we take a look around?'

'Of course, of course.' Perryman leant close to them and looked around furtively before asking in a whisper, 'Are you looking for a dead drop? You think the gang has got a secret dead drop in the cathedral, don't you?'

Palmer looked at him. 'A dead drop?'

'Yes, a place where the dealer picks up his stash and leaves his wad.'

'A *dead drop*, a *stash*, and a *wad*.' Palmer looked at Perryman sympathetically. 'Mr Perryman, I think you've been watching too much Netflix. Come on, give us the tour.'

Perryman did just that, from the cellars with unknown clergymen's sarcophagi stacked on top of each other, through the Knave, the North and South Transepts, Lancelot's Link to the Archaeological Chamber; and then the Harward Chapel, Sanctuary the Choir, into the Herb Garden, and finally a trip up the Bell Tower, whose one hundred and twenty two steps didn't do Palmer's sciatica any good. All the while, he and Gheeta had their eyes peeled for boxes; small boxes.

'And that just about does it,' said Perryman. 'Very impressive, eh?'

'Yes, and very exhausting too,' said Palmer. 'How many of those tours do you do a day?'

'Oh no, weekends only – unless it's a school party that has to come in school time.'

They walked slowly along the side of the knave towards the main entrance and past the confessional.

'I'll wait outside if you want to unload, guv,' said Gheeta, nodding towards it with a cheeky smile. 'I've got an hour to spare.'

'Take a look.' Perryman pushed open the clergy's door to the box and Palmer poked his head inside.

'Small, isn't it? I wouldn't fancy being sat in there for any length of time; claustrophobic.' Then he spied the small stack of shoe box size cartons under the Clergy's seat and his heart missed a beat. 'What's in those boxes?'

Perryman pulled a box out and opened it. 'Candles, altar candles. We go through quite a few boxes of these every month. They come all the way from the Vatican.'

'Pound Shop would be cheaper wouldn't it, or Amazon?'

'That would be much cheaper, yes,' Perryman laughed. 'But our candles have to be blessed by the Pope.'

'Are you kidding?'

'No, once a month the Pope visits the warehouse of the Italian manufacturer and blesses all the stock before it can be sent out around the world.' He pulled out two candles from a box and gave them to Palmer. 'Here, a memento of your tour.'

'Thank you.' Palmer gave one to Gheeta. 'Quite hefty, aren't they?'

'Ten inches tall and three inches diameter, twenty to a box,' Arbuthnot Perryman volunteered.

'And they are sent all round the world, to all the Catholic places of worship from the one factory in Italy?'

'Well, promise not to tell anybody, but not to *every* Church – logistically impossible. But all the cathedrals and main churches, yes.'

'Nice contract for DHL,' said Gheeta.

'Oh no, the Vatican has a diplomatic bag.'

'If they are sent all around the world, you'll need a few hundred diplomatic bags,' said Palmer.

Perryman laughed. 'It's just a generic term, not actual bags. It means that the Vatican can send stuff worldwide avoiding time-consuming Customs checks and paperwork if the Pontiff's seal is on the parcel, or in the case of these candles, on the crate. We get a crate every month.'

If the alarm bells ringing in Palmer's head were audible, they would have drowned out the ones in the cathedral belfry had they been pealing at that time. 'No Customs checks?'

'No, none. Means our courier this end can pick up the crate straight from the plane when it lands. Keeps our costs down.'

Palmer and Gheeta were looking straight at each other by now, amazed at what they were hearing.

'How often does a crate come in, did you say?' Palmer asked as calmly as possible.

'Once a month. In fact, one's due in on Sunday on an Alitalia flight from Rome to Heathrow.'

Gheeta had a question. 'Do you actually keep a stock check on the candles?'

Perryman was taken aback. 'A stock check? No, why? Do you think somebody might be taking a couple home to save on the electricity bill?' He laughed at his own comment.

Gheeta laughed back, a false laugh.

'Right then, things to do, people to see, places to go!' Palmer smiled at

Perryman. 'Thank you for your time, Mr Perryman. A most interesting tour.'

'You are very welcome, Detective.'

'It's Detective *Chief Superintendent*,' Palmer said gruffly as he turned and walked away towards the entrance.

'Oh dear.' Perryman looked apologetically at Gheeta, who smiled back sympathetically before following her boss.

Arbuthnot Perryman sat down on the nearest pew once they had left. He was starting to shake.

****

'Amazon Prime,' said Mrs P. 'Get things the next day, guaranteed. You didn't know that, did you? Thought it was just the TV channel and free books.' She was standing beside Palmer in the bedroom that evening, looking at an assortment of men's clothes arranged on their double bed and more on the bedroom chairs.

'Have you bought a whole shop?' asked Palmer.

'Five suits, all different colours; two sports jackets – unfortunately I couldn't find a Prince of Wales check one...'

'I bet you tried really hard,' said Palmer sarcastically.

'...four Fred Perry jumpers, four shirts, two pairs of leather shoes and two ties.'

'What if they don't fit?'

'Justin, you've been the same size for the last twenty years – they will fit. If I could find the secret of how you stayed the same size and weight for so long, I'd make a fortune!' She waved a hand over the assembled clothes. 'This, Justin Palmer, is the new you – welcome to the twenty-first century.' She gave him a peck on the cheek.

Chapter 6   SATURDAY

Weekends count for nothing when an investigation is ongoing, and when the investigation is as high profile as this one evenings and nights are often forfeited in the name of progress as well. Palmer quite liked working Saturdays as it made a change from the weekly supermarket shop, or at the first sign of spring a weekly visit to a garden centre to follow Mrs P. around, trying not to drop one of many 'bargain' pots of plants she loaded onto him.

Reg Frome was waiting in the Team Room when Palmer arrived.

'Blimey Reg, you're up early for a Saturday aren't you? Wet the bed?'

'Oh, very funny.' They shook hands. 'No, I thought you'd like to know the forensic results on what we found at the murder scenes.'

Reg Frome had started at the Hendon Police College the same year as Palmer and they had remained friends and compatriots in the fight against crime ever since. Frome had taken the path into Forensic Science and was now the top man in the

Yard's Murder Forensic Unit, whilst Palmer had stayed on the normal police path into CID and then the Murder Squad, and now as boss of the Serial Murder Squad.

Gheeta and Claire arrived as Palmer was taking off his coat, as did Johnson and Simms who had taken breakfast in the canteen; they all had their usual cups of coffee in one hand.

'Aah, that's very kind of you Sergeant,' said Frome, kidding them and holding out his hand to Gheeta for her coffee. She sheltered her cup from him and put it down on her desk.

'I'll pop up to the fifth floor and get you a cup Mr Frome if you like?' said Claire.

'I wouldn't, Reg,' Palmer advised him. 'Coloured water with ten spoons of sugar.'

'You've got a machine on this floor, what's wrong with that?' asked Frome.

'Coloured water with twenty spoons of sugar.' Palmer noticed Gheeta staring at him. 'What? What's wrong? It's dishwater by another name.'

'Nothing. Nothing's *wrong with the coffee* – it's you, guv. Something is different and I've just noticed – you're wearing a suit. A *new* suit.'

They all looked at Palmer.

'My God, so you are,' Frome expressed amazement. 'What happened to the Prince of Wales check jacket, the one with the ink stain on the lapel – did it finally fall apart? And where are the gray flannels?'

'Her indoors gave them all to a charity shop.' Palmer was a bit taken aback; he hadn't realised his 'ink stain' was so famous.

'A charity shop? No, Victoria and Albert more likely!'

Gheeta was impressed. 'Love the colour, guv. Deep blue suits you.' She covered her mouth as though in shock. 'And no turn-ups, my God. I never thought I'd see the day.'

Claire joined in and pointed at his feet, snug in a pair of patent leather shoes. 'The suede shoes, sir – have they gone too?'

Palmer thought he'd better end this conversation before his whole past wardrobe was slandered. 'All right, all right, that's enough. We have a case to solve here so let's get on, eh? Right Reg, carry on. What have you got for us?'

They all sat down as Frome opened his file and passed round copy photos as he spoke. 'Two guns used at the car shooting: one we don't know, haven't come across it before – we've done an analysis of the bullet and it doesn't look like this gun has been used in any previously reported crime either. The other is an old favourite of ours, we think it's a Glock 19; holds fifteen 9 millimetre rounds, and this particular one has been used in three major robberies and two street murders in different parts of the UK, so it looks like it's a rental or belongs to a travelling hitman.

'So, the bottom line is that if we get a gun seized with ammo that matches the bullets used in these murders, we can link the owner to the case. That doesn't really push the case on much, but this might; the back seat and the road outside the rear nearside passenger door had traces of cocaine on them. Quite a fair amount too, as though somebody was carrying a quantity out of the car in a bag and it was leaking.'

'That could square with the candle boxes Dawn was carrying from the cathedral being in the back of the car when the hit took place, and maybe taking a bullet.'

Frome raised his eyebrows and checked his notes. 'The *candle* boxes? No boxes in the car.'

'Don't worry about it, Reg; take too long to explain and it's just a lead we are looking at,' Palmer dismissed it.

'Okay.' Frome passed his file to Palmer. 'There's a number of photos of the scene in there, including the bodies in situ. The car and guns that the three men with Dawn had in their coats have gone down to ballistics to test fire and see if we can't match any of them to recorded crimes. As you know their bodies are now over in the Murder Morgue; Organised Crime have identified them and we are waiting for families to positively ID.

'Now, the gun that shot the fatal bullets into Alfred Dawn at the Hospital is the same Glock 19 used in the Walworth Road; so it looks like the killer went straight from the car shooting to the hospital, and that's it.'

'That timeframe works, guv,' said Gheeta, checking her screen. 'As far as I can work out there was a forty-five minute gap between the first 999 calls being received about the Walworth Road shooting and the discovery of Alfred Dawn's body at the hospital.'

Palmer nodded. 'Just about spot on for a scooter to do the journey. Thanks Reg, the cocaine bit is very interesting – could tie a few things together nicely. Right people, back to work – Simms and Johnson, you two keep tabs on Eve Dawn, see who comes and goes at her place. Something will break soon, I'm sure of it.'

****

The tyre and exhaust business was doing well. Stan Dawn sat in his glass-fronted office at the back of the premises off the Stockwell Road and watched as his mechanics worked on several vehicles raised up on the hydraulic ramps for a new exhaust or up on jacks for new tyres. Saturdays were always busy and today was no exception. In the customer waiting area the punters sat reading the papers and magazines Stan provided each day and helped themselves to his free tea and coffee machine. In the corner his two minders sat sipping their third coffees of the day and playing cards, their presence a visual warning to anybody questioning Stan's exorbitant bills.

Stan sat back in his swivel chair; it was all going to plan, so far so good. He hadn't been sure what might happen when he had first approached Jack Dooley with his plan.

'Hang on Stan, let me get this right.' Dooley had been taken by surprise by the offer. 'You want to team up with me and hit James and Dad, take over the South London manor, combine it with my West End and run it together as partners?'

'Yes.'

'You actually want to kill your own brother and son-in-law?' Dooley found it hard to believe what he was hearing. 'Are you for real?'

'Yes. I've had enough, Jack. They've never appreciated me, never. I should have been given the top spot when Alf got ill, but James got it. I built this manor with Alf – any problems along the way, any nasty business needed doing, who got called to do it, eh? Me. And now what have I got? Shunted into the sidings playing second fiddle to my son-in-law – I was handling fifty dealers when he was in short trousers.

'I've had enough, Jack. It should be mine by rights now, and if the only way to get it is this way then so be it. I'm getting on a bit Jack, and it's time I got my proper recognition. You can be in or out Jack, but one way or the other, I'm taking over in South London.'

'What about Eve?'

'I don't kill women – especially ones you're knocking off.' He gave Dooley a knowing stare.

'How long have you known?'

'Right from the start. I thought it was bloody obvious, watching you two at the charity boxing evenings that Alf sponsored – you couldn't take your eyes off her. I could have had a quiet word with James back then and you'd be brown bread by now Jack, you know that.'

'Why didn't you? You and him could have used it as an excuse to hit me and go for my patch?'

'No, not in my plans, Jack. I've told you my plan and it's going to happen with or without you. Make your mind up. Oh, and one other thing – James knows about Harry Jones skimming money to give to you. He's not exactly happy.'

Jack Dooley thought for a few moments. If Stan went ahead and took control of South London then he might get ideas about adding the West End, so Dooley would have to be continually watching his back; safer to be in the tent than outside looking over your shoulder all the time. But he needed to cover his back in case it all went wrong. And then there was the skimming of the Dawn money; James would certainly want retribution for that. He could only really come to one decision.

'Okay, I'm in. But we use outside people for the hits, or I'm going to obviously be suspect number one, aren't I. Make it look like a drug deal with another firm went wrong. And Eve stays safe.'

Stan nodded. 'Eve stays safe.'

And so far, it had all worked out perfectly. Now Stan had to think about what to do about Eve. He'd tell Jack to work on her, keep her in line; get any notion of 'being in charge' out of her head. He was now in charge with Jack and she had to accept it.

His thoughts were interrupted by the roar of two scooters coming in off the road. They halted beside each other outside the office. In the waiting room the minders' hands moved inside their bulky jackets. One of the pillion riders swung off the scooter and walked into the office; all kept their helmets on. Stan nodded to his minders who relaxed, sat back down.

'Any problems?' Stan asked.

'No,' said a muffled voice from inside the helmet. 'All good.'

'Those aren't the scooters you used, are they? I gave you a scrap yard address to take them to.'

'No, don't worry. We took them to the yard and watched them crushed.'

'Good lads.' Stan stood up and went to a wall safe behind his desk, keyed in the code on the keypad and opened it. The rider's hand was quickly into his jacket, which movement had the minders up on their feet and their hands snaking inside their jackets too. Stan held a hand up, waving it side to side to diffuse the situation.

'Steady on son, steady. I'm getting your payment out, that's all – no funny business.'

The rider kept his hand inside his jacket as Stan drew out two brown envelopes from the safe, closed it and put them on the desk in front of him.

'Twenty grand, used notes – as arranged.'

The rider picked them up and pushed them inside his jacket. 'I'll check it later. Better be right, or we'll be back.'

'It's right, I may need your services again soon. I'll be in touch.'

The rider turned to go.

'Hang on.' Stan's voice was serious. 'You have something for me?'

'Don't panic, just going to get it.'

He walked out to the scooter and fetched the two candle boxes from the panniers and handed them over.

'One took a hit. I patched it, but it will be a bit short.'

Stan took the boxes. 'Okay, I can wear that.' He slit the boxes open with a knife from the drawer and checked inside. 'Looks good.'

They gave each other a curt nod of approval and nothing more was said as the pillion rider took the back seat on his scooter and both scooters drove out onto the main road.

Stan sat back and looked at the boxes and a big smile crossed his face. Life was looking good, the plan was coming together. The tie-up with Jack Dooley had been taking a chance, it could have gone either way; Dooley could have slipped the word to James that Stan was looking to oust him and take over, and he would have been well rewarded for the tip off. But he hadn't; it was working so far. Dooley would be the main police suspect as the one who arranged the hits, even though the scooter boys were outsiders; the police would be concentrating on Dooley.

So that just left Eve to take care of now. His thoughts turned back to her; he didn't trust her, even though Dooley said he could control her. No, if she thought she was taking over she could think again – get her out of the picture and then it was plain sailing, and with South London and the West End under one banner they would be a major player in the game; Stan would get the respect he thought he deserved, and then, sometime in the near future, he would take Dooley out as well and become invincible. Well, that was Stan's plan.

So engrossed was he in those thoughts that the two scooters had roared back in off the road and screeched to halt in front of his office and the customer's area before he realised. A hail of bullets from the pillion rider he'd done business with slammed into his upper body and head. Stan's plan was dead.

The two minders were getting to their feet and reaching in their coats for their guns as the second pillion rider's scooter rode through the customer area doorway and he loosed off nearly a full magazine into them. Both scooters were out of the premises and away down the road before most of the mechanics and customers had realised what was happening.

****

The police crime scene tape stretched along the front of Stockwell Tyres and Exhausts and swayed in the light breeze. Two uniformed officers kept control of the growing number of the public who were attracted by the presence of the police cars, the flashing lights and the media activity. Crime screens had been erected across the front of the property. Media vans were arriving in convoy and their rooftop satellite dishes were opening up like oysters.

Palmer had his driver drop him and Gheeta a little further down the road and they walked along to the tape, which was held up for them to duck under. The press shouted questions.

'How many dead Mr Palmer?'

'Is it Stan Dawn, Mr Palmer?'

'Was it another drive-by?'

'Have there been any arrests?'

Gheeta pointed to a uniformed DI who seemed to be supervising the crime scene. 'Looks like he's the OIC, guv.'

They walked over and Palmer introduced himself and Gheeta. DI Coleman from Brixton Uniformed Branch was glad to see them; he was more used to traffic accidents than multiple murders. He brought them up to speed.

'We got the call about an hour and a half ago, or should I say calls – the phone lines went red hot. Three bodies, all shot dead: one in the office and two in the public waiting area. Seems that two scooters were ridden into the premises and the pillion riders did the shooting. Apparently they'd been in a few minutes before doing some business with the owner, they knew who to target. All three dead are known to us; Stanley Dawn seems to have been the main target and the other two were minor players in the organised crime scene and it would appear they were his minders, only on this occasion they didn't do a very good job.

'Obviously we are aware of the Walworth Road shooting of his nephew and the hospital murder of his dad, and as this has the same MOD I had my CID give the OC unit at the Yard a call and they passed it through to you. Sorry, I didn't realise that you'd got it – I naturally thought Organised Crime would be handling it.'

'That's okay,' said Palmer. 'They are a bit overwhelmed at the moment, so it landed on my desk.'

'Overwhelmed and understaffed you mean. Bloody stupid politicians – never learn, will they? I sometimes think they are on the side of the criminals.'

Palmer liked Coleman. 'I couldn't possibly comment,' he said.

That makes a change, thought Gheeta.

'What about witnesses?' asked Palmer.

'We've got five employees and two members of the public who were waiting for their cars. I've got them at the station giving statements.'

'Well done.' Palmer was relieved that he hadn't got to organise that. 'Any CCTV?'

'None.'

'Really?'

'Characters like Stanley Dawn are naturally camera shy.' Coleman smiled a knowing smile.

Palmer indicated the covered bodies of Stan and the minders. 'Anything been moved?'

'No, nothing, and nobody has been allowed into the office or the customer area except the medical first responders. They couldn't do anything for the victims so I had them covered up to wait for the doctor to legally pronounce them dead and then we can move them to the morgue. SOCO should have a clean area to work in. By the way, I haven't asked our Forensics to attend as I assumed you or OC would have your own team.'

'Yes, we have.' Palmer turned to Gheeta. 'Give Reg Frome a call and have him attend please, Sergeant. Right, well done Coleman, good job. Let me have copies of the witness statements when they are completed and keep us in the loop if you hear anything on the local grapevine please'

Gheeta was holding her mobile to her ear calling Reg Frome and had to twist her other hand to pull a business card from her tunic pocket, which she gave to Coleman. 'It's a direct line to the office.'

Coleman took it and remembered something. 'Oh, there was one thing – when our chaps got here there were a couple of the local crackheads stealing tools. One of them had two boxes of large candles as well, they're on the floor inside the office. We've got the pair of them in custody and I'll send their fingerprints through so you can eliminate them. I don't think they'll have anything to do with the murders – the only thing they shoot is cocaine into their veins.'

****

It was just over an hour before Reg Frome and his team arrived in a SOCO van. Palmer was itching to get into Stanley Dawn's office and had to be patient and wait. Gheeta had fetched coffees and cakes from the local coffee shop and the pair of them had settled in the back of a local patrol car to wait. Palmer suggested Coleman had the crime scene extended a good fifty metres either side of the tyre shop to get the public and media back out of the way, which Coleman did before officially handing over the crime scene to

Palmer, who would hand it over to Frome when he arrived.

When he did arrive, Palmer was round to the rear of the SOCO van pulling on a pair of plastic overshoes and gloves like a flash.

'What kept you?' he admonished Frome. 'Take the pretty route?'

'You cheeky bugger, we haven't stopped since I left you this morning,' said Frome. 'You're lucky you didn't have to wait until tomorrow. Two more kids knifed in Hackney, one DOA and another fighting for his life – that's seven in that area so far this month, and right in the Shadow Home Secretary's constituency, so you can imagine that the proverbial has hit the fan at the Home Office. PM will get roasted at the next PMQs.' He looked at Palmer's feet. 'You've got them on the wrong feet.'

'What?'

'Wrong way round, the overshoes are on the wrong feet.'

Palmer bent down and started to undo one and then realised that Frome's SOCO officers were stifling laughter. He stood back up, realising he'd been had; it didn't matter, one size fits all.

'Oh, very funny.'

'Come on.' Frome led the way onto the crime scene. 'Take large steps and don't move anything without telling me.' He sent his team to the far end of the unit and told them to work their way in line up towards the office doing a fingertip search, picking up anything loose on the floor and bagging it in evidence bags; ninety-nine point nine percent of the items would be of no consequence to the investigation whatsoever, but you never knew.

In the office, Palmer pointed to the two open boxes of candles Stan Dawn had put by the door and called Frome over.

'Reg, I'd like your people to take out one of those candles and have a look inside it. I suspect it's going to be hollow, with either coke or crystal meth inside. Can you do that here?'

'Yes, can't do them all here but can take a sample from one.'

'That will be fine.'

Frome went to the SOCO van and returned with a small battery powered drill. He took out one of the candles and carefully placed it just inside the opening of a plastic evidence bag and drilled halfway into it. Pulling out the drill, they could all see the white powder in its twists.

'Looks like you are right, Justin. I'd say cocaine.'

Frome gently shook a very small sample off the drill head into a five-by-ten-centimetre plastic envelope that had small ampoules of chemical liquid inside it. He finger-crushed one and the clear liquid mixed with the powder and turned blue.

'Cocaine it is. If all those candles are full of the stuff that's a big money haul, Justin.'

'That's only part of it – there's a crate of them coming into the UK tomorrow on a commercial flight. I think we'd better meet and greet.'

'You think this is what the Dawn family deaths are all about, drugs?' asked Frome.

'Looks that way – somebody's expanding their empire, or somebody hasn't paid for what they should have paid for. Who knows? Okay that's fine, thank you Reg – let me know if anything else turns up. The picture is still a bit fuzzy, but it's building nicely.'

He turned to Gheeta as Frome went off to rejoin his team on the fingertip search. 'Right Sergeant, I don't think we can do anymore today – give Claire a call and tell her to knock off. I think we might as well do the same.'

'There's a wall safe, guv. Might be interesting contents?' She pointed to it.

'Is it open?'

'No but it could be.'

Palmer smiled at the coded implication of 'could be'. 'Okay, let's take a look.'

They walked round the desk to where the safe was located at head height on the back wall. It was shut and had a keypad lock. Palmer carried a pair of lock picks on his key ring which had come in useful in past cases, but keypad code locks were beyond him to open; but he knew a person who probably could.

He looked at Gheeta.

'Shame it's not open,' he hinted.

Gheeta took out her iPhone and pulled up an app that was blank. She looked at the safe's keypad; it was two numbers across and five deep, ten in all, numbered one to nine and zero. She keyed that format into the app, which divided into a ten digit blank template that matched the keypad, and then held the phone screen against the keypad and took a close-up photo. Palmer watched as Gheeta pressed a string of commands on the phone.

'There you go, guv.' She held the screen so they both could see it.

'There you go what?' All Palmer could see was a screenshot of the keypad.

'Can you see that four of the digits are much darker than the others?'

'Yes.'

'That's the patination on them – in other words, the very fine coating of oil left on them from years of being pressed by fingers. It has ever so slightly discoloured them; hardly noticeable to the human eye, but the app has enhanced them. So the code on this keypad is made up of the numbers 2941.

'Okay, so we stand here and put in all the combinations of those numbers? Be here for days.'

'Ten thousand possible combinations, guv.'

'Sergeant Singh, I can tell by your smile that we aren't going to stand here for days going through ten thousand combinations, are we?'

'Maybe guv, but I hope not. If Stanley Dawn falls into the normal way of doing these things, then it's going to be 1942 or 1924.'

'Why?'

'Because ninety-five percent of people using a keypad number use their own or somebody else's birthday year as the code. Stanley Dawn and all his family and friends will have been born in the nineteen hundreds, so the first two digits, hopefully, will be 1 and 9, and that just leaves two options for the last two. Fingers crossed Stanley followed the crowd.' She waved her hand at the safe. 'After you, guv.'

Palmer hit the buttons, 1, 9, 2, 4 and turned the handle. The safe swung open. He was impressed. 'Don't tell me you wrote that programme?'

'No guv, not one of mine – it's a prototype they're working on at PITO. I still have my contacts.' She smiled knowingly.

The Police Information Technology Organisation works at the cutting edge of modern technology and is part of the Cyber Crime Technology Department that Palmer prised Gheeta away from to join his Squad; the best move he ever made.

The safe housed a few large office ledgers and a tin. Palmer reached in and took out a ledger. Laying it on the office desk, he opened it and looked through the first few pages.

'This is Harry Jones's financial dealings, money in and money out. Why would Stanley Dawn want that?'

'Depends whose money is going in and who it's going out to, guv. Jones was put away for laundering; bottom line, it tells the story of his business dealings with the Dawns. I don't think he'd want HMRC to get hold of that.'

Palmer closed the ledger and pulled the others out as well. 'They could be interesting, might give us a lead as to why Harry Jones took a one-way trip to Panama. I think I'll get Reg to have that forensic accountant chap of his to take a look.'

'DS Atkins,' said Gheeta. She reached inside the safe and pulled out the tin. 'This is heavy.' She shook it. 'Sounds like metal.'

'Careful,' said Palmer. 'Could be bullets.'

It wasn't bullets. It was forty Krugerrands; solid gold South African one ounce coins.

'That's a nice little nest egg,' said Palmer. 'Each one is worth about a thousand pounds.'

'You think they are from a robbery, guv?'

'No, I think they've been bought with drug money. It's a well-known way of washing small amounts of money: buy the coins for cash from coin dealers or at auctions, sell them onto the jewellery trade at spot price for smelting and get paid with a bona fide cheque which can be banked legally. The original stolen banknotes have disappeared, and the cheque amounts to near enough the same as the original notes, or more if the gold price has gone up.'

The phone on the desk rang. They looked at each other.

'Answer it, probably somebody wanting to book their car in.'

Gheeta picked up the receiver. 'Hello, can I help you? Hello? Hello?' She turned to Palmer. 'Whoever it was they rang off, guv.' She replaced the receiver and dialled 141; taking her notebook from her tunic pocket, she wrote down the number that had called. 'I'll check the number out back at the office.'

Chapter 7 SUNDAY

'Is it on time?'

Palmer and Gheeta had been met at Heathrow by Robert Vale, Senior Team Leader at Border Force Control, who was taking them through the baggage carousels where returning holidaymakers and visitors to the UK waited patiently for their luggage to appear through the flapper vents onto the circling carousels.

'It landed a bit early actually,' said Vale. 'Unusual I know, but it does happen sometimes when the plane gets a good tail wind pushing it along. Through here please.'

He led them to a plain door at the back of the public area and tapped in a code on the keypad; Palmer couldn't resist a sideways smile at Gheeta. Vale held it open as they walked through onto a steel platform at the top of one side of a massive warehouse-type building, with baggage handling conveyor belts criss-crossing each other mid-air as they carried luggage up to the right carousels in the public area. From the platform, an enclosed metal staircase zig-zagged down to the floor. It was noisy and the staff who made sure everything ran smoothly wore ear defenders and overalls. At the far end the electric tractor units that pulled the trailers of luggage from the aircraft into the warehouse bashed their way through the large entrance, pushing aside the weather protection hanging strips of thick plastic, and then stopped to have their heaped contents pulled off and put on the scanner feeds, one for each carousel.

Vale led them through and past the scanners into a back room where the silence was a merciful relief. The Air Italia crate was sitting on the conveyer belt feed to a solitary scanner sat in the middle of the room where two operators in blue overalls waited. They nodded acknowledgements when Vale introduced Palmer.

'Okay,' Vale gave the order. 'Let's have a good look at it then.'

One of the operators pressed the button and the crate moved slowly into the scanner until its X-ray was showing in full on the screen where he stopped it. The operator, who Palmer took to be the senior of the two, pointed to the scan on the screen which was showing the outline of the crate and the candles packed inside it clearly as oblong shapes.

'Right,' he said. 'You can see the outlines of the contents...'

'Candles,' said Palmer.

'Oh, really? We did wonder... Anyway, you can see there's six boxes in the middle of the crate where the candles are a distinctly darker shade than the rest. That brown shade usually means an organic material.'

'Like drugs?' asked Palmer.

'Very much like drugs, and it usually is.'

Vale looked at Palmer. 'If you would like us to open the crate and test one of the candles we can do, but I'll have to have it taken to the secure bio room to do that. Can't do it here.'

Palmer thought for a moment. 'No, no I don't think that is necessary – we have a good idea what's in them. You chaps have confirmed what we thought would be inside the crate. If you could move it out and turn it on its side, please.'

As they did that a uniformed security officer came in and spoke to Vale, who turned to Palmer.

'The courier who's picking this up is getting agitated. It's diplomatic label so should be first off the plane.'

Palmer nodded. 'Stall him for a few minutes if you would.'

Vale understood. 'Tell him it went with the public luggage by mistake and is on its way back down,' he said to the officer, who left to relay the news.

Once the crate was back out and on its side, Gheeta took a five centimetre metal button tracker from her pocket and removing the cover of the adhesive on its flat back, she pressed it firmly onto the inside of one of the wooden strengthening ribs of the crate where it stuck fast.

'That's it, she's all yours Mr Vale. Thank you for your time, gentlemen.' Palmer shook their hands. 'Job well done.'

Vale was surprised. 'I take it the button is a tracker? Bit small for a GPS unit, isn't it?'

Palmer turned to Gheeta to answer.

'It's not GPS, Mr Vale. It's an LAHD, a limited area homing device. The signal can be picked up within about two hundred yards; a bit like the key fob signal on your car key, but a little stronger.'

Palmer added, 'You see, we know where the crate is going but we need to know that it's there. No good doing a raid and it's not there.'

Gheeta took her laptop from its satchel and turned it on. 'Just want to check it's all functioning, sir.'

It was, she picked up a strong signal.

****

Palmer pulled his beloved eight-year-old Honda CRV into his drive and parked up. It was Sunday, so there would be a nice meal waiting for him; a roast, or one of Mrs P.'s steak and kidney pies. His stomach rumbled in anticipation as he opened the front door and was met in the hall by Daisy with her lead in her mouth, looking expectantly to be taken for a run around Dulwich Park.

Palmer patted her and stepped over the row of charity bin bags and hung his trilby and coat on the hall stand. 'Later, let me have my meal first and then we'll go out.'

Daisy understood; in fact, like most dogs she understood a great deal more than her master gave her credit for. She dropped the lead, padded back to her bed at the bottom of the stairs and curled up to wait.

'We are in the kitchen,' came the call from Mrs P.

We? Visitors? Probably somebody from the WI or her Gardening Club. It was too early in the year to plant seeds, but already Mrs P. had been planning what would go where and which vegetables she was going to grow and which not. Palmer put her great interest in gardening down to her childhood; like him she'd been brought up in a semi-detached council house in South London, with a small garden that her elder brothers had requisitioned as a football pitch in the winter and a cricket pitch in the summer.

So as Palmer's salary had progressed upward in line with his promotions, they had moved up from their first marital home of a Brixton flat to the detached four-bedroom Victorian house with large garden in Dulwich where they now lived. It was too big really now that the children had fled the nest, and Palmer was in favour of downsizing; but Mrs P. insisted that the next move would be their final one, and favoured a large modern bungalow on the coast with a large garden to potter about in. Palmer couldn't argue with that.

The visitor in the kitchen was Benji. He was sat at the table, tucking into Mrs P.'s steak and kidney pie.

'Oi! I thought you were vegetarian?' Palmer's first thought was that it could be his portion of pie on Benji's plate.

Benji feigned surprise and stood up. 'Hello, I'm Benji, and you must be Justin's twin brother.' He turned to Mrs P. 'I didn't know he had a twin, and such a well-dressed twin!'

Palmer realised Benji was being sarcastic about his new suit. 'Ha ha, very funny,' said Palmer drolly. 'If that's my portion of pie you'll be under arrest for theft.'

'It's not yours,' said Mrs P. 'There's plenty in the oven. Benji came over to pick up the charity bags and take them to the council shop.' She opened the oven and dished up Palmer's plate, as he took off his hat and coat and put them on the hallstand outside before sitting at the table.

'I was going to pick up a takeaway on my way back, but your good lady wife insisted I have this.'

'It's meat, you don't eat meat. You went vegetarian a couple of months back. Or has all that gone by the board now?'

'No, no, but a little diversion now and again doesn't hurt, does it. You know I've lost nearly a stone since I went veggie Justin – does it show?' He sat up and patted his stomach.

'No.'

'Yes it does,' said Mrs P., glaring at Palmer.

'And I feel much fitter,' added Benji.

'Good, then you can carry the charity bags out by yourself.'

'You know, I couldn't believe it when Mrs P. said you'd actually got rid of that awful Prince of Wales jacket – you know, the one with the ink stain on the lapel. I thought they'd have to operate to get that off you!'

Chapter 8 MONDAY

'I hate working weekends,' was Palmer's opening salvo as he arrived in the Team Room on the Monday morning. The rest of the Squad were already there plus one other, all with their usual coffees in their hands. 'You lose track of which day it is.'

'Crime doesn't take days off, guv,' said Gheeta, who was sitting at a table with Claire and a young man whom Palmer recognised.

'Detective Sergeant Atkins – how are you, young man?'

They shook hands. DS Atkins was a Forensic Accountant attached to Reg Frome's department; his skill was in analysing financial crime and dismantling the complicated frauds that many city types build for their own enrichment: the Ponzi schemes and equity release rip-offs.

'I'm good sir, thank you.' He pointed to the ledgers from Stan Dawn's safe on the table in front of him. 'You seem to have uncovered a can of worms here, sir.'

'Really?' Palmer slipped of his coat and trilby and sat down at the desk. 'Right then, what have we got?' He purposely ignored the exaggerated looks of approval Claire and Gheeta gave to his new brown suit and brown brogues.

DS Atkins took them through the ledger's contents. 'Harry Jones, disgraced solicitor who your sergeant tells me you know all about; he came out of jail and promptly flew to Panama – again, you know all this. But what you may not be aware of is the extent of his financial dealings in the criminal world. The pages in this ledger are his accounts of monies lodged with him by various organised crime gangs, which he has entered under various pseudonyms as clients' deposit money into his company's client account, listing them as property funds belonging to fictitious property buyers and sellers. This meant he could put say a hundred thousand in as the buyer's deposit and then transfer it out to another account as payment to the seller at a later date, making the transaction look like a normal property purchase, less his commission – and he certainly charged a hefty commission. It's a clever and clean way to launder money; it appears all above board until you check on the properties and find they never existed, which is what the Fraud Squad did and why Jones was originally arrested. But I don't think the FS knew the extent of his fraud because there was a fire at his offices before they had searched it, and they assumed all the financial records were destroyed. I checked their case file and all they could get him on was one transaction, and that was a plea bargain. He agreed to plead guilty to that one if all the others were dropped, and as most of the others relied on circumstantial evidence, it suited the FS to drop them. If they had the ledgers and the information they contain in their possession at that time, they would never have offered him a plea; this information would put him away for a considerably longer period than three years, and take a few names down with him.' He pointed to one of the ledgers. 'This is the major ledger detailing all his financial dealings for the period of the last year before he was arrested. This is documentary evidence, not just circumstantial, and documentary evidence can be used to secure a conviction; it can't be dismissed by a judge, whereas circumstantial evidence can.'

Atkins took a deep breath. 'Now we come to the shifting of the funds themselves, and these entries throw up an interesting scenario. Jones's two biggest clients by a long way were the Dawn family and Jack Dooley; there are many more, but those are mainly bit players dealing in tens of thousands of pounds on an ad hoc basis. The Dawns and Dooley were shifting millions regularly; about a quarter of the washed money was being transferred by Jones to foreign bank accounts in Panama, Belgium and Spain as proceeds for non-existent London property sales, as I explained earlier. He was using the offices of Mossac Fonsec in Panama for the majority of the transfers – I'm sure you have heard of them, and the 'Panama Papers' which was an exposé of that company's criminal dealings. My experience in this type of crime points to those accounts probably belonging to the Dawns' and Dooley's suppliers of whatever narcotics they were buying at that time. The rest of the washed money, the Dawns' and Dooley's profit, went into various UK bank accounts and was either taken out in cash or transferred onwards to other business accounts, one being the nail bars that Eve Dawn runs, Stan Dawn's tyre business and a host of others, including property developments. A few thousand pounds moving in and out daily wouldn't trigger the laundering alarms at banks; and banking being a competitive and, in my view, a wholly corrupt business anyway, if it did set off alarms they would probably ignore them. Don't quote me on that.' He smiled. Palmer liked Atkins.

'And this is where an abnormality pops up. It seems that Jones was skimming more off the Dawns than the Dooleys, or any others. This wouldn't be out of place as he'd negotiate as much as he could and he may well have different rates between different clients two. But, the extra that he took off Dawn was transferred to Dooley.' He shrugged. 'I don't know why – all I've got are figures, not reasons. And that is about it. I've put it all in my report.' He passed a copy to Gheeta. 'Anything you need clarifying, let me know. I had a chat with the officer in charge of the Fraud Squad's case against Jones, and with this as evidence he's minded to go for a Proceeds of Crime charge to seize money and property. But I can't see that he's going to get much as it's mostly gone abroad; cost more to chase it than he'd get back, but that's up to him.'

Palmer picked up his copy. 'I think you've given us a pointer towards what's going on and who's involved. Good job Atkins, thank you.'

Atkins left and Palmer summarised.

'Everything is pointing at Jack Dooley, isn't it; visits to Harry Jones in the Scrubs with Jones's wife, extra laundered money going from the Dawn account going to Dooley?'

'Dooley was a noticeable absentee at the funeral too,' added Simms. 'You would expect him to be there, or at least send a wreath. We checked the wreaths and there wasn't one from Dooley.'

'What about the North London lot – Robinson. Did they send one?'

'Yes, and Johnny Robinson was there with a couple of his men,' confirmed Johnson. 'The snapper got a few pictures of them.'

'I don't understand why Jones wasn't hit,' said Gheeta. 'The Dawns found out that he's scammed them for a lot of money and yet they put him on a plane to Panama to be with his wife?'

'Perhaps they need him,' suggested Palmer. 'He was the top man for laundering, he's got all the contacts to set it up again quickly. Perhaps the Dawns had a plan to take out Dooley after seeing the ledger and needed Jones. If they took out Dooley and added the West End to their South London patch, they'd need to be turning their drug money into laundered cash pretty quick to pay their bills to whoever is supplying them; and Harry Jones could do that, so they needed to protect him whilst they took out Dooley and then bring him back.'

'But Dooley got wind of the plan and attacked first,' said Gheeta. 'That checks.'

'So why didn't they take out Stan Dawn at the same time, why wait a week?' Simms asked. 'Stan could have retaliated in that time, so why wait?'

Palmer sat back in his chair, pondering that. 'Why indeed? There is another scenario to look at that puts Dooley out of the frame, and that is that Stan Dawn was making a play himself to take over the family business.'

'Why would he do that?' Gheeta couldn't see the sense in that.

'Well, Peter Long at Organised Crime told me that Stan was upset when Alfred Dawn decided to take a back seat and handed over to his son James, without involving Stan in that decision. In the family pecking order, I can see that Stan – being Alfred's brother – would have assumed he'd take over. He was a violent man with a short fuse, so maybe he decided to take control of what he saw as rightly his; after all, he built it all up from scratch with Alfred. James was brought in later.'

'He would have taken out Eve Dawn as well, wouldn't he?' suggested Simms.

'Perhaps he was going to at a later time,' said Gheeta. 'Perhaps he was being clever and making it appear that Dooley had hit them – have a war with Dooley and win, and then take out Eve and be in control of an even bigger turf; two birds with one stone. He would have absolute power of a bigger manor?'

'I think we might be jumping a bit ahead of ourselves here.' Palmer wanted to concentrate on the facts. 'Stan was taken out by the scooter boys, same MO as the car and the hospital killings. I think we concentrate on Jack Dooley for now and run the case as a straight-forward multiple murder investigation before we get into the world of fantasy. Facts, facts, facts – stick to them, and they point to Dooley, so we concentrate on him and his organisation. What would he be planning on doing next?'

'Getting Eve Dawn out of the picture, guv?' suggested Gheeta.

'Yes, she's an unknown quantity to Dooley. If she suspects him, what's her next move – could she rouse the troops to go for him? So he has to decide whether to hit her or not; and if he does, would the Dawn people work with his organisation? So, Johnson, you keep track of Eve Dawn, and Simms, work your lowlife contacts on the street and see what's happening there. Dealers need to make money, so they won't hang around in limbo for long; if Dooley is our killer, then his people will be making offers.'

'And I think I might go to church, guv,' said Gheeta. 'Check on our crate and maybe have another word with Arbuthnot Perryman.'

Palmer raised his eyebrows questioningly. 'Mr Perryman interest you?'

'The phone call to Stan Dawn's office the other day, remember it? The one that hung up?'

'Yes.'

'It came from the Bishop's Office, Southwark Cathedral.'

****

Johnson had found a nice warm cafe opposite Eve Dawn's apartment block that gave a good view of the entrance. He parked his plain squad car outside and settled himself in a window seat with a coffee and a jam doughnut. He smiled to himself: can't be bad, on expenses *and* being paid overtime.

His second mouthful of jam doughnut was stopped in its tracks with his hand halfway to his mouth. Eve Dawn was leaving the building. Johnson watched her coming down the large steps from the entrance foyer as he wiped the jam from his chin onto a napkin – why does the jam in doughnuts always have a secret escape route that finds a way out for the jam to go anywhere except in your mouth!

He hurried from the cafe and got in the car. Eve Dawn was waiting at the kerbside – meeting somebody? No, she hailed a taxi. Johnson followed it at a discreet distance. Damn! He'd got jam on his fingers and now on the steering wheel. He tugged out a tissue from a box on the driver's seat and wiped it. Never again, he told himself, jam doughnuts were off the menu from now on. The taxi wound its way through the traffic to the South London Crematorium where Eve Dawn left it, bought two cones of flower blooms from the stall at the gates, and walked in.

Johnson parked fifty metres down the road and radioed in. 'Johnson to all, Eve Dawn has taken a taxi to the crematorium and looks like she's visiting the remembrance garden. Instructions?'

'Palmer here, Johnson. Keep her in view, we didn't think she was the grieving widow type. Stay on her. Out'

'Will do, Johnson out.'

Palmer came on the radio again, 'Simms, unless you are on a good lead with the dealers, get over and liaise with Johnson. Take over from him at the crematorium in case Eve Dawn is on the lookout for tails.'

'Nothing doing on the streets, sir, nobody new making any offers so will get over with Johnson. Simms out.'

****

Eve Dawn placed the flowers on the grass between the two remembrance plaques, one for James and one for Alfred.

'Do it with feeling,' said a voice from ten metres away along the row of plaques. She looked towards it and caught a glimpse of Dooley out of the corner of her eye, and smiled as he knelt and placed flowers on a plaque. 'Going to get expensive when Stan's plaque is added – three lots of flowers.'

'You took care of him pretty quick, didn't you?' said Eve

'After our phone chat I had second thoughts about a partnership with Stan. I've always believed in attacking before you are attacked, so I did.'

'They haven't released the body from the morgue yet. I'm supposed to go and identify it but made excuses.'

'Are you not worried about a picture getting in the tabloids?'

'No, the public don't know him like they knew James and Dad – his death mask wouldn't sell papers. Anyway, I think you made the right move; ties everything up neatly. Whose plaque are you putting flowers on?'

'No idea, some lady called Daphne Hunt; passed on age 96 in 2005.'

'Is all this necessary, meeting like this? All a bit James Bondish.'

'Yes, just for the time being – best we aren't seen together, or people might put two and two together. It's just until the initial media interest dies down, then the police will shift it onto the back burner and we can carry on with the plan. It seems to be working perfectly, doesn't it?'

'Stan was always gullible, I'm amazed he really thought you'd be his partner in taking out James and Dad; his lust for power must have been incredible to take a chance on you. A few of the men will be quite angry, you know, if they ever find out you called it. James was very generous with his managers – they won't be happy, and now Stan's gone too there's nobody to keep them in order.'

'Nobody will find out I called it. Stan was the man who wanted to be boss; he came to me for a partnership, he organised the scooter boys from Manchester to hit James and Alfred. Just unlucky for him that they were part of the Roonans' firm and I do a lot of business with them, so they tipped me off and I added one more person to the hit list contract.'

'Stan.'

'Yes, it's just business, Eve. I could see the opportunity, and as you said, it ties things up neatly, so I took it. We always said he'd have to go at some later date, didn't we? Believe me, he would have hit you next and probably had a go at me sometime in the future. Don't worry, I have arranged to have meets with the Dawn gang masters; we've put out a rumour that the hits were organised from abroad because money hadn't been paid for supplies. As long as they are getting product to move, gang masters aren't bothered where it comes from, and I've enough product to keep them going as well as my existing dealers. The only ones who could have caused problems were in the car with James, and we know what happened to them. The rest are like sheep, they'll follow one another; once one comes across, the rest will too.'

Eve could see a problem. 'What about Johnny Robinson? He can't be very happy; he must feel threatened.'

'He'll keep his head down – any firm that can take down the Dawns can mop his outfit up in no time. He won't be any trouble, and when he hears it might have been ordered from abroad he'll fade into the shadows crapping himself.'

'What happens now?'

'Play it just like we arranged. You are now the Dawn boss, so we put the word out that you are looking to join with me to keep everything moving and not leave a hole for our Romanian friends to jump in, and we act like it's a business deal. You've been slaughtered by people unknown and need the protection of an organised firm, and that's why we are talking.'

'And Harry Jones?'

'He'll be back in a couple of days. I spoke to him earlier.'

'Good, I've got a lot of cash to be moved.'

'If Harry hadn't got caught and sent down, James wouldn't have got hold of those ledgers and none of this would have happened. Once James saw the ledgers and the details of the scam between me and Harry with the Dawn money, it was only a matter of time before he hit me.

'You think so.'

'I know so. He told Harry at the airport that he was going to take care of me later; and then he would have told Dad about it, who would have felt guilty because he was the one who told James to use Harry for laundering, but only because I recommended Harry to Dad. So James and Dad would have come to the conclusion that I did that so Harry could cream off some of the Dawn money to me. Stan knew that, and that was his lever to team up with me – kill or be killed. Oh yes, sooner or later James would have hit me'

'If he'd found out about our affair he'd have hit you sooner, not later,' Eve laughed.

'Well, that's the bonus of it all – once it settles down, we don't have to hide it.'

'Or keep meeting in cemeteries – not exactly romantic, is it?'

****

Johnson got a flash from Simms's car as it parked up a few cars behind him. He gave him a call.

'Johnson to Simms'

'I'm parked four cars behind you.'

'Yes, I saw you. I'm going into the cemetery to keep an eye on Mrs Dawn.'

'Okay, I'll wait here.'

Johnson left his car and walked into the cemetery grounds. He spied Eve Dawn standing at the far end where the latest remembrance brass-engraved plaques were laid in line. A few other visitors were standing paying respects along that line or milling around the gardens. She seemed to be talking to the plaques. Johnson moved round so he could get a better view of her face. The lips were definitely moving; so were the lips of a middle-aged man about ten metres further along who placed flowers on the plaque in front of him. Johnson flicked his eyes between the two of them; no doubt about it, they were having a conversation! He turned his back on them and walked away.

'Johnson to Simms.'

'Go ahead, Johnson.'

'She's had a meet – middle-aged man in brown overcoat, swept-back jet black hair. He's sort of ringing bells with me, but I can't put a name to him. They're talking at a distance, trying to avoid being seen together.' He took a look round. 'She's on the move now – looks like she's coming back to the gate. He's staying put at the moment.'

'Okay, you stay with him and I'll follow Dawn. Where's her car?'

'She didn't come in one – took a taxi, so she'll probably hail one to go wherever she's going to next.'

'Okay, yeah, I've got her – she's just come out and she's waiting by the gate. Looks like she's waiting for a cab to come along. Yes, she's flagging one now. I'm on it, over and out.'

The man who Dawn had spoken with was on the move towards the main gate as well. Johnson had all the training he needed for covert surveillance and headed towards the gate well in front of him; trailing somebody doesn't mean you have to follow behind if you know where they are going.

He got into his car just as the man came out of the gate and walked towards him; he passed without a glance as Johnson

140

made as though he was making a mobile call. In the nearside wing mirror he saw the man get into the rear door of a KIA Sorento. Shit! There must be a driver – had he seen Johnson and put two and two together? The Sorento pulled out and passed by as he carried on his pretend phone call; it had tinted glass, so he couldn't see if anybody inside was taking a lot of notice of him.

He pulled out the mugshots Gheeta had given them in the Team Room. The man stood out a mile, the swept-back black hair was a giveaway: Jack Dooley. Johnson pulled out and followed at a distance, keeping three or four cars between them. He had better make a call on the radio and bring the team up to date.

'Johnson to Palmer.'

****

Being a Monday afternoon, Southwark Cathedral had quite a few tourists milling about the precincts and inside. Palmer waited by the main door with Gheeta as she pulled up the tracker on her laptop.

'Well, the crate has arrived guv,' she said, as the tracker flashed its presence on the screen and beeped, causing tourists nearby, who were already wondering what a uniformed police officer was doing at a cathedral, to take even more notice. 'It seems to be at the rear of the cathedral.'

'Where the Cathedral offices are, probably in a store room. Lead on.'

They followed the tracker's light through the main nave and into the choir section. Gheeta's radio came on loud and clear.

'Johnson to Palmer.'

She quickly turned the volume down. As usual, Palmer's radio was turned off.

Gheeta answered, 'Go ahead Johnson, he is with me and listening.'

'Eve Dawn met Jack Dooley at the cemetery; they had a conversation and left separately. I'm on Dooley and DS Simms is on Mrs Dawn. Over.'

Gheeta looked at Palmer for an instruction.

'Stay with them and let us know where they end up,' he said quietly.

Gheeta passed the message on and signed off. 'Well, the plot thickens. What's she doing meeting the enemy?'

Palmer gave a knowing look. 'Perhaps he's not the enemy?'

They returned their thoughts to the flashing bleeper that led them through the choir and out into the south churchyard, following it round to the rear of the cathedral and the office building.

'It's in there, guv.' Gheeta pointed to the flashing light.

'Okay, let's see if anybody is home.'

Palmer led to the door marked 'Private' and opened it slowly. Inside was a large office with several desks, each with a computer and monitor. The place was empty.

The sound of wood splintering reached them through an open door at the end of the room. Quietly they made their way to it past the desks and carefully peeped inside. Arbuthnot Perryman and one other man were using claw hammers to pull the top off the crate. Palmer didn't recognise the other man, but the heavy build, six foot-wide shoulders, smart suit and broken nose didn't point to him being a person of the cloth.

Palmer stepped into the room, holding his warrant card in front of him.

'Good afternoon, gentlemen...' was as far as he got when a claw hammer flew through the air towards his head. It missed and made a sizeable hole in the plasterboard wall behind him, as Mr Broken Nose who had thrown it was out of a side door, with an amazing turn of speed for someone of such bulk, and away. Gheeta made to chase after him.

Palmer called her back. 'Don't bother with him, Sergeant. He's a minor player.' He turned to Perryman. 'While you, Mr Perryman, would seem to be a major player.' The cold stare he gave Perryman was the one Mrs P. said could frighten horses at a hundred yards and bring the Grand National to a halt. 'Read him his rights and cuff him, Sergeant.'

****

The Metropolitan Police Drug Squad are a 24-hour on alert team and the call from Palmer had them down to the cathedral within twenty minutes. They sealed off the offices, took the CCTV discs from the exterior cameras in the hope they would recognise Broken Nose, and took a handover of the scene from Palmer who promised them a report on the whole 'crate' affair as soon as he could. He didn't mention it was a side result of the Dawn ongoing murder enquiry, as having been a young detective constable in the Robert Marks team that cleaned up the bent CID officers in the late seventies, he knew only too well that the amount of money in drug trafficking these days would undoubtedly turn a few coppers' heads, and one of them in the Drug Squad may well be involved with the Dawns.

Back at the Yard Palmer got AC Bateman on the phone from the Team Room as Gheeta roughed out a report which they knew he'd ask for. Palmer was going to do this strictly by the book, and telling a bishop that his staff were drug mules was above his paygrade. And anyway, Bateman would relish talking to a bishop!

'You're absolutely sure about all this are you, Palmer?'

'Hundred percent sure sir, yes.'

'Run it past me once more.'

'The cathedral candles are made in Italy and shipped worldwide under the Vatican's diplomatic immunity code. We have the manufacturer's name and address in Madrid from the crate's label. A certain number of the boxes in the crate have hollowed out candles stuffed full of narcotics; definitely cocaine and could be others as well. Because of the diplomatic immunity the crate sails through customs without being scanned and ends up at the cathedral, where one of the bishop's assistants, Arbuthnot Perryman, is the receiver this end and distributes them to drug gangs in London from the confessional. Clever, eh? I have him in custody and will hand him over to the Drugs Squad, and as soon as I can.'

'This all sounds quite incredible, Palmer.'

'I know, like something on Netflix.'

'Where?'

'Never mind.'

'And you don't think this is part of the Dawn family murders?'

'No sir, I think we basically stumbled on this just because James Dawn picked up a couple of boxes of the narcotic candles on his last journey and we saw it on the ANPR camera and decided to take a look. I think it's just a part of a major drugs trafficking scheme operating through the Vatican's diplomacy code; probably the Italian Mafia run the factory in Madrid, but that's for the Drug Squad and NCB Interpol to look into. We've enough on our plate with the murders without getting into all that – unless you'd like me to pop off to Italy, sir?' He knew what the answer would be on that offer.

'No, no, you concentrate on the Dawn case – that's the important one for us.'

'So I can take it you'll have a discreet word with the bishop then sir, unless you want me to pull him in for questioning?'

'Don't you dare, Palmer! Yes, yes, I'll have a word with the Home Secretary first and see what she recommends.'

'Well, whilst you're at it you might recommend to her that Border Security starts slipping a few of these diplomatic bags through the scanners, sir.'

'Not a bad idea, Palmer. I didn't realise they weren't allowed to.'

'Leave it with you then, sir. Must get on.'

'Right, yes. Okay Palmer, well done. Written report tomorrow, please.'

'Of course.'

Click, Bateman rang off.

Palmer replaced the receiver and turned to Gheeta. 'He's going to run it past the Home Secretary.'

Gheeta knew what was coming next: Palmer's impression of Bateman fawning.

'Hello Home Secretary, madame, it's AC Bateman here, B. A. T. E. M. A. N. Just to report I've uncovered a major organised drug importing scam – yes, I work weekends, of course I do. Crime doesn't take weekends off, ma'am, and neither do I... I did it all myself and I'm getting on very well with the Walworth Road murders too... Palmer? Yes, he had a little to do with it.'

Thankfully Gheeta's radio interrupted. 'Johnson to Palmer.'

Palmer took hold of the radio. 'Go ahead, Johnson.'

'Dooley has been dropped off at Eve Dawn's apartment block. His car has driven off – it's not waiting for him, so looks like he's here for a while.'

'Hang on a minute, Johnson.' Palmer looked at Gheeta. 'Does Dooley live in that block as well?'

Gheeta scrolled down her laptop. 'No guv, got a gated pad in Bromley.'

'So he's either got a key to Eve Dawn's place or he's going to wait there for her then?'

'Seems they are a bit closer than we originally thought then.'

'Yes, we wondered about that, didn't we. A bit of a picture is emerging here.' He clicked back to Johnson. 'Okay Johnson, call it a day. Good work today, you and Simms. See you tomorrow. What's happening with Mrs Dawn, Simms?'

Simms answered, 'We are in the Victoria Bridge Road. Her taxi dropped her off at one of her nail parlours and waited; she was only inside a few minutes and now they've come over the bridge and looks like she's going home.'

'Okay, if she goes inside that'll do for today then Simms, well done, see you tomorrow.'

****

'Some of them don't like it. I've spoken to a couple of the gang masters, they've put two and two together and worked out you're the one most likely involved. They're not happy – you've got to remember James was a very generous boss.'

It was evening. Darkness was closing in outside Eve Dawn's apartment block; the lights from London Bridge were shimmering in the mirror of the Thames waters as she took a sip from her glass of wine and turned to Jack Dooley, who was sat on the sofa looking through the evening paper for any mention on how the Walworth Road investigation was going: no mention, just the usual editorial comment on London becoming a crime capital and what was the Home Secretary going to do about it, with opposition MPs on their soapboxes seizing the opportunity to get some exposure, blah, blah, blah.

He tossed the paper aside. 'Well, they're just going to have to get used to it, aren't they. Let me know who's not happy and I'll get a couple of my men to have a word. Who are you talking about, Henry Wright and John Holland? They're the only two of James's right-hand men left – the others were in the car with him.' He laughed. 'I'll have a word and sort them out.'

'You'll do no such thing,' Eve glared at him. 'You sorted out Stan and couldn't even arrange it to happen somewhere a long way away from here. All that did was put more pressure on the police to up their game. No more killing, understood? I'll clear the air, put them at ease that everything will get back to normal soon; last thing we need is more violence. Now hop it, I've got a lot of book work to do – call your driver to pick you up.'

'No, he'll be home now. I'll get a cab on the street.'

'Okay, you go down and I'll call one for you.' She picked up a mobile as Dooley gave her a peck on the cheek.

'I like this partnership.' He patted her bottom, which she didn't like at all, picked up his coat and left. Eve speed-dialled a number. It was answered. 'He's on his way down. Use the black cab, and Henry – no mess, understood? Good.'

She walked from the lounge into the master bedroom, whose windows gave a wide view of the road in front of the apartment. She watched Dooley wait on the pavement; she hoped no black cab other than her own would come down the road. A couple of minutes went by and one came along. She watched as Dooley hailed it and got in the back. A Range Rover pulled up behind and in no time at all the two rear seat passengers left the Range Rover and got into the back of the cab from either side. The lit 'for hire' sign went out and the cab pulled away.

Eve Dawn turned and poured another glass of wine and talked to herself in a wall mirror. 'Don't you just love it when a plan comes together.' She raised her glass and toasted herself.

****

The speed of the attack had taken Dooley by surprise. He sat in the back of the cab with Henry Wright on one side and John Holland on the other; a Walther PPK was pressed up under his chin. It all became clear; the partnership with Eve Dawn was about to be dissolved.

'The bitch.' He spat the words out as a hood was pulled down over his head.

Chapter 9   TUESDAY

Simms and Johnson took up the surveillance the next day; Simms was at Eve Dawn's apartment and Johnson outside the large gates to Dooley's Bromley home. Palmer met Singh at the Team Room. He stood in front of the big white progress board on the wall at the far end looking at the mugshots of the deceased and the felt tip lines Claire had drawn linking them to each other, with the dates of their death and whether they had been in the car or the hospital.

'It's all a bit slow, Sergeant – it's all too quiet. I'm wondering whether to bring in the Fraud Squad; Atkins said they'd have enough to pull accounts from the banks and charge Dawn and Dooley with money laundering. Let's face it, the killings were almost certainly done by a couple of pros hired in from way out of town and we aren't going to get them unless they are arrested somewhere else; and the matching guns are in their possession. But if the FS start agitating and stirring things up a bit, somebody might break cover.'

Gheeta had to agree; he was right. They'd fed all the information into the computers to try and find leads, little threads that could tie a person into the actual killings, and nothing had surfaced. It was obvious why the killings had happened, Dooley was taking over the Dawn manor; but Dooley's fingerprints or DNA weren't on anything. Frome had dusted the car, Stan Dawn's office, the candle boxes and found nothing. Dooley was either very lucky, or very clever.

'I don't know guv, the meeting in the cemetery of Dooley and Eve Dawn has baffled me; and then the visit to her apartment – what's he there for? Warning her off any retaliation? Forming a partnership? Something's going to break, it always does in the end. Anyway, if you push it over to the FS the lawyers for Dooley and Dawn will get them off a prison sentence; probably just accept a Proceed of Crime Order and pay a couple of million to the court. They can only set the amount on known funds, and who knows what this lot have stashed away offshore?'

Palmer agreed. 'That wouldn't really be a good outcome for us, would it? Nobody charged with the murders. I doubt we will ever get the actual lowlifes who pulled the triggers, but we might get the ones who ordered it, eh? I think I hold back on bringing in the FS.'

'Yes guv, early days yet.'

'Soldier on then.'

'Yes.'

'Anything from the lads?'

'All quiet, I think. I'll check.' She used her radio.' Singh to Simms, anything happening?'

'No, all quiet. She's still in her apartment, unless she shimmied down a drainpipe round the back somewhere.'

Palmer smiled at the image as Gheeta answered. 'Okay. Singh to Johnson, how about at your end?'

'No, all quiet at Dooley's place,' Johnson answered. 'Middle-aged lady came out of the gates with two large dogs and walked them round the block and back inside, but no sign of Dooley.'

'OK, both of you stay put for now. Over and out.'

Gheeta switched her radio off. 'Crack and Meths,'

'What?' Palmer didn't understand.

'Dooley's two dogs, he calls them Crack and Meths. It's in the file.'

'Bit cheeky, isn't it? I seem to remember Kenneth Noye did that after the Brinks Mat robbery; he had two dogs, called them Brinks and Mat.'

Nothing happened at the Dooley residence or Dawn's apartment for the rest of the day. Palmer thought that everybody needed to take a break, so unless something big broke he gave the team Wednesday off.

Chapter 10. WEDNESDAY

The day off didn't happen.

Palmer didn't like having to visit the Met's morgue once a week, let alone twice. The call had come from Gheeta just as Palmer had sat down to his breakfast, and was deciding whether to go to the office and take another look at all the evidence and reports and see if they'd missed anything. Usually by now they would have a name or names in the frame to put pressure on; but so far, in this case, they had their suspicions – mainly about Jack Dooley – but nothing strong enough to start a programme of harassment to try and make him show his head above the parapet.

All that had gone by the board as he listened to Gheeta on the phone.

'Jack Dooley's body has been fished out of the Thames, guv. It's been taken to the Murder Morgue; there's a bullet-hole in his head.'

****

'Fuck me, you got here quick didn't you?' was Professor Latin's greeting to Palmer. 'We only got the body an hour ago.'

Palmer was changed into the required green overshoes, white overall and hairnet.

'I wanted to have a look before the family collect it. I think they'll be in pretty quick for this one.'

'Not another of your Muslim converts, is he?'

'He might be. Different family, but tied in with the last lot.'

'Well, as I told you before, it's definitely *foul play* so they can't have it until I release it, Justin. And with a bullet hole in the head I can hold it as long as I please. How is he of interest to you then?'

'We had our eyes on him for being implicated in the Walworth Road murders.'

'That lot, eh? Yes, well this one would certainly tick the box for a gangland hit: single shot to the head. Who was he?'

'Jack Dooley, main man in the West End drugs scene.'

'Over here.' Latin led Palmer across the morgue to a steel table on which

Jack Dooley's body lay covered by a plastic sheet which he turned down, showing the single hole to his forehead.

Palmer winced a bit at the sight; it was large and not at all circular, with bone and flesh hanging from it. 'Exit wound?'

Latin nodded. 'Yes, shot through the back of the head – bullet came out at the front, always makes a mess. Pulled from the Thames by the River police at six this morning; they identified him, and he's on your current list of 'people of interest' which is why you got the call, I expect.'

'Any clothing?'

'None that came in with the body.'

'Time of death?'

'I haven't checked the water in the lungs as yet, but from the permeation into the skin and the eye colour I'd say he'd been dead in the water about ten hours.

'Shot late last night then. Any other marks – cuts, bruises?'

'No, none. You expecting some?'

'Not really. If there had been it would point to him being in a fight before getting shot; the lack of any points to an execution-type killing. Okay, I'm done.'

****

Back at the Team Room Claire was uploading the details of the finding of Dooley's body in the river from the River Police report into the computer programmes. Gheeta had printed it out for Palmer to read and added a 'dead' note below Dooley's picture on the white board. The report didn't throw any new light on the case, but Gheeta had something that could.

'Harry Jones and wife flew in from Panama last night, guv. Just got the Border Security note through; we'd flagged him up on a *report entry but don't detain basis*. He's booked into the Hilton Park Lane.'

'He wasn't away long, was he?' Palmer thought for a moment. 'So him returning would seem to point to whatever threat sent him away having now disappeared – and that would point to James and Stan Dawn.'

'Or Dooley.'

'No, he and his wife would have been well in-flight before Dooley was shot.'

'So he thinks he's safe with Eve Dawn?' Gheeta was puzzled.

'He must think he is, or he wouldn't come back. And with our suspicion of her being tied in with Jack Dooley, who Jones was scamming the Dawn money to, it could all tie up with Dooley being hit.'

'You mean Eve has taken revenge on Dooley for the scam or the killings? So why was she all pally with him in the cemetery, before he went to her apartment?'

'If he was responsible for the killings, he could have made her an offer of a partnership; he needed her to keep the Dawn people in order, either that or hit her too. She's a clever woman – she could have agreed to a partnership with him, amalgamated the South London and West End turfs, and now, once it was all up and running, had him put out of the picture and brought back the one person she would need to launder a much bigger cash take: Harry Jones.'

'You wouldn't take a partnership with Dooley, the man who probably killed your husband, father-in-law and uncle-in-law, would you? More likely think that you'd be next on his list as the remaining Dawn and go to war with him. Partnership doesn't make that much sense.'

'What if the partnership was pre-arranged with Dooley?'

Gheeta thought for a moment. 'You mean Eve Dawn was the one who set this whole thing up, including the killing of her own family and then brought Dooley in? That would make sense; and most of all, would keep the peace.'

'Yes, so why not? After all, who is the last man, or should we say woman, standing?'

'Eve Dawn.'

'Correct.'

'Christ, she must have had a big grudge against her husband to have him hit.'

'And her father-in-law and Stanley.'

Claire, who had been working at her computer, interrupted. 'I might have found that grudge.'

Gheeta and Palmer turned to her.

'Go on,' said Palmer.

'James Dawn was suing Eve Dawn for divorce. The papers were lodged with the court a month ago: adultery, uncontested.'

'You are kidding.' Palmer was astounded.

'No, it's all here in black and white. Due to be heard in court in five weeks.'

'Adultery with whom?' asked Gheeta.

'Doesn't say – probably wouldn't have to name him as it's 'uncontested'. In other words, she admitted it.'

'Got to be Jack Dooley, hasn't it? He seems to be pretty close to her.'

'Playing on dangerous ground if it was him,' said Palmer. 'Dawn seems to have been the kind of man who wouldn't have taken kindly to a competitor playing around with his wife; if that became common knowledge in their world he'd be a laughing stock. No, if he knew it was Dooley he'd just have taken him out – end of the affair. So why go for all the legalities of a proper divorce?'

'Well,' Gheeta had an answer. 'If the marriage had broken down and couldn't be patched up guv, a divorce would work in

James Dawn's favour financially. She's admitted the charge, so he could walk away with everything – wouldn't have to split anything with her.'

'I can't see the woman we interviewed accepting that – she definitely isn't the type to roll over easily,' Palmer made the point.

'Looks like she rolled over easily for Jack Dooley,' said Claire, bringing smiles to their faces.

'There is another angle,' said Palmer. 'If it was Dooley, Eve Dawn could have come to an agreement with James not to whack him if she goes quietly – no property, no money. For all we know Dooley might have been the love of her life and she wants to protect him. It's all agreed and then, when all this Harry Jones scam on the Dawn money going to Dooley comes out, that alters the picture, doesn't it? Dawn's got a big reason to whack Dooley now, other than his affair with Eve.'

'So Eve tells Dooley that the scam is out, and Dooley takes the initiative and strikes first,' said Gheeta. 'Self-preservation – makes sense.'

Palmer nodded. 'Yes, and he'd have to take out Alfred and Stanley to stop any retaliation.'

'Okay, that works so far. But who killed Dooley?' asked Gheeta. 'There's no more Dawn family left to do it as revenge.'

'There is,' said Palmer.

'Who?'

'Eve.'

'Eve?'

'Yes.'

'But she's got what she wanted. She and Dooley are away and in control of both manors.'

'Maybe she wanted that, and maybe not. Maybe she wanted the whole empire to herself and saw this as a way to get it. Maybe her affair with Dooley was just that, an affair, not something she saw as lasting; and when James Dawn found out about it and the divorce deal was made, it would have put her out in the cold financially. So the Harry Jones scam was a godsend – she tells Dooley it's out in the open and he's at risk, so Dooley gets rid of the Dawns, and then she gets rid of Dooley; she now has South London and the West End. Could be that was her plan from the start. So, two scenarios: she planned it all from the start and then brought Dooley in, or Dooley did it and then brought her in. '

'Whichever it was, if I was Johnny Robinson I'd be getting worried,' said Gheeta.

'Yes, he might well be. Are Johnson and Simms back on surveillance?'

'Yes, Johnson's tapping up the street dealers he knows to try and find out what the word on the street is and Simms is at Eve Dawn's Nail Bar in Victoria where she's inside.'

'Okay, pull Johnson over to join Simms. I think the killer is either being controlled by Eve Dawn or is Dawn herself – that's the only scenario that makes sense, and puts her firmly in the driving seat now.'

She clicked on the radio. 'DS Singh to Johnson.'

'Johnson, go.'

'The guvnor would like you to join Simms at Victoria please. DS Simms, you copy that?'

'Simms, yes, copy that. One thing that I've noticed – the taxi that brought Eve Dawn here was the same one that she went to the cemetery in, and he's waiting for her here now. That's two and a half hours on the clock waiting time so far; seems a bit peculiar as most cabbies I know want to get onto the next fare and the next tip. There's little or no money in waiting time.'

Gheeta looked at Palmer who said, 'Check it out.'

'Give me the cab number Simms, and we'll check it out.'

****

It took an hour for Transport For London to check the cab's registration number and come back with the information that it was registered to a cab company who had thirty black cabs working out of a garage in Euston. Palmer sent Johnson over, and a quick chat with the manager there, plus a radio call to the actual cab, established it was a copy plate on the Dawn vehicle; the cab with the genuine number plate was at Gatwick Airport.

The scam was much used by criminals: you find a vehicle which is identical to the one you use on illegal work and put its number on yours; any police car with a ANPR system that automatically checks numbers will get information that it is the right plate for that vehicle, and as long as the tax is paid no alarm will be raised.

Johnson gave the news to the Team Room over the radio. 'It's the right number plate, but it's on the wrong cab – it's a duplicate.'

Palmer took the radio. 'Okay Johnson, go back and join Simms and the pair of you stick with the cab. Don't worry about Eve Dawn, just stick with the cab.' He turned to Gheeta. 'That cab is becoming a very important player isn't it, eh? Eve Dawn doesn't seem to have a car herself and uses it all the time. I'll lay odds that Dooley was taken to the river in it to be dumped.'

'You think he was killed somewhere else then, guv?'

'Not necessarily, no. He was either killed elsewhere and then taken to the river, or taken to the river and killed there. Either way, that cab has to be involved.'

'Once we get the details of the real cab's fares yesterday we can upload all the routes that the number plate made that registered on the ANPR system onto a map, and sift out the genuine cab's journeys, which will leave the journeys that Eve's cab made.'

'And one of them will be to the Royal Docks,' said Palmer. 'It has to be.'

****

DCS Johnson shifted his position next to DCS Simms in the plain squad car parked fifty metres up the road from the nail bar.

'Here he comes.'

In the side mirror he could see the cab driver walking towards them from the coffee shop with a takeaway coffee in his hand.

Simms looked up at the rear-view mirror. 'He's not in any hurry, is he? She can't have called him back to drive her somewhere.'

'I could do with that coffee,' said Johnson, as the driver passed them and got into his cab outside the nail bar.

'Eh up! I don't think he's going to have time to enjoy it now!' Simms nodded towards the nail bar entrance where Eve Dawn was talking to an assistant as she came out. The driver left his coffee in the cab, got out and came round to open the passenger door for her. A last few words were exchanged between the assistant and Dawn before she got inside, and the driver shut the door, returned to his seat and the cab drove off.

Johnson quickly left Simms's car and hurried back to his own parked another fifty metres behind. Simms started following the cab at a distance. Before long Johnson caught up and took over the lead, as Simms dropped back a few cars. They changed places every half mile or so depending on the traffic; if the cab driver was a professional wheel man, he'd be keeping an eye out for tails.

Simms kept the Team Room up-to-date as they went. Palmer and Singh followed their route on a road map Claire brought up on the big screen: over Vauxhall Bridge, then left through Lambeth and Waterloo to London Bridge, where Eve Dawn left the cab at the entrance to her apartment block.

'Do you want one of us to stay on her, sir?' asked Simms.

'No, we know where she is – no, you two follow that cab and see where it ends up for the night.'

'Will do.'

Chapter 11   THURSDAY

Five o'clock in the morning on a cold January day, hunched inside his overcoat and stood against a tall hedge in a Clapham side street is not Palmer's choice way of starting his day.

The cab had been followed to a lock up in a row of six behind shops in Clapham High Street. The driver had parked it inside, pulled down and locked the shutter and walked to a house in a nearby side street – the house that Palmer, DS Johnson and several AROs were about to enter, either with or without the resident's permission. Around the corner, DS Singh, DS Simms and another smaller ARO team would force open the lockup and secure it, until Reg Frome's forensic team arrived at a more reasonable hour to take over.

Nick Barber, forty-two, five foot eight, overweight and not the sharpest tool in the box was a wheel man, car thief, and ex-stock car racing driver. He decided not to put up any resistance when woken by the banging on his front door, and the shouts of 'armed police open the door' sent small shudders of fear through his brain; being out on parole, having served half of a six-year sentence for transporting and handling Class A drugs, he knew immediately that he would be going back inside to serve at least the rest of his term plus whatever this arrest led to. So did his wife as she left the bed to open the door.

'You stupid bastard, what have you done now?' were her angry words as she foresaw another three years of hard work bringing up three young children on the 'social'.

****

Back at the Yard, the Custody Officer read Barber his charge sheet: kidnapping, suspected involvement in murder, plus various vehicle tax and licence avoidance charges. Palmer made sure he was refused bail and was put in a holding cell awaiting interview later that day.

It was no surprise to Palmer that Barber's one allowed telephone call was to Eve Dawn's mobile.

'I've been nicked and taken to the Yard and charged.'

'What with?'

'Kidnapping and suspected murder.'

'Don't say anything – a brief will be on his way.'

Click.

As soon as Barber was taken off to the cell Palmer checked the number he'd called and immediately radioed to DS Singh to put an ongoing trace on it that would list all the calls to and from, plus their numbers.

****

Palmer decided to let Barber stew in the holding cell until the solicitor arrived, and then let the pair of them wait for ages in an interview room. He knew the only answers Barber would give to questions would be 'no comment', so the more fear he could engender into the man the better, and he needed solid facts to create that fear. Reg Frome could, hopefully, provide those facts.

He had given the team two hours off to go to the canteen, or leave the Yard to get some breakfast and relax after their early start, so was surprised to find

Gheeta in the Team Room working. The big plasma screen was showing a London street map with lots of roads overlaid red.

'Is that the cab's journeys?' he asked.

'Yes guv, but it's a bit involved at the moment because we've got the real cab and Barber's cab both with the same number plate. So I've got the ANPR clicks for that number plate for the twenty-four hours before Dooley was found in the Thames, and a print-out from the Euston cab company of the real cab's fares during that time; so now I'm deleting the real cab's route fare by fare from the map, and hopefully that will leave us with a map of Barber's cab's journeys that day.'

'Okay. Have you had breakfast?'

'I'll get any early lunch.'

'So the answer is no. I'm starving, I'm going over to the sandwich shop – what would you like?'

Gheeta was quite taken aback by that. Palmer was the one who usually forgot all about food and drink when a case was ongoing; for him to feel the need for food was unusual – he *must* be starving.

'Chicken salad would be nice, guv. With mayonnaise.'

****

The team re-assembled just as Gheeta finished the ham with mustard sandwich Palmer had bought her. She didn't comment – she knew that when a case was opening up Palmer's mind had only one thing in it, and that wasn't a chicken salad and mayonnaise sandwich. Palmer finished his two Big Macs; he couldn't resist, never could despite Mrs P.s warnings about cholesterol.

Reg Frome gave a perfunctory tap on the door and followed them in. He sat down at a table and opened his folder.

'Good afternoon everybody. Right then, I've got a preliminary report on the lockup and the cab inside it which looks interesting – but remember, this is just a preliminary one.' He gave Palmer a look to underline the 'preliminary' bit. 'Nothing of use found in the actual lockup, but the cab itself has revealed quite a lot. We did a luminol test; there's blood drops and splats all over the passenger area – not intense enough to suggest that any violence or shooting was done there, but they are probably secondary touches coming off somebody's shoes or hands who committed the attack – if it was an attack – or the shooting elsewhere, and then got into the cab having blood on the soles of their shoes or shoe. Blood is on the carpet on both sides just inside the doors where anybody getting into the cab would first place their foot, and then to a lesser degree in the middle of the carpet.

'In the trunk we found this.' He handed round a picture of the hood that had been put over Dooley's head. 'No blood or fingerprints on this, but plenty of DNA inside from whoever's head it was on.'

'Dooley's, got to be,' said Palmer.

Frome continued, 'The passenger department of the cab has numerous fingerprints which we lifted and sent off to be matched on the database, and the same goes for the driver's area: steering wheel, gear stick and door handles. Three names have come back to us whose prints are on file: Nick Barber, John Holland and Henry Wright. We can't tell whose blood is in the rear, but we can identify the type which might match your victim in the morgue, as may the DNA inside the hood.

'That's the preliminary stuff – and now we will dig deeper looking for fabric types, human hair and the rest. One interesting thing is that the blood samples from either side of the passenger compartment have a residue of some sort of crushed granules mixed in them. We've tested for drugs and that came up negative, so I'm having them analysed and will come back to you with the results.' He closed the folder and sat back. 'Does any of that make sense?'

'It will – I'm sure the names will make a lot of sense. Thank you Reg, that's a good start. We've got Nick Barber in custody already, his shoes are in an evidence bag downstairs with the custody officer; get them released to you and see if we can't get a blood sample off them, hopefully Dooley's.'

'Will do.'

They shook hands and Frome left.

'Right then, I'd better go and waste a few minutes with Nick Barber and his brief. Sergeant Singh, pull up all the information you can on John Holland and Henry Wright, and then you and Claire carry on with plotting the route map – that's going to be very important. Johnson and Simms, sorry lads but I think we need to keep an even closer eye on Eve Dawn now. Sshe'll be wondering about Barber and what he might say, so back to her please.'

****

Just as expected, the only answer Palmer got to his questioning of Nick Barber was 'no comment'. He started off with the simple questions.

'Who owns the cab?'

'No comment.'

'Who owns the lockup?'

'No comment.'

'Do you work for Eve Dawn?'

'No comment.'

'Were you driving the cab yesterday?'

'No comment.'

'Do you know Henry Wright and John Holland?'

'No comment.'

Palmer exhaled loudly. Oh well, he'd given Barber a chance and now it was time to stick the boot in and get him worried. He sat back as though weighing up the situation; he knew exactly what he was going to do next. He stood up and pushed in his chair.

'I don't intend to sit here with you and your lawyer for the next hour listening to 'no comment', so I will remand you in custody on suspicion of murder.'

The lawyer spoke. 'Detective Chief Superintendent Palmer, you have to have some evidence to do that. I insist my client be released on bail.'

'Oh, do you really? You *'insist'*, do you? Well hard luck, sunshine. Let me advise you and your client of my reasons for holding him. We have his fingerprints all over the cab; the cab has the blood of a victim of a gangland murder all over the inside of it, and your client's shoes have the victim's blood on them. We have an ANPR route of the cab's journey and CCTV of the occupants, including your client.' To be truthful that was a mixture of fact and fiction that Palmer hoped would all become fact as the CCTV emerged.

Barber's face was showing the mix of surprise and fear Palmer had hoped for. He stopped at the interview room door and turned to the lawyer.

'I'll give your client one hour to think about what I've said and decide whether he wants to see his wife again outside of visiting hours in prison once a month over the next thirty years, or talk to me and see if we can't organise something better. One hour, that's all, and then I'm going home – which is more than your client will be doing.'

Palmer left the interview room, shutting the door behind him, and gave instructions to the duty officer on the desk.

'George, I think they might want to see me again pretty soon – let them stew a bit if you would, say I'm out of the building or in a conference. Keep them in there for a good half hour.'

The duty officer smiled; he'd lost count of the times Palmer had used that ploy to loosen tongues. 'Will do, Justin.'

****

Back in the Team Room the route map had been doctored with the real cab's journeys being deleted.

Palmer stood and looked at it. 'So on the evening of Dooley's murder the cab went from Barber's lockup to Eve Dawn's, and then along the river embankment to the Royal Docks complex. That must be where they killed Dooley and dumped him in the river.'

'Sugar! It's sugar!' Claire sat back excitedly.

'What is?' asked Palmer.

'The granules in the blood on the cab's floor that Mr Frome said were in the blood and on the soles of the shoes. I bet it's sugar.'

'Why?'

'Tate and Lyle have a major wharf at the Royal Docks, sir. It's called Silvertown – thousands of tons of raw sugar being unloaded from bulk carriers into warehouses every day, I saw a documentary on it once – sugar everywhere.'

Gheeta was already putting on her coat. 'Let's hope they have CCTV.'

The internal phone rang. It was the custody officer.

'Your prisoner's lawyer would like to talk, Justin. Still want me to stall him'

'Thanks George, he'll have to wait now – things are moving a bit fast. Tell him I'm out and back tomorrow late morning

– and George, no way does Barber leave the building; new evidence has come to light linking him directly to murder. No bail.'

'Got it.'

Palmer fetched his coat and hat from the hanger in his office as Gheeta phoned for a squad car to meet them at the front. 'Claire, give Reg Frome a call and tell him your sugar thesis and ask him to meet us at the wharf as soon as he can.' He stopped at the door. 'Oh, and Claire, well done.'

Gheeta met Claire's look of amazement with one of her own; praise from Palmer was a rarity.

****

The Royal Docks wharf was cold and windy as the cold air off the Thames swirled around, with evening shadows lengthening as the winter sun fell lower on the skyline. Palmer waited in the squad car as Gheeta went inside the security office to check any CCTV. She was back quickly with bad news.

'They've got cameras, but not on the wharf side. The dock where the sugar is stored in great heaps is gated off at night, with security patrols doing their rounds every hour, but the part where the bulk carrier ships dock is left open as the crews come and go. That's the only part the public have twenty-four hour access to, so our cab must have gone there; it's a lorry access route for tankers picking up a load of treacle from the factory.' She pointed ahead of them and spoke to the driver. 'Just follow this road. Go easy – not a lot of light so we don't want to end up in the water.'

They drove on and came to the dockside where a bulk carrier moored against it towered above them, with the dockside cranes now still and silent looking like aliens from *The War of the Worlds* with their massive pincher scoops swinging slightly in the wind.

Palmer directed the driver to take them to the far end of the concrete dock beyond the tanker, where he and Gheeta got out.

'It's a bit parky out here,' commented Palmer, turning up his coat collar and pulling his trilby firmly down. 'Don't go too near the edge, Sergeant. Use your flashlight – bloodstains are what we are after.' He ground his shoe into the concrete and heard the crunching of sugar crystals being crushed. 'Claire was dead right, you know. Sugar everywhere.'

'I bet the Thames tastes sweet around here,' said Gheeta.

'Yeah, well that's something I don't want to personally find out.'

Headlights approaching signalled the arrival of Reg Frome's forensic Transit van and his team.

'One thing about working with you, Justin,' said Frome as he got out. 'You do take us to the best places in town.' He looked around. 'This is a God forsaken place isn't it, eh?'

They all shook hands as Frome's team of four, now clad in white overalls and overshoes, joined them.

'Your young assistant rang me earlier and she got it spot on,' said Frome. 'Sugar crystals it was, crushed and stuck to the carpet in that cab by the blood. Same on the soles of the pair of shoes belonging to Mr Barber.' He looked around, using his own flashlight. 'I take it this is where you think the murder happened?'

Palmer nodded. 'Yes, the cab came here according to ANPR, so it all ties together nicely. Now we need to find bloodstains from the same blood group as Dooley's somewhere on this wharf to pin-point the murder spot.'

'Well, we're not going to find it by torchlight,' Frome pointed out. 'The blood would have turned a muddy black and permeated the concrete; plus there's been rain showers since the time of the murder.'

'And the security chaps at the gate said the dockside gets a mobile sweeper along it every morning as well,' added Gheeta.

Palmer gave Frome a knowing smile. 'Which is why you are here, Reg – to work your magic.'

Frome spoke to his team and they went back to the van, returning with handheld sprayers.

'Mrs P.'s got one of them for spraying greenfly on the rose bushes,' Palmer said to Gheeta.

'She may well have the same type of sprayer,' said Frome, overhearing the comment. 'But she wouldn't have the chemical that's inside them.'

'Luminol?' asked Gheeta.

'So you were paying attention earlier,' Frome laughed. 'Correct – a light spray will illuminate any bloodstains, even old diluted ones.' He turned to his team. 'Okay off you go – just a very fine spray on the edge of the dock.'

Before long the blue phosphorescence of blood oxygen pigments reacting with the luminol glowed from the concrete; the team widened the spray area and a picture of the murder evolved like a photo developing in a dark room tray. There were no slides of blue to indicate a bloody body being dragged along from the cab to the dock edge; all the luminol blood reaction on the concrete was at the dock edge, suggesting the body had been shot there and then pushed in. Frome had his people photograph the scene in detail and take measurements before putting a crime scene tent over it, held secure against the wind by sandbags fetched from the sugar works that were usually used as ballast for keeping tarpaulins in place over the mountains of raw sugar.

Gheeta had the main communication room at the Yard request a couple of uniformed officers from the local station be sent to keep the crime scene undisturbed for twenty-four hours, in case Frome wanted any more samples or tests done in daylight. A river police dive team would attend in the morning and search the riverbed nearby for anything that might have dropped in, like a gun, but Palmer didn't hold much hope.

It was past midnight when they finally left the Royal Docks and headed home in separate squad cars. Palmer dropped into the Yard on his way to arrange early 6am starts for Johnson and Simms, together with an ARV back up team to raid Wright and Holland's homes. Once that was all in hand, he relaxed in the squad car and went home – he was quite looking forward to his second interview with Nick Barber in the morning.

Chapter 12 FRIDAY

The next morning Palmer had a reminder from the custody officer that Barber's lawyer had returned and they were in an interview room waiting for him. He kept them waiting as he had other fish to fry, and was in no hurry to start the interview as he knew he now had enough evidence to place Barber and the cab at the Royal Dock, and just needed Reg Frome to confirm the blood type on Barber's shoes matched that of Jack Dooley to support it; so he decided to wait for that before conducting the interview, knowing it would come in later that morning. It did, and it was. He smiled at Gheeta as she read the confirmation email off her screen.

'I hope you like prison food, Mr Barber,' commented Palmer when she'd finished. 'And once we get the results from our two raids earlier, you'll probably have company.'

The two raids conducted earlier on Henry Wright's and John Holland's homes had been successful, with backup from Frome's forensic people waiting to go in once the suspects had been detained – their main purpose being to seize any shoes in the premises to be checked for sugar and blood.

Wright and Holland had been read their rights by the custody officer at the Yard and had the charge of murder given as the reason for their detention and refused bail. Both had taken advantage of the one allowed phone call to call their lawyers; they had more sense than to call Eve Dawn like Barber had, as they knew that word of their predicament would be passed to her immediately by the lawyers. After all, she would be paying the legal bills.

So Palmer felt pretty good about the way things were moving along now as he settled into a chair opposite Barber and his lawyer in the interview room. He busied himself with making out he was studying papers, until Gheeta arrived with two coffees and passed him one; then he took a few sips before looking up at Barber, puffing out his cheeks and exhaling loudly.

'Mr Barber, your charge of suspicion of murder has been changed – you are now charged with murder.' He took a nonchalant couple of sips of coffee as Barber stiffened visibly and looked at his lawyer.

The lawyer addressed Palmer. 'I take it you have enough evidence to substantiate such a charge, Mr Palmer?'

'I do. The custody officer will put the new charge to your client after this interview.'

'What new evidence do you have?'

'We have the deceased person's blood on your client's shoes, with particles of a substance that can be attributed to the particular place where the murder took place. We also have your client's fingerprints amongst others in the vehicle used to take the murder victim to the place of execution, and corresponding blood and particles in the back of the vehicle that we found in Mr Barber's lockup which we can trace by CCTV back from there to the murder scene.' Palmer sat back, avoiding the glances of Barber and the lawyer. 'Interview ends eleven forty-eight...'

'Whoa...' The lawyer held up his hands. 'My client would like a moment with me, if we may, and then possibly we might be able to look at this in a different way.'

'You've had all night and this morning to as you say, *'look at it in a different way.'* Palmer wasn't giving an inch;

he knew that the lawyer would now push Barber to give information in exchange for a lesser charge like manslaughter to be brought – nine years instead of thirty. Palmer stood and made for the door as Gheeta scooped up the papers he'd left on the table and spoke into the recorder.

'DCS Palmer and DS Singh ending the interview at eleven forty-nine.' She clicked off the machine.

Palmer turned at the door. 'You've thirty minutes and then I'm activating the murder charge and putting your client into a remand holding cell at Wandsworth.'

He and Gheeta left the interview room.

'What do you think, guv?' asked Gheeta. 'I'll give them ten minutes before they're on the phone looking for a plea to downgrade the murder charge.'

'Yes, about that – but then they can wait again. This up and down the stairs is playing havoc with my sciatica.'

****

In the Team Room Simms and Johnson were taking a break with coffee and biscuits.

'Well done chaps,' said Palmer on entering. 'Job well done this morning. Are Wright and Holland both here?'

Simms emptied his mouth first. 'West End Central, sir – no room here. Apparently climate activists Extinction Rebellion had a march this morning and some of them decided to block Westminster Bridge and refused to move – the cells are full.'

'Bring back National Service,' said Palmer.

This was his mantra to all the ills of the country, Gheeta didn't really understand how the bringing back of National Service would stop climate protesters blocking a bridge, but it wasn't worth commenting on.

'Wright and Holland's shoes gone to forensics?' asked Palmer.

Both Simms and Johnson nodded.

'We had a look, sir, and it did look like blood and sugar on the soles.'

'I never had any doubt about that.'

'Their mobiles have gone to forensics too,' said Simms

'Good.'

Claire turned from her screen. 'There's some good and bad news from the River Police, sir.'

'Go on.'

'No gun and no clothes found is the bad bit; the good bit is they found a bullet.'

'Really? That is good, all we need now is the gun that fired it.'

'We may already have it,' Johnson said through a mouthful of shortbread biscuit. 'Forensics took one away from Wright's home earlier.'

'They did? Claire, give the River chaps a call and get the bullet sent over to Reg Frome's department straight away; then give Reg a call and ask him to run a ballistics identifying test on the gun and see if it matches. Well, we are beginning to motor along nicely now, aren't we?'

'Be nice if the gun matches any of the bullets from James and Stanley Dawn's killings too,' said Gheeta.

'It would be nice, but I don't think they'll match,' said Palmer. 'Kids on scooters doing drive-bys is more likely to be a contract job passed out to pros from another city. I don't think we will ever get the lowlifes who actually did the shootings, but we might get the person who ordered it if we are lucky.'

'That must have been Jack Dooley guv, surely,' Gheeta said. 'He was the only one to gain from it.'

'So why is he now dead then?' Palmer asked.

'I still think Eve Dawn took her revenge – we know Wright and Holland work for the Dawns. She could have told them to do the hit.'

Simms wiped his mouth on a tissue. 'Eve Dawn seemed pretty friendly with Dooley at the cemetery, and he did go to her apartment as well. How would that tie up with her having him killed?'

'That,' said Palmer, 'is a bloody good point. What if their friendship was a bit more than just a friendship? Dooley could have been the reason she didn't want to contest the divorce and admitted adultery – she didn't want his name out in the open because they had a plan. What if Eve Dawn was party to the murder of her husband with Dooley? What if the two of them had a master plan to merge South London with the West End? Be a pretty formidable turf.'

'Biggest in the UK,' said Simms.

'Both in the sale of drugs and the amount of money coming in,' added Johnson.

'So why then have Dooley killed?' asked Gheeta.

'Something must have happened, and things didn't work out as they should have. That must be it, because Wright and Holland are Dawn men, and so is Barber, and we now know all three were involved in Dooley's murder; and since the deaths of James Dawn all three would be taking their orders from Eve.'

Gheeta was following Palmer's train of thought. 'And if all three weren't aware of a liaison between Dooley and Eve Dawn, they would assume it was a straightforward revenge hit on Dooley for killing James, Dad and Stan.'

'Correct.'

The internal phone rang and Claire took the call. She turned to Palmer. 'Barber and his lawyer wish to talk.'

****

Gheeta clicked on the recorder in the interview room. 'Twelve forty-five, Interview Room 3, those present are Nicholas Barber, Roger Geffs from Geffs Solicitors, DCS Palmer and DS Singh.' She sat down next to Palmer who spread his hands in an 'Okay, what have you to say?' manner towards the prisoner and his lawyer.

Roger Geffs of Geffs Solicitors cleared his throat. 'My client has instructed me to put forward a suggestion that a reduced charge of accessory to manslaughter might be considered in view of his co-operation, were he to co-operate.'

'No.' Palmer was adamant.

'No?' Roger Geffs of Geffs Solicitors was surprised.

Palmer looked coldly at Barber. 'Mr Barber, I have unquestionable forensic and CCTV evidence placing you at the murder scene of Jack Dooley. I also have the bullet that went through his head and killed him, and the gun that fired it.'

A bit premature on that, thought Gheeta, but she was used to Palmer stretching things a bit when he was on a roll.

'The vehicle involved was found in your lockup with Jack Dooley's blood inside it', continued Palmer. 'The charge is accessory to murder, and if your prints are found on the gun it will be changed to murder.'

'I never shot him.' Barber was beginning to see a thirty-year stretch looming before him. 'I just did the driving – that's all I ever done, driving.'

'So who did shoot Mr Dooley?'

Roger Geffs of Geffs Solicitors held a restraining hand in front of Barber. 'Can I assume any answer my client may give to that question will be seen to be co-operation with the police and taken into consideration when a final charge is made?'

'You may.'

Roger Geffs of Geffs Solicitors sat back and nodded to Barber to answer.

'Henry shot him, Henry Wright. The bloody idiot – we said just knock him out and throw him in so he'd drown and it would look like an accident, but Henry had been with Mr Dawn and Mr Dawn's dad since he was a kid. He was really angry.'

'And John Holland? He was with you, wasn't he?'

'Yes, he went ballistic when Henry shot Dooley – said we should take the body down the coast, weight it, and drop it in the channel a couple of miles out. He knew somebody with a small motorboat.'

'Who ordered the killing?'

'What?'

'We have CCTV of your vehicle near Eve Dawn's apartment block, and we know Dooley was there that evening. That's where you picked up Dooley, wasn't it?'

'Yes.'

'Didn't it surprise you that Dooley was at Eve Dawn's? Most people thought it was him who put out the contract on James Dawn, his dad and Stanley.'

'Well, things had changed from that. We had a whisper that she was joining with Dooley to make one firm, and that it might have been an outside firm that did the hits on her family – the Manchester Doonans were in the frame. When she said pick up Dooley, I thought that was probably what was happening and she and him had had a meeting to sort it out.'

'And Wright and Holland?'

'I never knew they was there. I picked up Dooley to take him home and then the other two jumped in the back of the cab with him. I never knew they was there until that happened; then Wright said to go to the Dock.'

'You didn't question that?'

'You don't question orders from Henry Wright, not if you value your front teeth.' A quick smile etched with fear crossed Barber's mouth.

'You had been to that Dock before though, hadn't you?'

'Yes.'

'Dumping bodies in the Thames?'

'No, no!' Barber showed fear. 'No, picking up drugs off the ships – crystal meths looks a lot like sugar crystals, a few kilos of them hid amongst a thousand tons of sugar and nobody will notice.'

'Okay.' Palmer gave Barber a small smile. 'I'll get this recording transcribed and then you and your solicitor will have to sign it as a genuine transcript of our conversation made without duress, agreed?'

'Yes.'

'Once you've done that, the charge will remain on file as one of Accessory to Manslaughter, and the defence lawyer your solicitor instructs should be able to argue that successfully in court when the case comes to trial.'

'Okay, thank you.'

Palmer nodded. 'Always pays to tell the truth, Mr Barber.' He flicked off the recorder after giving the time and 'interview terminated' procedure, then rose and left with Gheeta, who organised a pen and a witness statement form to be taken into the interview room by a uniformed custody officer.

'I have to admit it's beginning to look like Eve Dawn is moving into prime position on the major suspect list, guv,' said Gheeta as they mounted the stairs to the third floor.

'Certainly does,' Palmer replied, stopping to rub his sciatic left thigh. 'So it's either love gone wrong, or a well-thought out plan to take over the South and the West End without raising suspicions. She's either dropped into being the boss by other people's actions, or she's pulled off a great crime takeover scoop.'

'Barber's statement gives us enough to hold Wright and Holland in remand on murder charges,' said Gheeta. 'With a bit of persuasion Holland might buckle and give up Wright as the killer as well.'

'I'm sure he will when given the choice of nine years for accessory to murder or thirty years for murder.' Palmer smiled, and then winced as sciatica struck again.

****

The first phone call Roger Geffs made from his mobile after leaving the Yard was to Eve Dawn, giving her the news that Barber had gone for a deal and put Wright well and truly in the frame for Dooley's murder, but also put her partly in it too.

'How loyal is Holland? Will he look for a deal too?' he asked. 'He's got a duty solicitor, so he will probably advise him to take one if Palmer offers it. Do you want me to get in and take over?'

Eve Dawn thought for a moment. 'No, I don't think so; if you do that it does begin to look like I'm involved a bit too deep. If Holland cracks, he'll only be looking to save his own skin and put Wright in the frame as well for the shooting. I can't remember the number of times I used to tell James that Wright was a bomb waiting to go off – him and his bloody temper.' She had to keep up the pretence of not knowing that Wright would kill Dooley after being told to *'take him to the dock.'*

'What about Wright, will he put you in the frame?'

'He's got no proof that I had anything to do with it. If I'm questioned, I'll say he was always a loyal worker and very close to James, which he was, and that he must have emotionally flipped and taken it on himself to take revenge.'

'Okay, as long as you're sure you are bomb proof?'

'I'm sure. Remember, I am the grieving widow after all.'

'Yes, but in the mind of Mr Palmer you might well be the grieving widow who is intent on revenge. He brought your name up during the interview.'

'Really?' Alarm bells started ringing in Eve Dawn's head. 'Okay, let's wait and see.'

She ended the call a little worried; it wasn't going exactly as planned. By now all the gangmasters and their street dealers should be on side, things should be running smoothly; it was time to prepare in case the ship hit the rocks.

It had been the master plan of all master plans. For years she had wanted to get away from James; the money didn't mean so much now. Admittedly it had turned her head in the beginning; coming from a single parent family she had worked her fingers to the bone to keep herself, her mum and an older brother together as a family; sadly the brother had fallen in with a bad lot and ended up dead when a post office raid went badly wrong and the police were waiting. Stupidly he'd taken on the AROs and paid the final price.

The funeral was paid for by the Dawn family and only then had she found out her brother's involvement with them. James had paid her a lot of attention from then on, and pretty soon they were an item; this led to a wedding and her current life of luxury. To the outside world a very happy couple, but all wasn't well on the inside; more than once Eve had to explain away the bruises or the black eyes to her staff at the nail bars as 'accidents' whilst horse riding, or give some other credible excuse. James Dawn had a temper and it didn't take much for him to lose it; and behind all this growing dislike and distance between them simmered the fact that it was on a Dawn job that her brother had been killed.

When Jack Dooley had come into her life at one of the many charity boxing evenings James insisted she attend with him, she had been flattered and surprised at her obvious appeal to him and his attention to her; it was nice, and something she wasn't used to from James. The affair developed quickly; she had no real love for Jack, he supplied a need and that was all; if it had ended as quickly as it had started, she would just have shrugged and forgotten Jack in no time at all. But it hadn't, and when he told her in confidence of Stan's offer and the plan to hit James and Dad, it ticked all the boxes whirling around in her head and her masterplan had been born. It was so simple; James and Dad would be gone, but that would leave Stan. Why not go persuade Jack to go along with Stan and then get rid of Stan too? The soldiers would naturally think it was whoever hit Jack and Dad just cleaning up.

Knowing Stan as she did, she planted the idea in Jack's head that Jack wouldn't be safe as long as Stan was alive; she told Jack it could already be in Stan's mind to get rid of him too and reign supreme. He couldn't trust Stan. Jack could see the sense in this; could he ever really trust Stan? No, she was right – Stan had to go. So Jack arranged it; and that just left Jack – poor gullible Jack, how on earth he got to be in control of the West End beat Eve. Get rid of him, and all would be hers. She knew she would have some very loyal Dawn soldiers on her side, and if she told them Jack Dooley was the one who arranged the hits, they would take this as a suggestion they take revenge. At least Henry Wright would – and had.

But now Nick Barber was doing a *'Bertie Smalls'*, and if Holland did the same that would put Henry Wright firmly in the frame for murder, and he would seek a deal for a reduced term. That deal could only be to name who ordered the hit on Dooley, and that was Eve.

She stood looking over the Thames for a minute or two and then opened the wall safe, taking out an envelope of four Canadian passports with photos of the ladies on the passports that looked a lot like Eve Dawn but with a different name on each. She put on her coat and left the apartment. Once outside she ordered an Uber to pick her up and crossing the road to a large council waste wheelie bin, she broke her mobile in two and dropped it in.

****

'Isn't it nice when things start to fall into place?' Palmer had a big smile on his face. He was in the Team Room looking at a printout Gheeta had passed to him; it was from Reg Frome: the bullet found in the river had indeed come from the gun found in Wright's house, and Pathology had confirmed that the bullet that killed Dooley was probably of the same calibre.

'You'll like this too,' Gheeta said and passed him call printouts from the mobile networks for Eve Dawn and Henry Wright's mobiles. 'The highlighted calls are the ones of interest, guv – they are the calls made from Eve Dawn's mobile on the day of Dooley's murder and those received by Henry Wright's mobile in the same time period.

She pointed out the relevant ones to Palmer. 'A call from Mrs Dawn at eight forty-five to Nick Barber's mobile.'

'That will be the one asking him to pick up Dooley from her apartment block.'

'Yes, and then almost immediately after that a call to Henry Wright's mobile.'

'Telling him that Dooley's leaving her place and it's time to make him disappear.'

'Nice way of putting it guv, but yes, we must assume that's right.'

'So, we have Barber's statement giving Wright as the one who pulled the trigger; we have Holland in remand who might well substantiate that when he knows Barber has already pointed the finger at Wright, and then he'll be looking to get an accessory to manslaughter and not a murder charge; plus we have all the forensic and ANPR evidence putting the three amigos and the cab at the dockside.'

Gheeta and the team smiled at Palmer equating Wright, Barber and Holland as three comedy fools.

'And now we have telephone records implicating Eve Dawn as the puppet master pulling the strings.'

'We need Wright to confirm the order to hit Dooley came from Eve Dawn,' said Johnson. 'Otherwise it's all circumstantial on her.'

'He's not likely to do that, 'said Gheeta. 'He's up for murder and no way will him implicating Eve Dawn lessen that charge.'

'No,' Palmer agreed. 'And he's probably looking to her to look after his family's welfare when he goes down.'

'What if she didn't? What if she hung him out to dry?' Gheeta had a thought. 'After what Barber said about Wright's temper and going off the handle quickly, maybe if we dropped a hint that his family might not be getting any help from Eve Dawn – think it might loosen his tongue?'

Palmer showed a false expression of shock. 'Detective Sergeant Singh, am I to think that you are proposing we plant a thought in a prisoner's head that those he trusts may not be as trustworthy as he thinks they are – something that we have no indication is true?'

'And no indication it's false either, guv.'

'Sounds good to me,' said Simms.

'I like the idea,' said Johnson.

****

'What do you mean?' Henry Wright had so far answered every question Palmer had put to him in the interview room with the usual '*no comment*,' but the last one had stirred his mind into action.

'I mean exactly what I said, Mr Wright. If you think that your family will be, shall we say, *looked after*, if you go down for a long time, which you will, then think again. Because I think I know who you think your benefactor is, and if it is the lady I think it is then you may be in for a shock.'

'A shock?

'Yes. You see, she seems to have disappeared.' Palmer told a little white lie. 'Could be the Proceeds of Crime order on all her properties and possessions, and all the Dawn family bank accounts being frozen has something to do with it...' Another white lie. 'We can't seem to be able to contact her. You wouldn't happen to know where she is, would you?' No answer, so Palmer turned to Roger Geffs of Geffs Solicitors. 'You wouldn't happen to know would you, Mr Geffs? After all, she is supposed to be paying your fees I assume? Maybe she got wind of our interview with Mr Barber and Mr Holland and decided to go while she could – a far-off tax haven, maybe. Pure speculation on my part, of course.'

Gheeta was surprise that Geffs hadn't raised an objection, but perhaps his mind was concentrating on not getting his exorbitant fees paid if what Palmer had implied was in fact true.

Palmer rose and gave a parting shot. 'I've got a meeting to go to now. Have a good think about your position, Mr Wright; your solicitor will be going home today – you won't. You won't be going home for a number of years, but what that number is depends on what you decide to tell me. In my long experience, judges look kindly on people who have co-operated with the police when it comes to sentencing. I'll be back in thirty minutes and that will be my last interview with you. Think hard, son – think very hard. Interview ends fourteen twenty-five.'

He clicked off the recorder and followed Gheeta out.

****

Harry Jones didn't show any surprise when he opened his hotel suite door to Eve James.

'I can't say I wasn't expecting you,' he said.

'How are you, Harry?' she asked as she stepped inside.

'Alive,' said Harry, with a hint of surprise. 'That seems to be a bonus for people associated with you lately.'

'Been keeping up to date then, have you?'

'Of course, I'm a founder member of the Self Preservation Society. Tea or coffee?'

'Neither. All I want are a few numbers – the ones I asked you to get for me when we spoke on the phone to Panama.'

'We also spoke about the deal – the deal that got me back here, don't forget that, I get twenty-five percent of the washed money once you are up and running; that's the deal, and I won't testify about the ledgers if the police pull me in.'

'That stands, Harry – everybody is dead, you're safe. Where's your wife, is she here?'

'At the villa in Cyprus. She's my insurance.'

'Insurance?'

'Damn right she's my insurance. Lilian has a set of photocopies of the ledgers, all signed and witnessed by my Cypriot lawyer; a full account of all the financial activities of the Dawns, the Dooleys and everybody else I ever dealt with – amounts, dates, deals, it's all there. I knew the value of those ledgers – of course I did, I'm a solicitor – so copies were made. If our deal goes wrong or I get whacked, they go to Peter Long at the Yard.'

'He's not on this, Palmer is.'

'Really? Palmer, that old terrier – he won't let go until he's got it all tied up and passed to the CPS.'

'I know, hence my need of the account numbers in Panama. Things are getting a little too warm for my liking and I may need to take a holiday.' She held out her hand.

Jones went to a drawer in the central table and pulled out a small notebook.

'I've listed them in numerical order and then the password for that account –

four different banks and eighteen accounts in all. You are a very rich lady, Eve.'

'How rich?'

'Twenty-two million rich.'

Eve Dawn smiled. 'That should just about keep me in the luxury I aspire to, Harry. I take it your cut has been taken already?'

'Of course.'

'Fifteen percent, not thirty.'

'I don't make mistakes twice.'

'Good. I may not have a firm anymore, but money can buy most things in our circle of contacts.'

They both laughed.

'You'll enjoy Panama, Eve – good people. They mind their own business, and with your money the elite there will welcome you into their social circle.'

'I don't think so, Harry – not my scene, and I don't intend to be very visible. Once I organise things the way I want, I'll be moving on.'

'You will? Where to?'

'Never you mind. It's been a pleasure working with you, Harry.' She put the notebook into her shoulder bag, at the same time pulling out a gun and firing a bullet into Harry Jones's forehead before the brain inside it had registered what was happening.

She stood over the body. 'Twenty-five percent, Harry? You must be joking.'

****

Henry Wright took the bait after Palmer's parting remarks about Eve Dawn missing and was a worried man. Roger Geffs of Geffs Solicitors had left his client for a few minutes to make a phone call from outside the Yard to Eve Dawn – no connection, her phone was dead; no message, nothing. Dead. Roger Geffs was himself now getting worried. As usual with solicitors, he wasn't so much worried about the fate of his client as the fate of his bill. He went back inside and gave the news to Wright, advising him to sit tight until the situation with Eve Dawn became clear one way or the other.

Palmer's thirty minute deadline and then a last interview before being remanded on a first degree murder charge trumped his solicitor's advice; Wright sacked him, and a duty solicitor was called to sit in on the statement Wright had decided to make. It took an hour for one to arrive, which gave more time for Wright to put things in order in his mind. There was no need for Palmer to be present, so Gheeta sat in with a typist and prompted Wright when necessary as he recounted his long association with the Dawns and the final phone call from Eve Dawn, suggesting Dooley be taken to the Dock; no, she didn't say to kill him in so many words, but why else would she say 'take him to the dock', for a swim? Both he and Holland took that call to mean don't bring him back.

When Wright had finished, the paper was a stone-cold witnessed affidavit that would stand up in court against any defence lawyer's claims of 'witness duress', and without doubt put Eve Dawn in the position of ordering a murder. All they needed now was Eve Dawn.

****

AC Bateman read the CPS request for a warrant to arrest Eve Dawn, signed it and passed it back across his desk to Palmer.

'I don't think any jury couldn't pass a guilty verdict on her with those signed witness statements. Well done, Palmer.'

Palmer picked up the paperwork. 'I'd still like to have the lady in custody, sir. She's obviously a very dangerous person – no saying what she's planning next, but I'd say it looks like she wants total control of the London drug market, and nothing's going to stand in her way. The sooner we get her locked up the better.'

Bateman agreed. 'Anybody prepared to murder their own family wants something very badly. By the way, what's happening with the cathedral candles thing?'

'I brought the bishop in, got him on remand in Belmarsh.'

Palmer wished he'd been able to take a picture of the shock registering on Bateman's face.

'Only kidding, sir. We handed it over to NCB in Manchester and they are liaising with NCB in Madrid. It's basically a by-product of the Dawn case; not really relevant to our line of enquiry, so I hived it off.'

'Good, good. I had a quiet chat with the Home Secretary and she had a chat with the bishop. They thought it best to keep the whole thing under wraps as only one of the clergy was involved.'

'Probably best,' said Palmer. 'Media would love that story. Right then, I'll go and see if we can't find Mrs Dawn.' He started to leave.

'By the way,' said Bateman. 'Don't think it hasn't been noted how you seem to have smartened yourself up, Palmer. I don't think I have ever seen you in a suit before. Well done, sets a good example – smart clothes, smart mind.'

Palmer didn't have an answer to that; well, he did, but it would have had him reprimanded for gross insubordination, so he just smiled and left.

****

Back on the third floor he found himself subconsciously straightening his suit jacket before entering the Team Room.

'So what's she up to then?' he asked Gheeta and Claire, who were working at their computers.

Before he'd gone down to the interview rooms that morning to talk to Wright for the first time, he had sent Simms and Johnson out to tail Eve Dawn. He had prejudged what Wright would do, with the odds being very much in favour of him crumbling and putting Eve Dawn in the frame for organising the murder. Palmer's judgment of the man and his actions had been right.

'Visiting Harry Jones,' said Gheeta in answer to his question. 'Short visit and now back to her apartment. Did Bateman play ball?'

'He did, all signed and sealed.' He waved the warrant in the air.

'I can't get Simms and Johnson to arrest her without that,' Gheeta pointed out, flicking her eyes at the warrant. 'You want me to get over there with it?'

'No, tell the boys to just keep her in sight. I'm wondering what she wanted with Harry Jones; bearing in mind what Atkins told us about the deal Jones had with Dooley scamming some of the Dawn money to him, I wonder if she's bringing him back into the fold to launder again.'

'Going to be a lot of cash now, guv,' said Gheeta. 'South London and West End takings.'

'Yes, so she's going to want help washing that much. I think we'll pay Harry Jones a visit; maybe with a little persuasion he might stick another nail in Eve Dawn's coffin.'

'Not a good choice of words, guv, bearing in mind recent events.'

****

'He certainly likes the high life – who said crime doesn't pay, eh?' Palmer and Singh were on the second floor of the Hilton Hotel in Park Lane. 'What was the name of his suite?'

'The Albany Suite, guv, and I think the only people who say crime doesn't pay are the ones who get caught – the ones who get away with it say it does.'

Palmer smiled; he had a liking for DS Singh's sarcasm, it matched his own. 'Here we are then,' he said, stopping outside the door to the suite. 'We know you are in there Harry, so no silly games of not answering.' He knocked on the door.

They had checked at the desk in the hotel foyer and Jones's key was not there, so he hadn't gone out; or if he had then he'd taken it with him.

No answer. Palmer knocked again, loudly. Nothing. Palmer put on his serious voice.

'Mr Jones, open the door please. This is DCS Palmer, Metropolitan Police.'

Nothing.

'He may have gone out, guv,' suggested Gheeta.

'Well, I'm not going to hang around and wait for him to return,' said Palmer. 'Pop down and get the manager or somebody to come up with a master key.'

'There's an easier way than that, guv,' said Gheeta, and walked away along the corridor to where a housekeeper's trolley stood outside an open suite door. She went inside and was soon back out, together with a maid.

'This is Maria, sir. I've explained we have a warrant to search the room and shown her my ID. Would you show her yours?'

Palmer did and Maria inserted her master key card into the slot, and hey presto, the door clicked open. She called into the room, 'Mr Jones, are you in there?'

No answer. Palmer reached past Maria and pushed the door fully open.

Maria's screams were so loud they probably cleared the pigeons of Trafalgar Square!

Harry Jones's body lay in the centre of the suite's reception room; he was on his back, with the hole in his forehead making it quite clear why he was on his back – and quite clear he was dead. The blood from the exit wound at the back of his head had seeped around it and formed a small lake that was soaking into the expensive carpet.

'Well, well, well… Not exactly a surprise, Sergeant, knowing who his last visitor was.'

'You want Simms and Johnson to pull her in now, guv?'

'No, I don't want to risk them – she's obviously got a gun and knows how to use it. No, let's get this suite closed off as a crime scene first and get Reg Frome and his team up here; with a bit of luck they'll find something that proves she was here. Give

221

Claire a call and get the local boys in here to secure the site; then get an ARV and half a dozen AROs to meet us somewhere near, but out of sight of Eve Dawn's apartment.'

****

Back at her apartment Eve Dawn turned away from her picture window. It was one-way reflective, so she could stand and watch the street and beyond it the bridge and river without being seen herself.

The two cars that had followed her around for the past few days weren't anywhere to be seen, probably parked a hundred metres up the road. They were good, she gave them that; she had noticed how they swapped places and kept well back in the traffic behind her. But being married to a crime boss for thirty years she had picked up a few tips, one being to know when you are being followed. Odds-on it was the police – either them or another crime gang scouting the turf with an eye to moving in. Harry Jones's body would be found any time soon; latest would be when the house maid went in the next morning. Time to put the rest of the plan into action, get things back on the rails.

She took a burner phone from the drawer and dialled a number. A man's voice answered.

'Do you know who this is?' asked Eve.

There was a short silence. 'Yes,' answered Johnny Robinson.

'I have a business proposition, are you interested?'

'Going into business with you seems to be a very dangerous thing to do.'

'I have South London and the West End, and at the moment the dealers are all running around like headless chickens looking for product, which provides an attractive opening for one of the Manchester or Birmingham outfits to move in. If that happens, *you* would have a problem.'

'Maybe.'

'No *maybe* about it, Johnny. If an outside firm took over and had the strength of the South London and West End turfs operating as one, you'd be swamped and you know it. Now listen, I have no wish to be involved in the day-to-day running of things; I want to fade into the background as I did when James was running things. The gangmasters will rally round me and keep control of the streets, but I need a fallback person in case anybody steps out of line.'

'A fallback person?'

'A visible partner, a front man. I can handle the suppliers and the laundering and keep things running smoothly; I know all the contacts, I can run the back office while you take care of the soldiers. They know you, or those who don't know you have heard of you. And one more thing – I take it you are aware of the famous Harry Jones's ledgers, seeing he was your launderer too?

'Yes. They're a bit of a worry, aren't they?'

'Well, you don't need to worry about it anymore.'

'I don't?'

'No, Harry Jones is no longer with us so can't be used to collaborate the details in his ledger. Its now documentary evidence only – wouldn't stand up if used in court.'

'What about the copies? They could sink us – he told me they're witnessed by his brief and tucked away somewhere safe.'

'They will be taken care of too.'

'That would be a great weight off my mind. So, what sort of financial partnership are you offering?'

'I get twenty percent of the laundered profit, you get the rest.'

'That's a very attractive offer. Let me speak to my main people and see what they think.'

'Okay. I am away for two days and then I'm going to have a meeting with my gangmasters at the snooker hall next week. If you decide to come in, that would be a good time to meet them and get everything back on an even keel. When I get back, I'll ring for your answer. And one more thing, Johnny...'

'Yes.'

'I'm not going to run the turf on my own. If you say no, I'll be talking to Manchester.'

'Ouch.'

'Ouch indeed.' She ended the call and took a diary from the drawer and turned to the phone number page and dialled.

'Jamil?... It's Eve, are you okay?... Good. I know everything is a bit of a mess at present, but I'm sorting it and we will be back to normal in a couple of days... I've got plenty of product, so make sure your dealers don't buy elsewhere... If they do my people won't be happy, okay?... Good. I'm calling a meet at the snooker hall next week and I'm ringing round to the other gang masters with the same message. Just sit tight until then and everything will be explained and you can get back to the streets, okay?... Good man, I'll see you then.'

She rang off and then made a similar call to the other nine gang masters covering South London, and the five covering the West End. She needed to keep them onside for just a few days more; just a couple more things to take care of. She chose a passport from her shoulder bag. Eve Dawn was about to become Rachel Neil; the picture of Rachel Neil in the passport resembled Eve, but Rachel had long black hair and thick-rimmed glasses and was a Canadian national. The passport was Canadian because UK passports were now all digitally checked at Passport Control against the personal database of the Home Office in a matter of a few seconds by a scanner; a fake UK one would show up immediately. The Canadian database hadn't yet been integrated with the UK one; when it was the forgers would have to look elsewhere, but for now it was good to go. The wig of long black hair and the glasses were in a box in the wardrobe in the bedroom; the wig took five minutes to brush and fit over her shorter natural hair that she pinned up out of the way. She looked in the mirror as she put the glasses on; fine, all looking good.

The internal phone buzzed. Her heart missed a beat as she picked it up. 'Yes?'

'You have visitors,' said the foyer desk clerk, 'Boys in blue.' The phone rang off. James had sorted out a deal with the clerks who would ring ahead if any visitors that didn't want the Dawns to know they were coming up to the apartment appeared. The information was given in exchange for a brown paper envelope every month, and like most brown paper envelope deals it worked a treat.

Eve looked down from all the windows but couldn't see any activity. She hurriedly put on her coat and a headscarf, slipped the passport back into her shoulder bag with the others, opened the safe and took out ten packets of ten thousand pounds in used twenty pound notes that they'd kept for emergencies. She dropped these into a Morrisons bag before shutting the safe and leaving the apartment, checking the corridor was clear before stepping out.

The lifts were both stationary at the ground floor, not that she was going to use one of them. She went to the end of the corridor and through a door into the fire escape staircase; she opened the door to the roof and left it ajar. She had no intention of going that way, but it might give her more time if the police thought she had and checked it out. She then descended the stairs as fast and as quietly as she could.

****

Palmer's squad car pulled up behind the ARV which was parked up behind Simms and Johnson's cars in a parallel street to the apartment block but out of its sightline. He got out and an ARO sergeant joined him and Gheeta on the pavement. The ARO was in full black operational kit from the helmet and visor to the steel-capped boots and carried a Heckler and Koch MP5 submachine gun and a holstered Glock 17 pistol, as well as pepper spray, taser and double blade eight-inch knife. Heaven knows what other armaments the team carried in the vehicle.

'DS Mitchell, sir,' the ARO introduced himself. 'I have an eight man team with me.'

Palmer acknowledged Mitchell and introduced his team. 'Right Mitchell, we have a warrant for the arrest of one person, a lady called Eve Dawn. Now this may seem a bit of a heavy-handed approach to arrest just one female, but she has murdered or possibly been involved in the murder of several people, and she is armed.'

'Sounds like a nice lady,' said Mitchell.

'Yes, just the sort to take home to meet mum,' Palmer added. 'She has an apartment on the top floor and as far as we know is inside now. Over to you.'

'Right.' Mitchell looked at Simms and Johnson. 'Are you two armed?'

'No,' they both answered.

'Okay, well I've had a look at the layout of the building on our computer in the van on the way here and there are only two ways in and out, the main door at the front and the fire escape which comes down to the underground garage, which has an exit round the corner in a side street. I will be executing the warrant with six men, so, and as you two know what this lady looks like, I want one of you to stay in the foyer and one round the side at the garage in case she makes a run for it. You will both have an ARO with you. Okay?'

Simms and Johnson nodded acceptance.

'Right then, sir, if you're ready we'll get to it?'

Palmer spread his hands. 'Carry on, Sergeant.'

Gheeta had a memory flashback of films called *Carry On* that her father had sat and giggled at when she was a child. She hoped this arrest wasn't going to end up in a similar vein.

The AROs got out of the van and hugging the walls of the office buildings, they made a line with Palmer, Singh, Simms and Johnson bringing up the rear and snaked their way towards the apartment building. Once beside it, Simms was pulled away by an ARO and they disappeared around the corner to the garage exit.

The uniformed commissionaire at the front desk was taken aback as Palmer led the AROs quietly through the front doors and came to a stop in front of the reception desk, his ID in hand.

'I am DCS Justin Palmer of the Metropolitan Police and I have a warrant to arrest Eve Dawn who is a resident at this address. We have information that the lady is in her apartment at present and therefore I intend to execute that warrant.' He softened his tone, 'You got a problem with that?'

'No, no – executive apartment's top floor.'

'I know, the one with DAWN on the door – thank you. One of my men and an armed officer will wait here.' And with that he and Gheeta took a lift with DS Mitchell and one other ARO to the top floor, whilst the other AROs took the stairs. Johnson and the last ARO stood by the desk, watching the lifts and stair entrance.

The commissionaire reached for the wall phone.

'Ah-ah,' Johnson shook his head. 'No calls.'

'I'm going to ask the manager to come down.'

'Okay.'

The commissionaire tapped in a number; a few seconds later he spoke into the phone. 'You have visitors, boys in blue.' He hooked the phone back on its rest and smiled at Johnson, who smiled back.

Reaching the basement of the staff staircase, Eve stood and caught her breath before easing the door to the garage parking basement open very slightly; it was all quiet. She passed through and walked slowly towards the exit, stooping so she was masked by the parked cars. Then she saw Simms and his ARO at the bottom of the exit slope; there was no way past them without being seen. She edged as near to them as she dared, and taking out her car key fob from her bag pressed it. The beep and flashing lights from her car parked towards the back of the garage caught their attention and they made their way towards it, shielding themselves behind other cars as they went.

Eve kept to the side shadows as she hurried up the ramp and out into the street, where she turned away from the building and quickened her pace. After putting two streets between her and the apartment building, she called for an Uber.

****

On the top floor of the apartment building Palmer and Gheeta held back whilst an ARO crept to the side of the Dawn apartment door and placed a listening bug on the door. The bug looked very much like a doctor's stethoscope, with leads to earplugs that the ARO had in place. The standard procedure was two minutes; if no sound or sound of movement had been heard by the,n it was deemed the apartment was empty or those inside asleep. The ARO signalled from the door with a thumbs down.

'It's empty,' Mitchell told Palmer, and they moved silently to the door.

'I'll just check that, 'said Palmer. 'I don't want to force entry and find her sitting reading a book.'

He knocked loudly on the door. No answer.

'Do you want us to force it open, sir?' asked Mitchell.

'No, no need. Would you like to do the honours?' Palmer said to Gheeta, pointing at the keypad.

Gheeta took out her iPhone, pulled up the keypad app and putting it over the Dawn entry keypad, set it in motion. After a few seconds it beeped and she read off the numbers. 'One, six, nine, guv.'

'Only three numbers? Should be four, surely?'

'One of them will be in the number twice. The six is the one with most patination.'

'So it's one, six, six, nine.'

'Yes.'

'And using your theory about people's birthdays, it would be one, nine, six, six then?'

'Yes.'

'World cup,' said Mitchell.

'What?'

'The year England won the world cup, 1966. This lady a football fan, is she?'

'I doubt it, but her husband might have been. Okay, let's go.'

Gheeta keyed in the numbers and the door lock clicked. Mitchell waved Palmer and Gheeta away down the corridor and his men formed up three each side of the door, their submachine guns raised in attack mode as he gently turned the handle and pushed it open.

'POLICE, this is armed police, anybody inside show yourself with your hands above your head NOW!' Mitchell shouted, peering inside.

No movement inside.

'This is the armed police, show yourself!' One last try, but still no movement.

Mitchell waved his men in and they moved quickly inside, checking the rooms off the hall and shouting 'Clear!' as each one was found empty until all had been checked.

Mitchell signalled Palmer to come forward. 'All the rooms are clear, sir, nobody home.'

Gheeta grabbed Palmer's coat sleeve and pointed to the open service door at the end of the corridor. 'There's your answer, guv. She's used the fire escape stairs.'

Mitchell held them back. 'Hold on, you wait here while we check it out.'

He called two of his men out of the apartment and they slowly approached and entered into the stairwell.

'Door to the roof is open too, sir,' reported Mitchell to Palmer. 'Hang on while we check it out.' The rest of his team joined him and they moved onto the roof, leaving one ARO with Palmer and Singh.

It took a good ten minutes for the roof search to come back negative, during which time Palmer radioed Simms and Johnson to see if there was any action at their end. Nothing happening was the answer – no sign of Eve Dawn at either exit. The AROs checked down the stairwell and Gheeta radioed for a local uniform officer to be sent to secure the apartment as a crime scene until forensics could give it the once over in the morning.

'That's disappointing,' said Palmer as they travelled down in the lift. 'I think it's time we put a stop and detain on Eve Dawn now we have a warrant. Circulate to all border areas, airports, ferry terminals and the rest; she obviously knows we are after her, and either she'll go to ground or go abroad. What's your guess?' he asked Gheeta.

'Abroad – nothing to stay here for and you can't go to ground for ever. Get a reward out for her and somebody will grass; she'd know that and wouldn't take a chance. No, I think she'll go abroad, guv. Let's face it, judging from Harry Jones's ledger she will have enough money in offshore accounts to give her a good life, and if she was thinking of carrying on the family business here she'd have sorted things a different way, wouldn't she? She wouldn't have brought the searchlight onto her with a murder charge for a start, would she?'

'I think you're right.'

The lift jolted to a stop at the second floor. Mitchell pulled Palmer back and behind him as he unlocked the Heckler.

The doors slid open and an elderly lady stepped in; she reminded Gheeta of Miss Marple. She froze at the sight of DS Mitchell in his ARO gear and the firearms.

Gheeta gave her a smile. 'It's alright ma'am, police business, nothing to be alarmed about.' She showed her ID card.

The lady pressed the ground floor button and stood as far away as she could. 'Is he under arrest?' She pointed at Palmer half hidden behind Mitchell.

Gheeta laughed. 'No, ma'am.'

'He looks the suspicious type, perhaps he should be. Get a few like him knocking on our doors trying to persuade us into Equity Release; mostly his age and smart suits. Load of spivs if you ask me. They're not supposed to allow them into the block, but I think the boys on the front desk get a bribe. Perhaps you should take a look into that.' She nodded at Palmer. 'Are you taking him in for questioning then? I would, he looks the type.'

Palmer was about to come to his own defence when they reached the ground floor and the doors opened. The lady scuttled off to the main exit doors as Palmer, Mitchell and Gheeta joined Johnson and the other AROs who had come down the staircase.

The commissionaire laughed. 'Oh, I see you met Miss Lampard then.'

'Yes, interesting conversation too,' said Gheeta. 'Where's she going this time of night?'

'The library, so she says.' He gave a knowing wink.

Gheeta checked her phone. 'Libraries aren't open this late, are they?'

The commissionaire laughed. 'No, and I don't think they sell bottles of gin either.'

****

It was now a waiting game. The hope was that Eve Dawn was running and would be picked up by Border Force at one of the UK's exit points. Palmer was waiting for that, and waiting for anything useful from forensics at Jones's suite and Eve Dawn's apartment that would tie her unquestionably to being part of the murders. Waiting was not Palmer's game, he was impatient; he could see the trees from the wood now, the scenarios were falling into place, and he was champing at the bit to get Eve Dawn in custody and put the case to the CPS to start prosecutions. But without Eve Dawn in custody he couldn't move – just wait. So he gave the team the weekend off with instructions to keep their mobiles on, just in case.

Chapter 13 SATURDAY

The lady who arrived at Larnaca International Airport in Cyprus on a JET2 flight from Birmingham with a passport in the name of Rachel Neil looked every bit a businesswoman. The business this woman had in mind wouldn't take her very long – just long enough to visit Harry Jones's wife, Lilian, in their Mediterranean beachside villa, stab her to death with a locally-bought knife and return to the airport hotel for one night before taking her pre-booked seat on a flight back to the UK the next day, carrying an extra piece of hand luggage: that extra piece being Harry's signed ledger copies – the copies that had not proved to be such a good life insurance policy as Harry had thought they would be.

Eve had found them in a bedside cupboard, pointed out to her by Harry's wife after the first stab of the knife went into her thigh. The second stab had been aimed to open the jugular vein on Lilian Jones's neck; she was dead in twelve seconds. Eve had thought that a man with Harry's experience would at least have lodged them in a safe or a local bank deposit box. 'Tut, tut, Harry. Big mistake.'

Chapter 14 SUNDAY

Once back in the UK, Eve collected the Morrisons bag from the left luggage locker she'd hired at Birmingham Airport and made her way by National Express to London, booking herself into a second-rate hotel in Victoria. She just needed to make sure everything was in place for the final curtain. First thing to do was to make sure Johnny Robinson was definitely in; she pulled her mobile out and made the call.

'I'm back. Just checking – you in or out?'

'In.'

'Good – that's the right decision, Johnny. I'm going to arrange a meeting with all the gangmasters on Thursday at two in the snooker club; if you can make it with your main men, we'll sort out people's responsibilities.'

'Sounds good to me.'

'I'll be there from one thirty and we can have a chat first.'

'Okay.'

Eve finished the call and smiled. Things were falling into place nicely.

Johnny Robinson also finished the call and smiled. Things were falling into place nicely.

Chapter 15 MONDAY

Gheeta handed Palmer a wad of 10 x 8 colour photographs taken by the Cypriot police inside the Jones's holiday home, complete with the body of his wife on the floor with her head in a pool of blood.

'They reckon she disturbed a thief who turned on her, guv. But they aren't aware of Harry Jones's death and the connection to the Dawns or the rest of it.'

'When did it happen?'

'Their pathologist puts the time of death down to between twenty-four and thirty-six hours ago.'

'That's within the timescale of Eve Dawn being off our radar then?'

'Yes, she could have flown out or paid somebody on the island to do it. Claire's checking the passenger lists of all the flights to Cyprus in the two days prior to the killing; no Eve Dawn, so we are checking for all single ladies travelling.'

'Right. So how did *we* come to get notified?'

'Spanish police contacted the British Embassy to find the next of kin for Mrs Jones and it listed Harry Jones in the UK;

and of course, when the Home Office was alerted they noted that we'd flagged him up as '*person of interest*' and passed it to us.'

'Why would anybody, including Eve Dawn, want her dead?'

'Well, the only assumption I can make is that she knew something that was dangerous to whoever killed her, and we have to assume it was the same person or people who killed Harry – somebody doing a bit of tidying up the loose ends maybe?'

'Well...' Palmer sat down and leafed through the photos. 'We know Harry's ledgers could have worried some top people if they knew about them and the information inside them.'

'So you think that somebody wanted the ledgers and went to Harry for them, who didn't have them but maybe said his wife had them in Cyprus? So whoever it was killed Harry and then went to his wife, who also didn't have them, and decided to kill her too?'

'Which points again to Eve Dawn – she's the only one left who knows the ledgers weren't burnt in the fire at Harry Jones's office.'

'And the only one who knew they were in Stan's safe, and would now be in our hands.'

'Quite so, and she would know that they wouldn't count for much in a court of law without Harry or his wife to substantiate what's in them; purely documentary evidence, and if you remember the lessons on evidence law at Police College....'

Gheeta interrupted him and quoted: '*Before documentary evidence is admissible as evidence, it must be proved by other evidence from a witness that the document is genuine.*'

'Correct. It's called 'laying the foundation', and without the Jones's swearing on oath that what's in the ledgers is the truth, they have no foundation as evidence and a brief wouldn't have much trouble in having them thrown out.'

'Two murders to prevent one piece of evidence?'

'Yes, why not? The information in those ledgers with Harry or his wife backing it up in court would be enough to put an end to the business of Eve Dawn and just about every organised crime boss, dealer and money launderer in London, and put them all away for quite a long time – a stick of dynamite that has now had its fuse cut out.'

'By Rachel Neil,' Claire said, turning from her computer towards them.

'Rachel Neil?' Palmer asked, turning towards her. 'Who's Rachel Neil?'

'I don't know yet, but we will do in an hour or so. I think she might be Eve Dawn.' Claire lent back and read off her screen. 'A female called Rachel Neil left Birmingham Airport on the early bird JET2 flight to Larnaca, Cyprus last Saturday morning, and returned the next day on the first flight back.'

'Why her, why do you think she's Eve Dawn? Was she the only female on flights to Cyprus that day then?' asked Palmer.

'No, there were lots of females, but most were travelling with family members with the same surname; there were also eighteen single females travelling from Birmingham and London Heathrow that day as well. So, looking for a match with Eve Dawn I could get rid of any under the age of thirty-six – Dawn's age – and that left me with five. Now, seeing that we have a 'stop and detain warrant' with the Border Force, if she was the one going to Cyprus to kill Mrs Jones, she wouldn't be travelling under her own name or she would have been stopped; so she would have to have a false passport and not a UK one, 'cause they are easily detected and stand out a mile. Which left me with one lady: Rachel Neil, age thirty-eight, single lady travelling on a Canadian Passport.'

'Canadian?' Palmer questioned.

Gheeta explained. 'Their passport system isn't integrated into the UK one guv, so a fake wouldn't automatically set off an alarm.'

Claire continued. 'And, as I said, Rachel Neil returned to the UK the next day Sunday on the first flight back – that's got to be suspicious in its own right, hasn't it? Anyway, we will soon know as I've emailed the Border Force at Birmingham Airport for copies of the boarding CCTV for the outward flight – they're sending a file ASAP.'

'Odds on it's Eve Dawn,' said Gheeta.

Palmer stood and walked to the progress chart. 'If it is, what's she up to then?

Gheeta joined him and pointed to the board as she spoke. 'Her masterplan, guv.

She's the one left standing – James, Dad and Stan out of the picture, as well as their loyal lieutenants killed with Dawn in the car and with Stan at his tyre business; Dooley gets the blame and he's hit, which just leaves Eve as the top dog, with enough knowledge of the business to keep things ticking over. I'm betting Harry Jones put a threat on her, that he'd tell the police he'd verify the information in his ledgers unless he was cut in as a partner or similar, and Eve decided she didn't want him; and both he and his ledger threat had to go.'

'But why go to all the trouble of going to Cyprus and killing his wife?'

'I don't know, guv. Perhaps there was something in Cyprus that needed sorting out?'

'Copies. I bet he had copies of the ledgers out there,' said Palmer.

'So he's demanding a partnership or a big percentage and she's refused, and he's threatened to back up the ledger contents as a witness unless he's in.'

'Yes, signing his own death warrant with that threat though, so I can't see he'd do that.'

'Yes, unless he tells Eve it would be pointless to kill him because he's got copies.'

'In Cyprus.'

Gheeta nodded. 'And if they were in the holiday place in Cyprus, that would make her trip make sense. She went to get them and silence Jones's wife; any threat from the ledger's content is now gone.'

'Okay, that all makes sense. But the business has got a lot bigger with the West End added, now she's lost her launderer and her main men.'

'Eve's still got control, guv.'

'Okay, I get that. But what if somebody else fancies the turf? There's no menace protecting it now like the Dawn brothers or Jack Dooley could exert, you wouldn't think of going to war with them – but with Eve Dawn?'

'So you think she's going to have some trouble?'

'Not necessarily so, but if she stays on her own, then yes. I'd expect a takeover battle from Johnny Robinson or at least one of the outside mobs – without some heavies on her team she's a sitting duck. She's a hard businesswoman and she'll have realised that, so I wouldn't be at all surprised if she pulls in a partner – somebody with a bit of clout who can kick back if need be.'

'The file's through,' Claire shouted to them. 'JET2's boarding CCTV for the Cyprus flight.'

They quickly walked back and stood behind her as Claire set the film in motion. It showed the boarding gate from the departure lounge with a stream of people walking through.

'Now which one is that woman you said, Claire?'

'Rachel Neil, thirty-eight – travelling alone.'

'There she is!' Gheeta pointed to the screen. 'Pause it.'

And there she was, the unmistakeable figure of Eve Dawn; only this Eve Dawn had long black hair and glasses. But Eve Dawn it undoubtedly was.

'Case proved, milord,' said Palmer. 'Proof she flew out the day Mrs Jones was killed, and no doubt there will be CCTV of her boarding the return flight the next day too. Claire, check the local hotels close to Larnaca Airport and see if we can't find where she stayed for the one night. If we can, and they have CCTV, then we have her bang to rights.'

'Bang to rights?' Gheeta gave Palmer a questioning look.

'Legal term,' he said.

Reg Frome entered. 'Good day, all.'

They all responded with greetings.

'Do you have good news for us, Reg?' asked Palmer.

'I'm afraid not,' said Frome, looking downcast. 'This Eve Dawn person seems to be a very astute lady.' He sat down. 'Nothing in the Jones's hotel suite to place her in there at any time, and I've just come from her apartment where we are drawing blanks too. I was hoping we might get some sugar particles to tie her into the Royal Dock murder, but none at all; but at least we were able to lift her fingerprints and DNA, although no matches in the Jones's place. And no matches of prints with any we have on file of the men killed in the James Dawn car or Stan Dawn workshop. Sorry.'

Palmer shrugged. 'Can't be helped – if there's nothing there then there's nothing there. I think we have enough circumstantial to nail her.'

'We've got a bit more now, sir,' said Claire, tapping her keyboard. 'At least Mr Jones had CCTV at his villa gate in Cyprus – Cypriot police have sent it through. I'll put it up on the big screen.'

They all watched the big screen as clear colour CCTV pictures showed 'Rachel Neil' arrive by taxi outside the steel gates of the Jones's villa and use the intercom after paying off the taxi that drove off. No sound was on the recording, but the pictures told the whole story as the gates automatically opened and closed after 'Rachel Neil' had entered. The screen then cut to her leaving by opening one of the gates by hand from the inside and closing it behind her. The date and time showed top right of the recording.

'Date and time is right, sir,' said Claire.

'She's not stupid, is she?' said Frome. 'I said she is a very astute lady – look, she's wearing gloves on a lovely hot Mediterranean day; no prints left.'

'No matter, 'said Palmer with a big smile. 'I think that is quite enough with the airline recordings to put Eve Dawn in the right place at the right time.'

'Bang to rights then, guv?' asked Gheeta with a cheeky grin.

****

Palmer strode through the Organised Crime Team Room to Peter Long's office at the back and tapped on the open door.

'Ah, come in Justin,' said Long, putting down a sheaf of reports he had been reading.

'I got a message to give you a look, Peter, 'said Palmer, taking a seat.

'Yes, a couple of my chaps on the street have got wind of developments in the Dawn manor; seems there's a big meeting going to happen on Thursday at the Dawn snooker hall in Camberwell. Word is that all the South London and West End gangmasters have been told to attend.' Long shrugged his shoulders. 'Your guess is as good as mine as to why, but it looks like things are going to be sorted out and normal service resumed. Both the turfs have had their street dealers running around like headless chickens trying to buy cocaine and crystal meth anywhere they can since the Dawn supply stopped.

'The small amounts they are getting is coming in from outside the capital, and to make it go round it's never been cut so much – which is a bit worrying as these idiots will mix it with anything, including poisons to get the weight up. My chaps on the street say you'd get a better high sniffing flour, and that the price of a tab has trebled.'

'Thursday at the snooker hall, eh? Well, I assume Eve Dawn will be there so it's an opportunity to nab her.'

'You'll have a riot if you go marching in there with a warrant. I'd have a couple of buses of TSG officers as back up if I was you.'

'No, if I decide to go for her I'll wait until she leaves and arrest her away from the place – low-key. What time is the meeting at the club?'

'Two o'clock, and to be perfectly honest Justin, it will be a good thing if some kind of normality resumed. We've had an increase in violence and stabbings as the street teams get protective of their postcodes and eke out their supplies. Sooner or later somebody outside the capital will see an opportunity and move in, and then all Hell could break loose; much easier for us to know who we are dealing with and who to target. If somebody like the Manchester gangs try to move in, they are pretty free with firearms use – and once the bullets fly, the public are in danger.'

'Have you got anybody inside – anybody who will be at that meeting?'

'Not as such, no. But we will get all the info on what took place pretty soon afterwards.'

'What's your reading of it then?

'I think Eve Dawn is either going to promote a couple of her bigger gang masters to a sort of partner status, or she's already got a partner lined up and this is the 'meet the new boss' meeting.'

'Any ideas who that might be?'

'No word on the street, but I'd put my money on Johnny Robinson.'

'The chap who runs North London?'

'Yes.'

'Well, that would make sense.'

'He's good at it – Teflon-coated is Johnny, old school. We know he's done a few nasty things in his time, disappeared a few people, but we've never been able to make any charges stick. Clever man – getting on a bit, but knows the business inside out.'

'So where the Hell are you, Mrs Dawn?' Palmer rubbed his chin. He was back in the Team Room where Simms and Johnson had joined Gheeta and Claire. They had all just finished looking at the Birmingham Airport CCTV of 'Rachel Neil' coming through arrivals and out of the main concourse into the wide world beyond. 'Where did you go next?'

'London,' Claire said. 'On the ten-fifteen National Express from the airport. Look.'

The big screen showed CCTV footage taken by the onboard camera of the National Express coach as passengers got on at Birmingham Airport. 'Sixth person on.' And Claire was right; the sixth person that got on and showed a ticket to the driver was Eve Dawn – the Rachel Neil disguise had been discarded. 'She's back to being herself.'

'She must have changed in the lady's room at the airport,' said Gheeta.

257

'There's a black wig and pair of glasses in a Birmingham Airport waste bin I bet.'

'I've emailed National Express to let me have a copy of the CCTV showing the bus arriving at Victoria Coach Station, and the bus CCTV of the passengers getting off. I would think she travelled all the way back to London, but if that shows her getting off then we know for certain she did.'

'Good, well done.' Palmer took it for granted that Claire would tie everything up nicely. 'So, where would she batten down the hatches in London? She can't go back to the apartment, and as far as we know the Dawns don't have another address.'

'The snooker hall?' suggested Simms.

'No, a lady like Eve Dawn isn't going to kip down on a sofa at a snooker hall – and she'd be aware we would probably be watching it. No, she's more likely to be in a hotel I would think.'

'But we are not watching the snooker hall, guv,' Gheeta reminded him.

'No need – but she won't go there in case we are.'

At times like that, Gheeta gave in to Palmer's experience.

'Well…' Gheeta was thinking hard. 'I bet there's a monthly or annual service charge levied on the Dawn apartment to pay for the commissionaire and other staff; and with a bit of luck it will be paid by direct debit.'

Palmer opened his hands. 'And?'

'If that's right then we can trace the bank account it comes from and get a warrant to have them release the card information and any recent payments.'

'Hoping that one is to a London Hotel,' Palmer said.

'Exactly.'

'Good thinking, Sergeant.' He turned to Simms and Johnson. 'Off you go, lads – have a chat to the manager at the apartment block and see what you can get on that. As soon as you find anything out call it in and we'll get a warrant for the bank.'

Simms and Johnson left the room.

****

'It's data protection laws.'
'It's a murder investigation.'

Simms and Johnson were stood inside the second floor management office of the Dawns' apartment block in front of a large expensive desk, behind which the manager was explaining his refusal to give them the information on the Dawn's service charge payments.

Simms tried again. 'You do understand me, don't you? This is a murder investigation, not some minor parking offence – a murder investigation.'

The portly manager in his smart suit with orchid buttonhole was beginning to sweat. Two six-foot plus plainclothes detectives leaning halfway across his desk with a threatening look on their faces wasn't a regular occurrence; it was easier dealing with elderly residents whose parking place had been taken by somebody else.

'I do understand, but since the tightening of the data protection laws my hands are tied.'

Johnson pulled a plastic hand restraint from his jacket pocket. 'Stand up and turn around.' He walked around the desk and heaved the manager into a standing position and twirled him around. 'Hands behind your back.'

'Wh-what are you doing?'

'I'm arresting you for obstructing the police in their line of duty. Anything you might say will be...'

The thought of being marched out of the apartment block in front of the staff and residents cuffed like a criminal was enough to turn the tide.

'Wait, wait, wait.'

Johnson relaxed his grip on the manager's arm, who reached over to a shelf of arch files and pulled one out. He put it on his desk, opened it, rifled through the papers and pulled one out. 'Here.'

Simms took it and looked. It was a chronological listing of the monthly payments for the service charge and other auxiliary charges for the Dawn apartment; all paid on time, and all paid from the same bank account. Simms took a photo of the page with the bank code and account number on his mobile and returned it to the manager.

'Thank you. That didn't hurt, did it?' He put his mobile back in his pocket. 'Have a nice day sir – and just remember, we were never here. Wouldn't want it known that you broke the data protection laws, would you? Heavy fine your bosses would have to pay, wouldn't be very happy with that, would they?'

And they left as Simms sent the photo through to Gheeta.

****

Banks can be very obstructive when it comes to disclosing their customers' account information; especially when their customer is a major criminal sending laundered money through their system. Banks have a lot of interest in profits, and no interest at all in morality.

Palmer knew this, so had Reg Frome get Pete Atkin to fast-track a warrant through the Forensic Accounting branch, forcing the bank to open the Dawn account under fraud investigation laws, which they are compelled to do. This includes use of any credit or debit cards associated with that account.

'She's been busy, guv,' said Gheeta as they pored over the recent dealings on the account. 'She's cleared it out except for a couple of thousand pounds – two hundred and sixty grand gone out in the last two weeks to Panama.'

'I wonder if she's thinking of doing a runner then?' Palmer pursed his lips in thought. 'It would make sense if she's had enough and wants out of the business entirely.'

'So why not just go at the start after the hits on James and Dad?' asked Gheeta. 'Why all this stuff with Dooley and Jones?'

'Changed her mind. Women do that.'

Gheeta held her tongue.

'Anyway, where is she now?'

'The Sidney Hotel – Victoria took a payment off the debit card for one hundred and forty pounds this morning.'

'Right, let's go. Claire, give Simms and Johnson a call to meet us there – park a hundred yards down the road from it.'

'Metres, sir.'

'What?'

'A hundred *metres* down the road. We went metric in 1972, sir – no yards anymore.'

'Whatever, just make sure they don't get seen.'

****

With Simms at the front of the building and Johnson covering the side, Palmer and DS Singh entered the Sidney Hotel and stopped at the reception desk. Palmer showed his ID, which was hardly necessary as DS Singh was in uniform. The young lady receptionist was very helpful.

'She paid and booked out this morning, sir. Just the one night.'

'A hundred and forty quid for one night?' Palmer was astonished.

'Includes breakfast, sir.'

'I take it the corn flakes are gold-plated then? Did she say where she was going?

'No, sir.'

Gheeta thanked the receptionist and they left.

'I wonder if she did the usual thing and nicked the bubble bath, guv?' Gheeta smiled.

'For a hundred and forty pounds a night I'd nick the whole flippin' bath!'

'What now, guv? We've got all the UK exits covered, so she can't leave the country as Eve Dawn or Rachel Neil.'

'She might have other aliases, other passports – probably has, she seems well prepared. Not a lot we can do except sit tight and hope she breaks cover, or else it's going to be Thursday's meeting at the snooker hall for our next move.'

****

'Shit!'

Eve Dawn sat in the Ford Fiesta she'd just rented from the Europcar branch at Victoria Station that morning in the name of Rachel Neil. She was driving past the Sydney Hotel on her way to find another one for the night when she saw Palmer and Singh coming out. That had been a close thing; how had they found out she was staying there? She thought hard; she'd changed her phone immediately after Barber had called from the Yard knowing it would be traced, so it wasn't that. It had to be the only other traceable thing she'd used: her bank card.

'You stupid fool,' she admonished herself. 'Of course they'd got her card number somehow and the Sydney Hotel would show up on her card statement. Idiot!' A Morrisons bag of money beside her, and she'd used a card! She had used it again renting the car so they'd be on that pretty quick too; and she had used the Rachel Neil cloned card at both, so she couldn't use that again. 'Stupid! Stupid! Stupid!'

She drove on into Belgravia and pulled up alongside Eaton Square Gardens, where there was little traffic and it was quiet. She needed to shake Palmer off; he was getting too close for comfort. She walked away from the square into Belgrave Road and into the Beverley Hotel, where she booked a single room for the night using her Rachel Neil passport and card. She left the Beverley and walked along the pavement until she saw a drain and dropped the car keys and Rachel Neil's passport and cloned card through the grill. She walked into the gardens and sat down, sorting through her handbag, and pulled out her next alias. She was now Margaret Hocking; the photo was Eve, so no problem with disguises.

She thought for a while about what to do next. She could find an internet cafe and transfer the remaining money in her UK account to Panama, but the police were obviously monitoring the account and would be at the cafe in no time, so she decided against that; she could do that from Panama when she was there. She needed to move fast; her payment to the Beverley would have registered on the account, and Palmer would be putting a ring round it pretty quickly. She hailed a black cab.

'Heathrow, please.'

She made a phone call as they moved off; if the police had a trace on this mobile, she'd be miles away from Eaton Square by the time they got there.

'Changed your mind?' said Johnny Robinson when he answered the call.

'No, no, not at all – things have got a bit too hot for me, I need to disappear for a while. I won't be able to get to the Thursday meeting, so you'll have to handle it. I'm sure you can.'

'How *hot* have things got?' Robinson wasn't stupid; no way was he going to get mixed up in a multiple murder case. 'Teflon' was his nickname, and he meant to keep it that way.

'Palmer's getting close, so I need a couple of months off the grid. I think it best if Eve Dawn disappears for good, so I'm going to spend some time in Panama and then come back with a new identity; I'll keep in touch by phone and Skype. It could be good for us as I can set up some new laundries and maybe more suppliers whilst I'm there – I have a few old contacts through James that I can look up.'

'Okay, when are you going?'

'Soon as I can get a flight – I'll call you when I'm settled in. If you want me to talk to the gang masters on the phone or by Skype on Thursday, we can do that.'

'We'll see how it goes. Good idea – that would present a united front from what my people have heard on the street. They just want everything to settle back to normal, so it shouldn't be a problem.'

'Okay, talk soon.'

'Take care.'

Click.

****

In the Team Room Palmer had mixed feelings. He was happy that the real time monitoring of Eve Dawn's bank card by Claire had thrown up the booking at the

Beverley Hotel almost as soon as it had been made; but he was unhappy because it was Mrs P.'s steak and kidney pie for tea, and by the time he got home his portion would probably be in the fridge; food never tastes as good reheated.

'If Benji comes round, he's not to have it,' was the explicit order he'd given Mrs P. when he phoned her to say he'd be late and didn't know what time he'd be home.

'There's plenty to go round, and anyway I'm not expecting him to come round tonight – he's had all the bags for the charity.'

'Don't bet on it – that man has an inner sense of when you've cooked a pie.'

'Don't be silly, and you take care.'

'I always do. Love you.'

'You too.'

Click

'She's hired a car.' Gheeta turned away from her screen towards Palmer. 'Used the same bank card as at the hotel. I'll ring Europcar and get the registration and put it on the ANPR System.'

'Put it as *'report location'*, I don't want any car to try and stop and arrest her – too dangerous. Right, let's get a team organised and pay the Beverley Hotel a visit.'

****

'I'm beginning to think we've been set up.'

The trap had been laid at the Beverley. Palmer had gone in alone at five pm and had a quiet word with the manager who had been very co-operative. Rachel Neil had booked in earlier and then left; she hadn't been to her room so they were expecting her back that evening, as an evening meal was included in the one hundred and eighty pound charge. Palmer had refrained from comment. Simms had been smuggled in through the staff entrance and kitted out with the hotel logo waistcoat and bow-tie and was now on duty in reception with the genuine receptionist at the desk.

Upstairs on the second floor, Palmer and Singh with two AROs were inside Eve Dawn's room waiting for word that she was on her way up, and they would then execute the arrest when she entered the room. Outside, an AROV blacked-out Transit sat two side streets away with the rest of the Territorial

Target Team ready to lockdown the hotel once Dawn was inside – just in case something worried her and she took flight without going to the room.

It was now eleven forty-five, and they had all been in position since five thirty. Palmer took another prawn and mayonnaise sandwich off the tray Gheeta had ordered around nine o'clock; the corners were beginning to curl and the pot of coffee had long since gone cold. 'We'll give it another hour. Is anything happening with the car?'

'I'll check, guv.' Gheeta called Johnson who was in a plain squad car in Eaton Square, with eyes on the Fiesta that the ANPR system of a passing patrol car had picked up earlier. 'All quiet, Johnson?'

'All quiet,' came back the reply.

****

Inside room 435 at the Hyatt Hotel, Heathrow, Eve Dawn alias Margaret Hocking was enjoying a very comfortable night's sleep after a superb medium rare steak meal and a long hot bath; all paid for in advance with cash, and the excuse that her card had been stolen in London earlier and she had put a

stop on it, but being a Canadian National –
and her passport confirmed this – she couldn't
replace it before her flight in the morning.
The hotel had been quite prepared to take five
hundred pounds cash as security against her
bill.

Chapter 16 TUESDAY

'You're a crafty so and so, aren't you?'

Palmer stifled a yawn the next morning as he stood looking at Eve Dawn's picture on the white progress board on the far wall of the Team Room. He had stood the team down from the Beverley Hotel at two in the morning and eaten his microwaved steak and kidney pie at two forty-five, having been unable to resist.

'Clever so-and-so,' said Gheeta, sitting at her computer. 'Very clever so-and-so.'

'She's out there somewhere,' said Claire in a hopeful voice. 'We've covered every angle so she must pop up sooner or later.'

Palmer had left Simms at the hotel all night, just in case Dawn had returned, and sent him home to get some sleep at eight that morning.

'We've hit the buffers, haven't we?' Palmer sat down beside them. 'Anything from Johnson?'

Gheeta nodded. 'No, drawn blanks so far.'

Johnson was out around Eaton Square showing Eve Dawn's photo to all the various hotel reception staff in the local hotels, hoping she might have booked into one using cash after setting the false trail at the Beverley with the bank card.

Peter Long tapped on the door and entered. He had a big smile on his face.

'And how is the Nocturnal Murder Squad this morning?'

'Ha ha, very funny,' said Palmer. 'Don't you forget that we are only handling this case to help you out.'

'I wish you could help us out a lot more, Justin – seems that the powers that be have got it into their heads that any little gathering of brainless young oiks with knives and drugs anywhere in London is now classified as Organised Crime; most of those thickos couldn't organise a piss-up in a brewery. Anyway, I think I might have some good news for you.'

'Could do with some of that. Go on.'

'Eve Dawn is flying out to Panama today.'

'How do you know?'

'Phone call ten minutes ago to one of my chaps from a contact – seems somebody wants us to know.'

'Could be another false trail, guv.' Gheeta was not going to be caught out twice.

'No.' Peter Long was adamant. 'This has come from a known source, I wouldn't have bothered you with it otherwise. One hundred percent.'

'Charter flight or scheduled airline?' asked Palmer.

Peter Long shrugged. 'No idea, all we were told is that she is flying out today.'

Gheeta turned to Claire. 'You take the charter companies and I'll check the airlines.'

They both hit their keyboards.

'Panama makes sense,' Palmer told Peter Long. 'We retrieved a few ledgers that listed accounts where a considerable amount of laundered Dawn drug money was sent off to somewhere in Panama.'

'Mossack Fonseca?'

'Yes.'

'Those two individuals and their company are responsible for aiding and abetting more organised crime money laundering, tax evasion and ruthless dictators stowing away their country's money than all the other bent lawyers put together; and still they haven't been charged.'

'The elite protect the elite, Peter. Was always so.'

'Right then, I have to go – time and crime waits for no man. Good luck with Dawn, keep me posted.'

Peter Long left the room and Palmer paced impatiently up and down to the sound of Claire and Gheeta's keyboard tapping.

After fifteen minutes Gheeta sat back. 'Air France, Heathrow – leaves at three this afternoon. That's the only commercial flight to Panama today.'

'Nothing booked in the charter flight plans registered with Air Traffic Control so far.' Claire carried on tapping.

'I'll get the passenger list for the Air France flight. Give me ten minutes.' Gheeta went back to her keyboard.

Palmer thought it best to leave the room as Gheeta worked. He knew she would be hacking into Air France servers; many of the programmes in the team's computers were from unauthorised sources that Gheeta's skill at IT had procured. He didn't ask questions, because if the proverbial hit the fan at any time he could honestly say he wasn't aware; then at least he'd keep his pension, if not his job. So whenever he could he left the room when Gheeta went on one of her hacking trips.

'I'll get coffees,' he said and left the room to make for the fifth floor; the executive floor, Assistant Commissioners and senior Home Office civil servants; the floor with the decent coffee machine that didn't spew out lukewarm dishwater like the machines on the other floors. He didn't take the lift, as its doors opened opposite AC Bateman's office and the last thing Palmer wanted was for Bateman to see him and ask for an update. So he took the stairs up the three floors, with his sciatica giving him a sharp jab in the right thigh every now and then reminding him of its presence, and the ongoing mantra from Mrs P. of 'It's your discs, go and get them checked over. Nobody has to suffer pain these days.'

When he got back, the look of success on Gheeta and Claire's faces told him they had good news.

'Go on, tell me,' he said, lowering the three plastic cups onto a desk and wishing he'd taken a small tray with him. Holding two cups coming downstairs was fine, but three was a problem – a problem resulting in some spills that showed on his new suit's trouser leg.

'She's on the Air France flight, booked an hour ago at the Air France desk at Heathrow under the name Mary Hocking, with Canadian Passport and paid by cash.'

'Well done, didn't take you long to hack that.'

Gheeta gave him a quizzical look. 'I didn't hack it, guv. I emailed Air France and they sent the information straight back.'

The sciatica pain and the spills on his new trousers that Mrs P. would go ballistic about hadn't been necessary; he made the best of it. 'Okay, good – well done. Better give British Transport Police a call and tell them we will be coming over to make an arrest.' Then he went off to the male washroom to find a paper towel he could wet and have a go at lessening the coffee stain on his trouser leg.

****

The British Transport Police Security Suite at Heathrow Terminal 3 was busy. It was a large room with banks of monitor screens that covered every part of the terminal from the entrance door to the boarding apron. Operators sat with each having four screens under their control.

At the back of the room Palmer stood with Gheeta and the local commander DI Conway. All the operators had been given a photo of Eve Dawn, and Simms and Johnson were out in the concourse keeping their eyes peeled as well. It was two thirty, and check-in for the Panama flight was happening. Margaret Hocking alias Eve Dawn had checked in via the internet from the hotel and downloaded her boarding pass, so they weren't expecting her to approach the desk and were concentrating on the departure lounge. The first call for passengers to assemble there for the flight had been made. She wasn't to be seen.

'Do you think this is another false trail, guv?' Gheeta was getting worried.

'I wouldn't put it past her,' Palmer acknowledged the possibility. 'I wouldn't put it past her at all.'

'We're stuck here watching, and she could be in a car going over to Gatwick or Birmingham and flying out to somewhere else.'

'Long was pretty adamant his information was good.'

'Let's hope so, guv.'

****

Eve Dawn kept to the crowded part of Terminal 3 concourse before making her way off to the left luggage counter, and using the Margaret Hocking passport as ID she put a small briefcase that she had bought five minutes earlier at WH Smiths into the system for three months, the maximum time allowed. She paid by cash from a small roll of notes, the rest of the cash being inside the briefcase; as she intended to transfer all her UK account money to Panama, she would need some working capital when she came back. At least if it was deposited here, it would still be there.

Adjusting the headscarf she had arranged to look like a hijab and give herself a Muslim appearance, she made her way towards the departure lounge. Without either of them realising it she passed within six feet of DS Simms, who didn't give her a second look. The last call for passengers for the Panama flight was made over the loudspeakers. She waited outside the departure lounge; not time to go through yet. She was pretty sure she had thrown Palmer off her trail with the hotel swap, but couldn't be too careful.

****

'She could have changed her mind, guv?' Gheeta was watching the screen like a hawk watches for prey. 'Boarding has nearly finished – all the passengers on.'

She's in seat 42G and that seat ticket hasn't been presented at the boarding gate,' DI Conway said, checking the ticket screen for the flight. 'She's not on it, and they'll close the gate in a minute.'

****

'Will passenger Margaret Hocking for Air France flight 32004 to Panama please make your way to the boarding gate. Margaret Hocking for flight 32004 – last call,' was the loudspeaker call that Eve Dawn was waiting for; it meant that all the other passengers were onboard and the way was clear. She hurried through the departure lounge at haste, her ticket ready. The staff at the check-in rushed her through, and in no time she was on the gantry for one last ticket check, and then across and into the aircraft, apologising to the stewardess with an excuse about M4 motorway delays. She sank into her seat, ignoring the glares from other passengers and clicked on the safety belt as the flight attendants went through the safety procedures at the front of the aircraft.

****

'That's her!'

Gheeta pointed excitedly to the screen as the lady in the scarf was seen running through the departure lounge and past the check-in gate, where a quick look at her ticket was made before waving her quickly on down the corridor towards more staff, who were waving her towards them in near panic mode and across the gantry to the plane.

'Keep her off that plane.' Palmer turned to DI Conway. 'Pull her off it.'

'I can't, that's French territory.'

'What?'

'Inside the plane, it's designated French jurisdiction – need to get a warrant from their Embassy.'

'Are you serious?'

'I'm afraid I am.'

'I've got a warrant.' Palmer pulled the Eve Dawn arrest warrant out of his pocket. 'It's a warrant for her arrest on charges of murder,' he said, which was a slight exaggeration as it was for '*suspected murder.*' 'Stop that bloody plane and stop it now, or you can explain to the Home Secretary why a known murderer – the subject of an arrest warrant signed by her – was allowed out of the country.'

Gheeta had moved to the big picture window that gave a panoramic view of the apron. The plane was moving slowly off the gantry, being pulled by a tow truck towards the runway. 'You need to do something quick, sir. She's being pulled to the runway.'

DCI Conway wasn't a fool and realised the seriousness of the situation. He went to the wall phone and rang the Control Tower and quickly explained the situation, then beckoned Palmer and Singh to follow him. He led them out of the Security Suite down a corridor, and then down a flight of stairs into an engineering warehouse and through that onto the airfield apron. His radio gave him the message that the tow truck driver had been told to stop, and the captain of the plane had been informed that a passenger was to be evicted by security and to warn the flight staff to expect police to board.

The plane's engines cut out and a mobile access steps vehicle drove alongside and the stairs telescoped up to come to rest outside the aircraft door.

****

Eve Dawn had watched all this from her seat; around her the other passengers were excited, and some a little frightened. The flight attendants had sought to calm everybody and the captain had spoken on the intercom about a *technical problem.* As the access steps audibly clunked into position on the door, she saw Palmer and a uniformed inspector and uniformed WPC make their way up. There was no point in playing the game anymore; nowhere to run. She left her seat and walked to the front of the aircraft where the flight staff waited for instructions to open the door. She gave them a smile as they were about to ask her to go back to her seat.

'I think you'll find that I'm the person they are coming for.'

An audible blast of hydraulics released the door security catches and it was slid sideways to show Palmer, Conway and Singh on the top platform of the steps, with several more uniformed British Transport Officers at the bottom.

Eve Dawn held out her wrists in submission. 'It's a fair cop, governor,' she said, with an awful Cockney accent that made Palmer smile for a moment, before reminding himself that this woman in front of him was responsible for several murders.

Gheeta walked forward and pulled Dawn's wrists behind her and coupled them with a plastic tie, while Palmer told her he was executing an arrest warrant in her name and read her the usual rights.

****

Up on Terminal Three public rooftop observation platform, one man stood out amongst the varied assortment of enthusiastic plane spotters clicking their cameras and outdoing each other with their engineering knowledge of the inner workings of every aircraft engine that came into view, down to the torque value of the smallest screw. He stood out because he wore a suit and a large loose overcoat that flapped in the breeze, rather than the well-padded body warmers and thick berets covered in aircraft related badges favoured by those around him. The binoculars held to his eyes above his broken nose were bog standard racegoer's type rather than the expensive Leica or Zeiss precision ones with night vision adapters favoured by the serious spotters around him. He let them drop and hang from the strap around his thick neck as he speed-dialled on his mobile.

'Yes.' Johnny Robinson had been waiting for the call.

'They've got her. Dragged her off the plane.'

'You sure?'

'Yeah.'
'Good.'
Click.

****

Johnny Robinson smiled to himself as he put his mobile down on his desk and looked across his office to where his three main men were playing cards. 'Don't you just love it when a plan comes together?' he said to himself as a smile came to his lips.

****

'I don't know how you manage it.'

Mrs P. shook her head in disbelief at the coffee stain on Palmer's trouser leg. 'You've barely had that suit a week.'

'I couldn't help it. I was trying to balance three coffees without a tray.'

'Is that a trick?' She wasn't amused.

'No, I just didn't think to take a tray to the machine.'

'Go and change – put the blue suit on, and hurry up. I told Benji we'd be there about eight.'

****

It was the evening of the re-opening of the local library and it was packed. Benji and other local councillors were doing the 'meet and greet' at the door as the Palmers arrived, having had to park a good two hundred metres away because of the amount of cars.

'Would have been quicker to walk from the house,' said Palmer as they walked up the wide stone steps of the library to a beaming Benji, who gave Mrs P. a peck on the cheek and shook Palmer's hand.

'Hello, hello,' he gushed. 'I was afraid you might not be able to make it with that awful shooting case going on.'

'We tied it up this afternoon. You can sleep safely tonight, Benji – the mob has been locked up.'

Benji gave a false laugh, and Mrs P. a scowling glare. 'Right…' Benji ushered them inside and through the crowd, most of whom said hello to Mrs P. and gave Palmer a smile. 'Well, do come through and I'll introduce you to our new librarian Finbar, who has purchased lots and lots of books with the money made from the charity donations from you and others.'

Being introduced to people at civic functions was not one of Palmer's favourite things. He knew that after being introduced as Detective Chief Superintendent Palmer, there would be the usual humorous, oft repeated, remarks of *'who have you come to arrest?'* and *'oh no, have I parked on a double yellow line?'*, plus numerous others he'd heard a hundred times that he replied to with a bored smile.

Benji spied the new librarian and called out: 'Finbar! Finbar, over here a minute.'

The new librarian was a middle-aged man that had the look of an absent-minded professor: corduroy trousers two sizes too big, a WWF tee-shirt that could do with ironing, sandals, and to top it off ,a ponytail like Benji's. The only thing that looked to fit was the Prince of Wales check jacket with an ink stain on the lapel.

AFTERMATH

A month later Peter Long, Palmer and his team, AC Bateman and officers from the National Central Bureau Unit sat in the media viewing suite at the Yard, and watching a video link from a drone high above a suburb of Madrid as armed units of the Policia Nacional led by the Spanish NCB raided a large candle factory on an industrial estate; workers were led out and onto buses and taken away. At the rear of the building two cars attempted to speed their way through a roadblock and were brought to a halt by a hail of gunshot from armed officers in full gear, who then dragged bodies from the wreckage. The video cut out.

The Yard's NCB Commander spoke. 'That's it, gentlemen. All happened at five this morning and was a complete success – our partners in Madrid are very grateful to you. The workers are mainly immigrant non-passport holders; the managers of the factory are known low-ranking Mafia people, of whom six were killed at the scene. At the same time a cardinal in the Vatican was arrested on narcotic smuggling charges.'

Closer to home, Eve Dawn was in remand at Bronzefield Women's Prison, Ashford awaiting a full trial at the Old Bailey. The CPS were sure that murder charges naming James Dawn, Alfred Dawn, Stanley Dawn, Harry James, Lilian James and Jack Dooley as victims would get a guilty result with all the video evidence available, plus the statements from Wright, Holland and Barber, as well as the avalanche of circumstantial and documentary evidence. Palmer and Singh were spending an awful lot of time with the CPS, putting everything into chronological order and tying up loose ends.

Palmer had given a major press conference once Eve Dawn had been remanded, and had been accompanied on the steps of New Scotland Yard by AC Bateman and the Commissioner, who had heaped praise on him and the Serial Murder Squad. Palmer in turn had praised his team and the British Transport Police; Bateman had waited for his name to be mentioned in the accolades, but it wasn't.

In the Team Room Gheeta, Claire, Simms and Johnson watched on the screen, applauded at the end, and gave each other high fives.

In the OC Team Room, Peter Long raised a plastic cup of coffee as a toast. 'Good man, Justin – good man, mate.'

At home, Mrs P. watched it with pride. What a smart looking man her husband was – blue suited him.

END

THE BLACK ROSE

WEDNESDAY

'He looks like he's sleeping, I can't see any wounds.'

DCS Justin Palmer moved around the steel trolley in the morgue to look at the rest of the male body laid out on it. The only 'wound' was the closed incision Professor Latin the pathologist had made for the post-mortem so he could remove the inner organs for weighing and examination. Palmer had taken Latin's call earlier that day and together with DS Gheeta Singh had made the journey across the river from the Yard to the morgue in Vauxhall at Latin's request. As usual when visiting Latin with a female officer, Palmer had apologised before entering the morgue for the professor's well known use of expletives. It wasn't often that Latin called in Palmer, so something unusual must have caught his attention. The Murder Squad morgue was not a place Palmer was keen on visiting, as the smell of dead flesh, formaldehyde and disinfectant has a habit of clinging to clothes, and even though he and DS Singh were in regulation white overalls plus hair and shoe coverings, Mrs P. would know as soon as he got home that evening that he'd been to the morgue, and would insist his clothes went into the wash and he went into the shower. Palmer looked around. No, it wasn't a very nice place. The four latest gang stabbing victims from the weekend's London drug wars were laid out on other benches, plastic sheets covering their bodies. Palmer guessed they'd all be young men in their teens or early twenties, lured into selling drugs by the promise of easy money. It didn't work that way. His attention was brought back to his own case by Professor Latin.

'There are no fucking wounds,' Latin said. He pointed across the morgue to another trolley carrying a middle-aged lady. 'None on her either. She's the wife, he's the husband – both found in the back of their family business Transit van parked at the back of the lorry park at South Mimms Services off the M25 three days ago. All dead, with a pipe attached to the exhaust and poked into the van through a floor drainage plug hole'

'A floor drainage plug hole?'

'The family business was a garden centre, the van would have been used to carry plants about. Plants need watering, hence the drainage hole.'

'So it's a family suicide then?' Palmer knew it wouldn't be. Latin wouldn't have called him out to the morgue for straightforward suicides.

'No, it's a fucking family *murder.*' Latin gave Palmer a beaming smile.

'Do we know who they are?' Palmer asked DS Singh, who stood nearby and had her laptop open and fired up. She was well used to Latin's language, which was nothing more than she'd hear in the Yard's canteen every day and was like water off a duck's back to her.

'The Hanleys, guv,' she read off the screen. 'According to the report from the local station the deceased are Geoffrey and Linda Hanley. Geoffrey Hanley has a garden centre business in Borehamwood. No other family members and no previous dealings with the police – they seem to be just an ordinary pair.'

'No children?'

'No, not according to BDM records. I checked.'

Palmer turned back to Latin. 'So it's a murder not a suicide then, is it, go on, explain?'

'Well, the first thing I noticed was an abnormal reading from the lungs. The toxicology test on his lungs showed no residue of CO or NO2. Same test on the female gave the same reading, no CO or NO2.'

Palmer spread his hands. 'Which are?'

'Carbon monoxide and nitrogen dioxide, the stuff that makes up most of car exhaust fumes and pollutes our streets.'

'Neither of them had any of that stuff in their lungs?' Palmer looked from one body to the other. 'A bit strange if they died by inhaling it from a pipe run from the exhaust.'

'There were very small traces, but we all have that in our lungs – can't avoid it if you live in or near a city or town. But they certainly didn't inhale enough to kill them, no way.'

'And no wounds on the bodies either, no bruises or strangulation marks?'

'No none.' Latin shook his head in an exaggerated manner to underline the point, 'None at all.'

Having worked with Professor Latin for many years, Palmer was well aware of his theatrical approach to post mortems; Latin knew perfectly well what had caused the Hanley's deaths, and was making Palmer wait for the final reveal like a Poirot final chapter twist. Palmer rolled his eyes at Gheeta, who was well aware of Latin's ways as well.

'So how did they die?'

'Poison.'

'Poison?'

'Yes.' Silence.

Palmer's patience was waning. 'Are you going to explain what happened to these people, or are we going to precede one word at a time? I've got Mrs P.'s steak and kidney pie for dinner tonight, and at the rate you're going it'll be cold or in the dog by the time I get home.'

Latin took the hint. 'Because the bodies exhibited a lack of exhaust fume damage to the lungs we examined all the organs and stomach contents thoroughly. In the stomachs of both deceased we found traces of the poison wolfsbane, which comes from the root of the deadly aconitum family of plants; a very pretty and popular plant you can buy at most garden centres. As are many plants with deadly poison attributes, like digitalis, belladonna and others.'

'What do you mean '*it comes from the root*'? Are you saying the Hanleys sat in the van and ate the root of a plant to kill themselves?'

'No, not at all the root has to be dried and crushed first, but it could then be put in a drink or on food – it's tasteless.'

'Hold on a minute, I'm getting confused. They were found in the back of their company van with the exhaust pipe pushed through, but were actually killed by this wolfsbane poison?'

'Yes.'

Gheeta interrupted as she read from her screen. 'No cups or drinking vessels found in the van, guv. It was completely empty in the back except for the bodies, fully clothed.'

'Where are the clothes?

'Forensics have them.'

'They were dead before they were put in that van,' said Latin forcibly, a little annoyed that the spotlight had been taken off him.

'They were? How do you know that?' Palmer asked.

'The amount of wolfsbane in their bloodstream and stomach indicates a very quick death. That poison paralyses the body's organs and overpowers the heart – the amount they took would have killed them within two minutes at the most. There's no way either of them could have driven that van after taking the poison.'

'And no cups or anything else in the van, so somebody else poisoned them, put them in the van, dumped it at South Mimms and fed the exhaust through to make it look like suicide.'

'That's for you to find out, Justin. All I can positively say is that it was the poison that killed them, not the exhaust,' said Latin, with all the solemnity of an actor delivering the final revealing line of a play. All that was missing was the sweeping bow at the end.

Palmer half expected all the bodies in the morgue to sit up and applaud.

****

'He gets worse every time I see him.' Palmer and Gheeta were in the back of the squad car outside the morgue. 'I'm surprised he hasn't had a stage put up in the morgue to make his pronouncements from.'

Gheeta was more interested in the local police report on the Hanleys than Latin's theatricals.

'If the family had no next of kin or relatives nobody will know they are dead, guv. There's nothing in the report to say their house or business has been visited by officers, or that anybody has made enquiries about them.'

'Strange, after three days you would think people at their business would be wondering where they were by now.'

Gheeta showed him a picture on her laptop. 'That's the Hanley's garden centre, looks a nice place, quite big too, just off the high street in Borehamwood.'

'Okay, let's go and take a look. Get onto the local force involved, speak to the OIC and have him or her transfer the case to us. And tell him or her to keep that information quiet too, if any local media gets wind of the Serial Murder Squad being involved they'll start getting interested, and I don't want that just yet. Then give Claire a call at the Team Room and ask her to contact the motorway services and get copies of their

CCTV recordings from the time the van arrived; and then get her digging into the Hanley's background, see if we can't come up with somebody harbouring a grudge big enough to kill for.'

'To kill *two* people for, guv.'

'Yes, bit like the Mary Celeste isn't it.'

'There weren't any bodies on the Mary Celeste, guv. It was empty.'

'Okay, the Titanic then.'

'No icebergs in Borehamwood, guv.'

Palmer searched for a retort but couldn't think of one.

'Clever arse.' That would do.

Gheeta smiled as she leaned forward and gave the driver the postcode of Hanley's garden centre.

****

'Looks busy doesn't it?' Palmer remarked as they drove off the main road onto the large car park at Hanley's Garden Centre. 'Park at the back driver, don't want the Sergeant's uniform to frighten the natives.'

Once parked up Palmer and Gheeta skirted round the perimeter of the car park to the centre's entrance, getting a few funny looks from shoppers on the way. Inside they found themselves in a very large glass house with rows and rows of benches laden with flower and vegetable plants and gardening requisites of all kinds; it was very tidy with soft classical music piped through the sound system.

'Better make ourselves known.' Palmer walked over to a lady assistant wearing a green company uniform with Hanley's embroidered on the front and back of the jacket. He showed his ID card. 'Hello. Nothing to worry about, just a routine call, but could you point us in the direction of the manager?'

The assistant's immediate minor panic attack at being confronted by police officers holding ID cards diffused as Palmer gave her his killer smile, the one Mrs P. had said could melt the Arctic – well, what's left of it – she relaxed and looked around trying to locate somebody. 'You want Jim, Jim Riley – he's not in here so probably out on the patio. We had some fruit trees come in earlier so I expect he's sorting them out.' She pointed to the back of the premises. 'Through the big doors at the back, if he's not there the office is out there on the left, big wooden shed – he'll be in there.'

Palmer thanked her and they made their way to the back of the glass house and through the big doors into a large open patio beyond where another large glass house loomed. Jim Riley was indeed sorting the fruit trees on the patio; he was struggling with a large potted conference pear, wiggling it into position in line with others and hadn't seen Palmer and Singh approach. Palmer waited until Riley straightened up, panting a bit with the exertion.

'Mister Riley?'

He was young, Gheeta estimated his age as early thirties, and he looked fit, but then if you were manhandling large pots of trees about all day you'd be fit too. Dark hair cut close and a face that had a chiselled appearance – all in all Gheeta thought Jim Riley to be quite handsome.

Riley was taken aback by Palmer's ID card and Gheeta's uniform. 'Yes, that's me. What can I do for you.'

Palmer flashed his fatherly smile this time, 'Nothing to worry yourself about, Mister Riley. Is there somewhere private we could go?'

'Yes, yes the office.' He pointed to the large shed on the side of the patio the assistant had mentioned and walked towards it, taking a key from his pocket and opening the door.

Inside was a bit of a mess; an old table that might be more at home at the local tip held centre stage, with a chair behind it and two in front that both Palmer and Gheeta felt inclined not to trust despite Riley offering them.

'Sit down, sit down please.'

'That's all right sir, I'll stand if you don't mind. Been sitting in a car all day,' lied Palmer, eyeing the chairs. 'I am afraid we have some bad news for you concerning the Hanleys.'

It was noticeable that the blood drained from Riley's face. He didn't speak, so Palmer carried on.

'Can you tell me when you last spoke to them?'

'Yes, yes, four days ago – they were going off on holiday the next day. Why, what's happened?'

'Where were they going for the holiday, sir?'

'Err, Scotland I believe. They often went there, hired a motor home and just toured. What's happened?'

'Well, there seems to have been an accident. I'm sorry to tell you that both Mr and Mrs Hanley are dead.'

Riley looked like Tyson Fury had punched his stomach; his mouth dropped open and he didn't speak for some time. Palmer and Gheeta noted his reaction – it was genuine. Or was it?

'Dead? How?'

'Well it's all a bit perplexing actually.' Palmer took a deep breath. 'They were found in the back of the Hanley Garden Centre Transit van parked at a motorway services, with the exhaust run into the van.'

'What?' Riley's reaction was disbelief. 'Suicide? No, no way.'

Palmer shrugged; he was keeping his cards close to his chest for the time being. 'Well it looks that way at present sir, but we have to wait for the post mortems. Can you think of any reason why they should take their own lives, if indeed that's what has happened – money troubles, family rows?'

Riley was regaining his composure, 'No, no not at all – no rows anyway. I don't know anything about the money, we have a bookkeeper in once a week who handles all that side – she does the books, wages and banking.' He pointed to a large solid safe in the corner. 'Daily takings are kept in there and she puts it all together; does the book work and wage packets, and we go to the bank together to put in the rest.'

'Are the books in there too?' asked Gheeta, nodding towards the safe which she was sure Palmer and his lock picks could open in a couple of minutes; a long career in dealing with criminals of all types had given Palmer a few extra skills.

'No.' Riley turned in his chair and pointed at a lever arch file on the shelf behind him. 'It's all in there, daily till receipts books and all that stuff. I put everything in that and she sorts it.'

Gheeta walked round the desk and picked up the file. 'I'll take it for our forensic accountant to take a peek at, just to make sure there weren't money troubles acting on the family's minds.'

'Yes, yes okay.'

'And do you have the bookkeeper's name and number? I'll give them a call.'

'It's only one lady, Alison. Her card's in my drawer.'

He opened a desk drawer and rummaged out a business card which Gheeta took.

Riley was regaining his composure after the initial shock at the news. 'What should I do now, close the centre? It's the Chelsea Flower Show on Sunday – business rockets after that, it's our busiest time. We've stocked up already, so if we close the stock will wilt and die, and so will the business.'

Palmer didn't want that; in fact that was the last thing he wanted. To close the business would put a stop on the one place that might hold the answer to why two people are murdered in a van at a motorway services with it made to look like suicide.

'No, no need to close. I'm sure you can run the day-to-day business of the garden centre and ask the bookkeeper to carry on keeping things in order financially. What I will do is have a word with the bank and explain the situation, banks are usually okay in emergency situations like this. Do you pay the staff in cash?'

'Yes, Alison sorts that out.'

'Good, then carry on as normal for the time being, and one thing I would ask is that you keep this to yourself. If you tell the staff what has happened it won't be very long before the local newspaper gets to know and then you'll be pestered all day long.'

'No, no I don't want that – no, not at all. The staff think they are on holiday so best if I keep it like that, don't you think?'

'Yes I do. Good, okay Mr Riley, I think that's all we can do for the present. My sergeant will give you a direct line to our office, use it if you need us – other than that we will be in touch as soon as we have more information, so for now carry on as before if you would. Now all we need is the address of the company solicitors if you have it? They will do a search just in case there is another director or silent partner we need to talk to.'

Riley nodded. 'I think that will be in here.' He pulled a large desk diary off the shelf behind him and leafed through it. 'Yes, here we are – Michael Whitley, Whitley Solicitors, 28 High Street, Watford.'

Gheeta tapped the address into her laptop.

Now,' Palmer continued as Gheeta passed her direct line card to Riley, 'Is there a back way out that we might take? A police uniform can be guaranteed to start tongues wagging and people getting the wrong idea.'

'Yes, yes follow me – we have a side path that takes you to a staff door into the car park.' He led them out of the office.

'Do you have any aconite plants?' asked Gheeta in an offhand way. 'My mother was looking for some online, apparently they are very pretty and ideal for a hanging basket.'

Jim grimaced. 'Aconite? Yes, but I wouldn't recommend them if there's pets around. They're poisonous, best keep away from them.'

Gheeta feigned surprise. 'Oh really? Right, we won't be buying those then – mum dotes on her cat.'

****

'I'm not sure about him, are you?' Palmer asked Gheeta as they settled back into the squad car.

'No. He seemed genuinely shocked by the news, but not as shocked as he ought to be – after all, it could be his career down the pan if the place closes.'

'Another one for Claire to take a good look at. Where's the Transit van now?'

'Secure pound at Paddington, guv.'

'Email Reg Frome to go and give it a forensic deep clean, see if we can't turn up some clue as to who drove it to the Services with two bodies in the back; and ask him to put a team into the Hanley's home and look for aconite, or anything that might make a man who seems perfectly at ease with the world suddenly commit suicide with his wife. Not that suicide is the main suspicion here.'

Reg Frome led the specialist Murder Squad Forensics team and as such worked with Palmer on most of his cases. They had both started their police careers in the same intake at Hendon College as teenagers, and whilst Palmer opted for the usual career path through the ranks in CID Frome had branched off into the science of forensics, where he had reached the equivalent high office as Palmer. You couldn't miss him; his shock of white hair stood out, making him look a lot like 'Doc' Brown from the *Back To The Future* films.

'Right, next stop the bookkeeper, Alison. Where do we find her?'

'Alison Burnley,' said Gheeta, reading from the card Riley had given her. 'Office is off the high street in Watford.' She passed the card forward to the driver who put the postcode in the SatNav.

****

Jim Riley sat for some minutes contemplating things before pulling out his mobile and speed dialling.

A female voice answered. 'Hello Jim.'

'What have you done?'

'What have I done? What are you talking about?'

'You know what I'm talking about. The Hanleys – what the hell have you done?'

'Jim, I really don't know what you are talking about.'

'Liar. They're dead – both of them, dead.'

There was a silence on the line for a few seconds.

'Hang up Jim, we will come and see you at home tonight.'

Click. The line went dead.

****

Alison Burnley's office, if that is the right name for it, was a small single room at the top of a steep flight of narrow wooden stairs that led off the high street in Watford beside an Indian takeaway.

Palmer eyed the stairs with worry; his sciatica had a habit of letting him know its presence when climbing stairs, especially steep ones. He motioned Gheeta to go first and took his time going up behind her. A knock on the old wooden door that had a bevelled glass panel that showed its age around the cheap, faded, adhesive letters that announced 'ALISON BURNLEY & Co. BOOKKEEPING' got a muted 'Come in,' followed by a bout of coughing.

The inside was an extension of the faded exterior. Miss Alison Burnley was a very large lady, the kind that wear smocks because their size is not stocked by ladies' clothes shops. She sat behind an old wooden desk that in its prime had a fine green leather top, but that top had been ravaged by time and neglect. The one thing that Miss Burnley was obviously good at, other than bookkeeping, was smoking; a cigarette hung from her lips, an ashtray on the desk overflowed with red lipstick-smeared dog ends, the room had a definite hanging fog of tobacco smoke and the ceiling showed the tell-tale amber tinge of many years of lingering smoke.

'What can I do for you?' asked Burnley, her fat fingers stubbing out the cigarette in the ashtray.

Gheeta looked but couldn't see a fire alarm on the ceiling, which was a bit worrying as there would be no way the rotund bookkeeper would be able to exit from around her desk in a hurry if need be. In fact, Gheeta wondered how on earth a lady of such bulk managed the narrow stairs up from the street.

Palmer held his ID out. 'DCS Palmer, Scotland Yard, and this is DS Singh.'

Burnley nodded. 'I wondered when you'd come along. Jim Riley phoned me with the news earlier, said you'd been there. How's he doing, is he okay? Did he take the news badly? He sounded pretty down.'

Palmer removed his trilby and decided to sit down on one of a pair of chairs that at one stage would have matched the leather desk. It was a toss-up which had the worst wear to the leather, the chairs or the desk, but the main reason for Palmer taking a seat was to get his head out of the smoke cloud that hung like a spider's web in the top half of the room. There was a large window looking out to the street below, but whether it had ever been opened was doubtful judging by the dust on the handle.

'He seems to be coping at present,' answered Palmer. 'But often the real shock of events like this takes a while to hit home.'

'It's ridiculous. Geoff and Linda were quite happy, the business was fine, there's no reason for it, none at all.' She leant back and lit another cigarette, offering the pack to Palmer.

'No, no thanks. You said the business was fine – there wasn't any financial problems, no creditors banging on the door that you know of?'

'No, none. The bank balance went up and down with the seasons as you would expect in a garden centre – down in the winter and then up when spring arrived and the gardeners flocked in. He did have a blip a few months ago but that was sorted.'

'A blip?'

'Yes.' She shrugged. 'I feel like I'm talking out of school. Geoff had an Achilles' heel: gambling. Most of the downs in the business finances were due to his gambling debts and not the seasons, although we never mentioned it to Linda.'

'We?'

'Geoff and I – he made me promise not to tell her. He tried to break the habit but he couldn't.'

'What sort of *blip* was it?' asked Palmer.

'An eighty thousand pounds blip. He did the cardinal sin of all gamblers: lost a bit and instead of writing it off and stopping for a while, he chased it, lost more and then chased that – a sort of never-ending spiral into more and more debt. I must have warned him several times that the bank might put a stop on the account, but he was a typical Mr Micawber, always saying '*something will turn up.*'

'You think that debt could have pushed him into suicide?'

'No, because something did turn up, it was settled. One day in the red, then the next day the account was back into the black. I asked him if he'd got a loan or something as I could claim the interest against tax, or at least some of it, but he said no; said he'd got a partner coming into the business who had settled it as part of the deal, for half the business.'

'Really? Who was this partner?'

'I don't know, he wouldn't say. Said the person wanted to remain anonymous – didn't even want to see the books.'

'Well, if he or she wants to see them now they'll have to come to us, we've got them. Will that impact on your work at the garden centre? Riley said you go in once a week to sort the wages and do the banking.'

'No, no that's all right – Geoff used to sign every cheque in the cheque book when a new one arrived, I've still got quite a few left in the current book so any bills falling due I can pay.' She took a long drag on her cigarette, letting it out slowly. 'What happens now?'

'Well, I've no reason to close the business whilst we investigate the reasons behind the Hanleys' deaths, so my advice would be to carry on as normal. My department will talk to the Hanleys' solicitor and the bank and try to contact this partner. Hopefully whoever it is will carry on the business as usual. Thank you for your time, Mrs Burnley.'

'Miss, it's *Miss* Burnley – not had much luck in the husband stakes.' She laughed and then coughed.

'Well, you never know what might turn up... *Miss* Burnley. If you do think of anything that may have worried Mr Hanley, please let us know.'

Gheeta stepped forward and passed her contact card across the desk to Burnley. 'It's a direct line, no infuriating menu to navigate.'

Burnley laughed as she took the card. 'Oh God, don't you just hate those?'

Palmer smiled, put on his hat and hurried out of the office and down the stairs to fresh air as fast as he could, without jogging his sciatica into action.

They stood on the pavement gulping in fresh air.

'So Sergeant, we have a mysterious benefactor-cum-partner emerging from the shadows. Funny how Jim Riley never mentioned that.'

'Maybe he isn't aware of it guv, but if there's a deposit of eighty grand it will show up in the bank accounts in the file we've got. I can do a trace on the bank code and account number and find out where it came from.'

'Maybe you're right and Riley doesn't know about the partnership deal, but the Hanleys' solicitor will – changing from sole owner to partnership involves legal paperwork. I think Michael Whitley will be our next port of call, may as well do it whilst we are in the area.'

Gheeta checked her laptop. 'Twenty-eight the High Street, can't be far down here.'

'Good.' Palmer walked away.

'Guv.'

He stopped and turned.

Gheeta pointed a finger towards their unmarked squad car parked opposite with the driver reading the paper. 'It's two forty-five, don't you think you should let the driver go and get a sandwich and a drink?'

Palmer looked across the road. 'Yes, yes of course. Time flies, doesn't it? Go and tell him to take a break for half an hour.'

Gheeta did so as Palmer wandered off down the road looking for number twenty-eight. She noted that as usual, no reference to either Gheeta or Palmer getting food and drink had even crossed his mind, but this was usual for Palmer. When a case was running his mind was totally immersed in it; any thoughts of food, drink and time were parked in a small back room somewhere in his brain.

Number twenty-eight Watford High Street was chalk and cheese compared to Alison Burnley's hovel of an office: a full glass-fronted state of the art modern build, with large automatic doors that slid silently open to let Palmer and Gheeta walk through into a spacious foyer where several receptionists sat using keyboards and manning several phone lines. All eyes turned to Gheeta in her uniform.

Palmer presented his ID card to a young man whose badge said he was *'PHILIP. CLIENT SUPPORT'*

'How can we help you, Detective Chief Superintendent?' Philip asked, reading from Palmer's card.

Palmer liked that; full deference, nice touch. He smiled at Philip. 'I wonder if your Michael Whitley could spare us a few minutes?'

'I'll certainly ask his secretary, sir. Might I ask what it is in connection with?'

'The murder of Geoffrey Hanley.'

That shook Philip speechless for a few moments; he wasn't sure what to say to that.

He regained his composure. 'One moment please.' He dialled an internal phone and spoke to whoever answered, explaining that Palmer was here and what his business was. There was a short wait before the answer came back. Philip smiled at Palmer and Singh. 'Would you both like to take a seat? Mr Whitley is with a client at present and will be with you as soon as he finishes. Shouldn't be long.' He indicated a row of plush seats in a waiting area.

Palmer and Gheeta sat down. Gheeta took advantage of the free coffee machine. 'Want one, guv?'

'No, I'm fine thank you Sergeant.' Palmer was a coffee man, but only French strength five, percolated for ten minutes; to be offered instant was an insult in his book. He looked at Gheeta's plastic cup as she sat down.

'Don't spill that onto your shoes, it'll take the shine off.'

Gheeta ignored him; it was very welcome, seeing that the last drink she'd had that day was tea with her breakfast at seven in the morning.

It wasn't too long before a call came through to *Philip. Client Support* who came over and asked them to follow him.

'Mr Whitley is free now and will see you.'

He led them through large double doors at the rear of the foyer area and down a wide, plush carpeted corridor with offices off each side. Michael Whitley's office bore his name on the door. Philip knocked before holding the door open for Palmer and Singh to go in.

They were met and greeted by Michael Whitley who stood up from his large modern desk and came round it, hand outstretched.

'Detective Chief Superintendent Palmer, how good to meet you.'

They shook hands and Palmer introduced Gheeta. Michael Whitley was in his forties, obviously fit, and immaculately dressed in solicitor regulation dark blue suit and brown brogues, with a Westminster College tie shouting out his elite credentials for the job.

'Sit down, sit down.' He waved them towards comfortable sofas around the walls and retook his own desk chair. 'Coffee, tea?'

'No, no we are fine, thank you,' said Palmer. 'We won't take up too much of your time Mr Whitley, and thank you for fitting us in at such short notice.'

'Mr Palmer – may I call you Mister?'

'Please do.'

'Mr Palmer, any officer coming into the office and asking to talk about the murder of one of our oldest clients isn't going to be turned away, I can assure you. Geoff Hanley murdered? Tell me more.'

Palmer recounted the story and the basic facts as far as he felt was necessary; he didn't mention poison, just murder.

'So you see Mr Whitley, we are without any suspects at present, although no doubt some will emerge as we dig deeper into the Hanleys' lifestyle. But neither Riley nor the company bookkeeper could give us any information on the new business partner. I was hoping you would have the identity, as being Hanley's solicitor you would have had to be involved with the legalities of the ownership change from sole trader to partnership?'

Whitley looked bewildered. 'I can't help you there Mr Palmer, this is the first I've heard of it. We've not been approached by Mr

Hanley to incorporate the company into a partnership. I can't think he'd use anybody else.' He shook his head in disbelief. 'Geoff Hanley was one of our original clients from way back when my father started the business. Dad only retired last year, he will be shocked by this news – they were very good friends, both mad on roses. Many a time Dad would pop over to the Garden Centre at Borehamwood for the quarterly health check on the accounts and come back with a boot full of roses. I never saw him raise an invoice for the visits either.' He gave a sad laugh. 'I don't suppose he'll get his Midnight Glory now.'

'Midnight Glory?' Palmer didn't understand.

'Yes, both bred roses, Dad as an amateur but Geoff was a master at it. Been breeding roses for decades, one of the top breeders in the country was Geoff, and like all of them the final goal is a pure black rose, never been bred. Dad said Geoff was near, but not quite there. You have to jump through so many hoops to get a rose listed as a genuine new type – I don't know much about it, I'm not a gardener like Dad, but apparently whoever gets the Rights Certification for a black rose from the Plant Variety Rights Office or whatever they are called, then that person is a millionaire overnight.'

'A millionaire?' Palmer couldn't believe what he was hearing, nor could Gheeta. A probable reason to murder two people had just appeared.

THURSDAY

Palmer knew the second day of the case would be probably the most important, or one of the most important days. It followed the usual path of every new case: day one you get acquainted with the case, the people involved so far and possible avenues for further investigation; day two you start to put the jigsaw together and start down those avenues of investigation.

With Gheeta's bespoke computer programmes and Claire's skill at shaking out leads with the determination of a dog with a rag, Palmer knew he was in good hands.

His first port of call on the way to the office was the Paddington Secure Evidence Yard where the Transit van was parked. Reg Frome was already at work in it and under it with his forensic team, all in white paper suits, overshoes, hats and gloves. Palmer stood away from them until Frome noticed him and came over.

'Good morning, Justin. Not going to be much help here I'm afraid.'

'No prints?' Palmer was disappointed.

'Some off the driver's cab and steering wheel but nothing in the back. Hardly surprising really when you realise it's a garden centre's van – probably been hosed out many times in the past. We've collected stuff from the drainage hole but it looks like it's mostly plant debris. I'll take the length of hose that was run from the exhaust to the plug hole back to the lab; it's not your everyday garden hose – about three times the diameter, but most likely common in garden centres – but you never know, we might get a print off it.'

'Okay. There's two people's prints I would like you to ignore, the garden centre manager and the bookkeeper. I don't think they are involved, but their prints will probably show up on things and you can eliminate them. I'll have my Sergeant get the local boys to go round and take their prints and DNA and pass them to you.'

'Yes, that's fine. I'll run them through the national database though. If one turns out to be a serial killer I'll let you know.' Frome smiled.

Palmer couldn't imagine Alison Burnley being able to swat a fly, let alone murder anybody – unless they'd stolen her cigarettes!

'Talking about your Sergeant,' said Frome, 'She gave me a call earlier. She wants to pass some bank papers from this case onto Pete Atkins to have a look at; apparently there's a large payment made to the deceased and she'd like to know who made it. I told her to give him a call.'

Pete Atkins was the forensic accountant attached to Frome's squad. Atkins's previous career was in the city, where he worked for a major bank in the acquisitions and takeover department handling the takeover of companies by other companies, before moving up into the wealth advisory department which basically was charged with finding ways for the rich elite to hide or transfer accumulated wealth that they preferred HMRC not to know about; in layman's language it's called money laundering, in bankers' language it's called wealth advice. Atkins, who came from a normal working class background, was not happy with the banking industries' deference to these elite rich and often major criminal types, and so he left behind the six figure bonuses and champagne lunches and moved into the legal department of the yard's forensic squad under Reg Frome. The poacher became the gamekeeper.

****

Back in the Team Room Gheeta and Claire were delving away into the back grounds of Hanley, Riley and Burnley. Nothing out of the ordinary or causing concern was showing up so far. But Gheeta had some interesting information from another source to pass onto Palmer as he took off his coat and hat and told them that Frome had drawn blanks on the Transit van.

'This rose breeding lark is big business guv,' said Gheeta. 'It's a bit like the music and publishing business. If you can breed a new rose and get a certificate, you get royalties on every one sold. It's policed by BARB – the British Association of Rose Breeders – who are responsible for collecting the royalties on roses that get a certificate. If Hanley was a top breeder like that solicitor said then they should know him, and maybe know others who he was competing with for the black rose. Maybe worth a chat with them?'

'Yes, you may be right. I'll give them a call later.'

A knock on the door announced the arrival of Pete Atkins. He still gave the impression of a young city type with his

Savile Row suits and Ralph Lauren shirts, topped off with a very handsome face and immaculately styled hair.

'DS Atkins, come in young man.' Palmer liked Atkins. 'Have you found our secret benefactor?'

Atkins sat at a table and opened a file as they gathered round.

'I have found your benefactor sir, and I think it might surprise you.'

'Go on.'

'Well, from the bank statement that DS Singh emailed me I was able to see that the eighty thousand pounds payment came from a Santander Bank account – it's pretty simple to find that out as all account codes relate to certain banks. Now, having got that information I was able to take the account number and work out which branch it was from, and it was a business account – so no branch, as all their business accounts come from a business hub. That's where it gets tricky, as other than hacking into the bank...'

Palmer covered his eyes, hoping beyond hope that Atkins hadn't.

'Don't worry sir, I didn't.'

Palmer breathed a sigh of relief.

'I rang an old mate at the City branch of Santander and he got the information for me. The account belongs to Edward and Janet Bloom, who trade under the name Bloom's Garden Centres with a Watford address. I think that ties in well with this case, doesn't it?'

Gheeta nodded. 'Yes it certainly does. Thanks Peter, that's really helpful.'

Atkins closed the file. 'I'll put it all in an official report and send it through.' He stood to leave. 'One more thing – I think you might find Mr Bloom interesting. I had a quick look on file and it seems we know him already.' He nodded to Palmer and left.

'I'll pull up all we have on Edward and Janet Bloom,' said Claire, returning to her workstation. 'Give me a couple of minutes.'

'Interesting eh, guv?' said Gheeta. 'Looks like one garden centre coming to the rescue of another garden centre, if the money came from the Blooms.'

'Good name for a garden centre, Blooms. They'll get a shock when the news reaches them that Hanley's dead; and if the partnership hadn't been registered the money's gone too.'

'Hang on a minute, I want to check something,' Gheeta said and sat at her keyboard and worked for a minute. 'No, nothing's changed. Company's House still has Hanley's as a sole trader; it's not been changed to a partnership and it's not in review, so there's not a change going through their system at present either.'

'So Blooms haven't a claim on the money they gave Hanley, or on half the actual business?' asked Palmer.

'Well, I'm not a lawyer guv, but it certainly looks that way.'

'That's enough to make you a bit angry, isn't it? Eighty grand down the drain and no legal right to claim it back.' Palmer raised his eyebrows.

'I wouldn't like to be the one who tells them,' Gheeta added.

Claire sat back. 'You might actually like to be the one who tells them, guv. Mr Bloom doesn't seem to be the helpful benefactor he comes across as.'

'Go on.'

Claire read from her screen. 'Edward John Bloom, aged 64. Numerous convictions for petty theft as a young man, seven years in and out of remand centres, finally jailed for seventeen years aged 32 for the armed robbery of a Securicor van in Manchester in 1995; five million taken in the raid and very little recovered. Let out on parole after 12 years, served his parole without any problems and not heard of since.'

'Until now,' Palmer stood and moved to behind Claire and read the screen. 'Keep digging on Mr Bloom, he's just become suspect number one. I think the Blooms' garden centre deserves a visit.'

'Garden centres, guv,' said Gheeta, pointing to the Bloom Garden Centres website she had pulled up on her screen. 'There's three of them, and they look pretty impressive too.'

'I wonder if Mr Bloom is a rose breeder?'

'You're thinking what I'm thinking, guv.'

'Midnight Glory.'

'Yes.'

'I think a call to The British Association of Rose Breeders might pay dividends. What's the number?'

The call to BARB did indeed pay dividends. The secretary was somewhat shaken by the news of Hanley's death; Palmer didn't go into details about the poison, just said that it was an accident and he was trying to find out as much about Hanley as possible because there didn't seem to be any relatives to take control of the business. He put the phone on speaker so Gheeta and Claire could hear.

'No, I don't believe there are any relatives. If there are Geoff never mentioned them,' said the BARB secretary. 'God, what an awful thing to happen – both he and Linda killed in one accident. Awful, he was a lovely chap.'

'And a good rose breeder so we are told,' said Palmer.

'Oh yes indeed, one of the top few. We have many named roses that belong to him. Quite a few breeders achieve double figures, and high double figures at that; Geoff was one of those. It's a long process to breed a new rose Chief Superintendent, eight to ten years from the initial crossing of pollen from selected plants, and then no guarantee of success. It has to be pretty nigh perfect to pass the National Institute of Agricultural Botany trials and tests and go on to the PVRO for intellectual property rights to be given.'

'I'm told Mr Hanley was determined to breed the first black rose.'

The secretary laughed, 'The Holy Grail of rose breeders everywhere. Yes, and he was damn near to doing it too. He sent an example to the NIAB two years ago and it was bloody close, but just not quite jet black. They were expecting another one next year from him – might well have cracked it by then.'

'Instant fame and fortune then?'

'Well, not instant, no. If the trials proved good and he got a certificate then Geoff would take cuttings and bud wood – that's small pieces of stem with a bud on – and grow them on and then repeat the process for a couple of years himself, and we would license growers to commercially grow on and multiply the stock until there was enough to go to market. The market for a black rose would be enormous; tens of thousands of plants would be sold through garden centres and mail order, and that's just the UK. But don't be deceived, as I said before it's a long haul – can be upwards of eight years to breed a rose good enough to trial.'

'I don't know whether you can answer this, but was Mr Hanley's income from rose breeding substantial?'

'Substantial? No. The market fluctuates a lot; one season everybody wants yellow and the next everybody wants red. Geoff's stable is a good one and would give him and Linda a couple of decent holidays every year, but you couldn't live on it unless you were very frugal.'

'I bet the chap who bred Peace lives on the royalties from that one.' Palmer felt quite proud that he'd remembered the name of at least one rose in Mrs P.'s garden.

'I'm afraid he doesn't. That entered commerce in 1945, long before Plant Breeders Rights were in existence; and even now rose royalties like other plant royalties only last twenty-five years, and then it's a free-for-all.'

'Are there many rose breeders then?'

'Not many individuals, it's more of a hobby than a good business proposition. Don't forget they are up against the professional business growers with massive greenhouses and hundreds of thousands of seedlings growing away; they can do very well on growing existing roses for the trade.'

'Ever heard of a grower called Bloom, Edward Bloom?'

There was a telltale silence on the line for moment.

'Oh yes, we've heard of Edward Bloom. I wish we had never heard of him. Why do you ask?'

'Well, and I must ask for you to keep this confidential, it seems that Mr Bloom may have made a partnership offer to Mr Hanley.'

'Geoff wouldn't touch him with a bargepole. Let me tell you about Edward Bloom. He first came to our notice some years ago when he worked for a lovely lady called Angela Robinson, who had a garden centre in Watford and another in Stanmore – two good centres too, and she bred roses as well. Bloom was an ex-convict who had met Angela when she visited the open prison at Pentonville to run a garden club and an allotment for the inmates. They hit it off, and when Bloom was released he began to work for her; a year later they married, and I have to say that everybody I know who met Bloom took an instant dislike to him and wondered what on earth had possessed Angela to marry him. Within a year she was dead, accident with a chain saw, and Bloom inherited the centres and moved in a young lady thirty years his junior who had recently graduated from the Pershore Agricultural College as his new wife and business partner. I have no need to tell you, Chief Superintendent, of the rumours that circulated within the business.'

'I can imagine.'

'It gets better, or maybe I should say worse. Angela had always bred roses and had quite a few licensed through us. Well after her death new ones were still coming into us for trials from the Blooms on a regular basis – nothing wrong in that, except after about three years we noticed a distinct similarity between the ones Blooms was putting in and those from other breeders. It's a close-knit community Chief Superintendent, very close-knit, and a lot of peer group support. We made a few discreet enquiries and found that the Blooms were often visiting other breeders on the pretext of asking for help with something to do with garden centres, or just simply turning up unannounced – '*we were just passing.*' Have you met Mrs Bloom, Chief Superintendent ?'

'No, not yet.'

'Well, when you do you'll understand why a late middle-aged gardener might well have his attention riveted on her – so much so that he might not notice a new bud wood growth or seedling disappear from the row on his bench into Mr Bloom's rucksack that he always carried over his shoulder. Anyway, to cut a long story short a trap was laid and sprung and the Blooms were thrown out of the Association, and I hope never to see them again. So you see, no way would Geoff have entertained a business partnership with them.'

Claire pushed a written note in front of Palmer. *They have 3 centres, not 2.*

'Where did the Blooms' third garden centre come from? Did they expand?'

'Yes, they bought Charlie Hilton's garden centre in Barnet. Charlie was getting on a bit – had a dicky heart, no family and looking to retire, so it suited him. All legal and above board as far as I know.'

You've been very helpful sir, very helpful indeed. Thank you for your time and once again I'd ask you to keep our conversation confidential if you would.'

'Of course, anything else I can help with just give me a call.'

Palmer ended the call. 'Well, the Blooms certainly have my attention now. Do they have an office?'

Claire scrolled her screen. 'The main garden centre is at Stanmore which has the main phone line.'

'Give it a call, see if we can get to see them in the morning'

****

'What did you do? What the hell have you done?'

Jim Riley let Edward and Janet Bloom into his bedsit. They had been waiting in their car outside for him to get home from work. Edward was mid-sixties, with greying hair and a paunch, wearing a dark grey suit and looking anything but a gardener. Janet, early thirties, slim and blonde (from a bottle) was in a designer trouser suit and ankle boots; she looked fit and business-like.

'Calm down Jim, it's all under control.' Edward motioned him to sit.

'Calm down? Under control? I've had the police round asking questions, they said the Hanleys had committed suicide in the back of the van, found in a motorway car park.' He sat on the edge of the bed as the Blooms took the two chairs beside his small table. 'You killed them, didn't you? You murdered them for the black rose!'

339

There was no answer.

'You did, you killed them! Christ, what's going on? The police have kept the van, said the exhaust was piped inside and killed them.'

'They robbed us, Jim.' Janet Bloom spoke softly. 'They broke their promise of a partnership.'

'What? What do you mean? How could they rob you?'

'They took the eighty grand that bailed them out of debt and kept the bailiffs away on the promise of a partnership, and then decided they didn't want a partnership.'

'So what? Take the money back and that's it, the end.'

'The money was gone, Jim – paid off the debts, all gone. We offered to let them pay it back bit by bit, but Geoff wouldn't. He laughed at us – he said he knew all along you'd been giving us some of his bud wood and seeds. He was going to press charges against us, and you.'

'What did you do, tie them up and run the exhaust until they were dead?'

'I poisoned them,' said Janet.

'WHAT?'

'It was a spur of the moment thing, it wasn't planned. They sat in our kitchen, Jim, and basically laughed at us – said we wouldn't get any of the money back, wouldn't get a partnership, and would probably get a prison sentence for stealing the rose, and so would you. They laughed at us. I was so angry I could have strangled the gloating pair of them, I was making tea at the time and the temptation was too great – I slipped a spoonful in their cups. It's tasteless.'

'What poison?'

'Aconite, I'd had it in the cupboard for ages. Made it to get rid of a few rats in the greenhouses ages ago.'

Jim sank his head into his hands. 'Oh for God's sake. They know, the police know.'

'No they don't, the police think it was suicide,' Edward Bloom said forcibly. 'And that's all there is to it. Just stay calm and this will all calm down. We will be able to prove we paid the money to Hanley, and then everything will get back to normal and we will have the centre.'

'Did you hear me?' Jim shouted at Bloom. 'I said the police fucking know! The Sergeant asked me if we sold Aconites – why would she ask that, eh? They know!'

They sat in silence for a few moments before Janet spoke

'Even if the police know they died from poison, it's alright. It just means the Hanleys took aconite before turning on the exhaust; after all they were garden experts, they would know it's a poison and so they used it to make sure of the suicide. The police can't tie it to us.'

'That damn black rose, eh? You have to have it, don't you? And now you've murdered two people to get it.' Jim stared coldly at Edward. 'I was so stupid, wasn't I? You played me all along. When Janet came into the centre I thought it was just coincidence – coincidence that the girl I loved at college had turned up again; coincidence that she spilled her heart out to me about a loveless marriage with you. It was just a sham, a ploy, wasn't it? A ploy to get to me and the black rose.'

Edward Bloom gave a sarcastic laugh and pointed to the bed Jim was sitting on. 'You didn't mind that when you were shagging her on that cheap bed, did you?

'He knows?' Riley looked at Janet.

Bloom laughed louder. 'Knew? Of course I knew, I planned it you fool! You think a girl as attractive as Janet would go for you without a good reason? I want that rose and I'll have that rose. You get our van over to Hanley's in the morning, load the plants – the bud wood and seedlings of the black rose – and get them over to Watford. That black rose is going to be unveiled at the Chelsea Flower Show next Monday for the press and the royal visit, and it will be there under the Bloom name.'

'It won't – I'm going to the police in the morning. I'm not getting involved in murder, I'll take whatever I get for theft of Hanley's roses, but not murder. No.'

Edward Bloom's mood got nasty. He leant forward face-to-face with Jim and jabbed a finger into his chest. 'You do that Riley, and you'd better get police protection for yourself, understand me? You just do as I say, you stick to your story – you're not involved, you don't even know about the partnership. You didn't tell the police you knew, did you?'

'No.'

'Good, then keep it that way and everything will work out fine. Here.' He took a key out of his pocket. 'This is for the door to the staff entrance at the Watford Centre. Put everything in the rose house.'

****

'What do you think you are doing?'

Mrs P. and Daisy the dog stood in Palmer's porch at his house in Dulwich Village, looking at him stumbling about in her front garden rose bed. 'Get your size elevens out of there before you do some damage.'

Palmer had got home and parked his CRV on the drive when the thought had struck him: *perhaps, just perhaps?* He looked over to the porch.

'I'm looking for a black one.'

'A black what?'

'Rose, a black rose.'

'Don't be stupid, you've got more chance of finding Shergar in there than a black rose. Your dinner's on the table – lasagne with burnt cheese topping.'

The thought of one of his favourite dishes immediately put paid to the rose bed search and he carefully made his way out of it, knowing that one broken stem would bring down fire and brimstone if Mrs P. found it.

He left his shoes in the porch in case they were dirty, padded his way down the hall, put his coat and hat on the hallstand, rescued his slippers from Daisy's jaw and went into the kitchen.

'Smells nice.'

Mrs P. carried on eating hers. 'I take it the foray into the rose bed has something to do with a case at work?'

Palmer gave her a brief outline of the case between mouthfuls of lasagne.

'So you think this Bloom character is after the black rose, which you don't even know exists?' Mrs P. had a habit of throwing water on the fire.

'Yes, it will exist, mark my words. Everything points towards its existence, otherwise why would two people be dead?'

'Did you enjoy that lasagne?

'Yes, lovely.'

'It was vegetarian.'

'Tasted awful.'

The ongoing battle in the Palmers' kitchen was Mrs P.'s attempts to get Palmer to eat less meat and onto a more healthy diet, both for his own sake and the planet's.

'I'll get a Big Mac later when I take Daisy out.'

'You'll do no such thing. She's on a diet, the vet said she should lose a kilo.'

'She's fine, she gets taken out for walks twice a day.'

'Once a day, with me in the morning – your so-called '*dog walk*' in the evening is up the road to Dulwich Park and back again.'

'Yes, so?'

'When you've done the one hundred metres to the park gate Justin, the idea is to go inside and walk round the park, not turn round and come home and then give her a large fatty treat for being a good girl. Anyway, talking about roses, Benji is going to make his front garden into a rose garden like ours.'

'He only had it paved over last year.'

Benji, full name Benjamin Courtney-Smith, was Palmer's next-door neighbour and nemesis. A retired advertising executive in his early sixties, spray on tan, ponytail, designer clothes and, in Palmer's estimation, of questionable sexual orientation, judging by the mincing walk and habit of waving a floppy hand about when talking. Too much money and too much time on his hands was Palmer's usual anti-Benji mantra; three or four continental cruises or holidays a year, a new motor every year, and Palmer reckoned a new nip and tuck every year too. But Benji was a great favourite with most of the ladies in the area, especially Mrs P. and her gardening club and WI, and this rankled a bit with Palmer who was their favourite until Benji moved in and knocked him off that plinth. Then, to cap it all, he ran for the local council elections and got voted in; he was soon elevated to Chairperson and became everybody's favourite by reinstating pensioner free bus passes and pool passes for the over 50's. He then had topped it off by twisting arms at the county level to secure funding to re-open the library that the previous council had closed due to financial cuts. But he was also prone to accidents, usually involving Palmer's property.

'He's got a mini-digger coming in the morning to take up the paving and some topsoil being delivered later on.'

'What about the roses themselves?'

'He wants me to go with him to a garden centre and choose some.'

'Don't go to Bloom's.'

'I'm not going all that way. We'll go local, there's a good one in Norwood. He only wants roses without thorns – he's allergic to pricks.'

'You could have fooled me.'

FRIDAY

'It's all very interesting sir,' said Claire, turning from her computer to Palmer who was reading the report from Pete Atkins. Gheeta was sticking photos of the deceased on the big white progress board at the far end of the room and drawing felt tip arrows to the names of the other people in the case: Riley, Burnley, the Blooms. Bit by bit those lines would grow into a pattern as the case progressed and a tie between the people shown became apparent; they always did.

Palmer raised his head from the report. 'What's all very interesting?'

'Breeding roses. It's a bit like sex.'

'How's your memory, guv?' Gheeta said from the end of the room.

'Very funny, Sergeant. Carry on, Claire.'

Claire turned back to her screen and read from it. 'Well, first you select the two roses you want to cross and take the petals off the flower of the mother plant, leaving the green outer petals which are called anthers, and then remove all the inside except for the stigma – that's the central bit. After a while that will go sticky, which means it's ready for the father's pollen from the other plant. Using a soft paintbrush you put the pollen from that one onto the stigma, then put a small paper bag over the flower and leave it for a few days for the pollination to take place. Then you grow it on until the rose hip develops, which is the seed pod, and when that's ripe you take the seeds out and leave them in a fridge to simulate winter conditions until the next January. Then plant them and cross your fingers.'

'And commercial growers do this thousands of times to get one good one?'

'They do.'

'And obviously nobody's hit on a black one yet.'

'Which is why it would be worth so much,' said Gheeta, joining them.

'And worth stealing,' said Palmer. 'Our chat with the Blooms is going to be an interesting one.'

Gheeta walked back from the board and gave Palmer an enquiring look. 'You think Hanley had bred one, don't you guv? You think the black rose is what this is all about, don't you?'

'I do.' He turned to Claire. 'Has the CCTV recordings from the motorway services come through yet?'

'Not yet, sir. They quoted the Data Protection Act so I've had our legal department issue an exemption notice – should be here soon.'

****

Palmer had asked DS Singh to be in normal clothes for the visit to the Blooms; he wanted to take a quiet look around before announcing his arrival.

The Bloom's Stanmore centre was obviously the jewel in the crown. It had five large greenhouses, a restaurant, child's play area, aquarium and gift shop.

'Impressive, eh?' Palmer said to Gheeta as they got out of his car and walked towards the busy entrance. Plain squad cars have a habit of standing out amongst others, so he had opted to drive to Stanmore in his own.

'Very impressive, guv. You know I was thinking about Edward Bloom's seventeen-year stretch for the Manchester robbery – hardly any of the five million was

351

traced and it was before the days of the Proceeds of Crime Act, so I suppose it was just written off by the insurance company?'

'Very probably, why?'

'Well, three very busy garden centres would be a good way of laundering quite substantial amounts of cash if it was still around, wouldn't they guv.'

'They would.' He thought for a moment. 'Have that Atkins chap take a look at the posted accounts of Blooms since he inherited it, and do a quick comparison with the years before and after. I take it HMRC would have them archived somewhere?'

'They have guv, and they show an increase of a hundred and twenty thousand on the first year of his ownership, rising to an increase of just on three hundred thousand pounds in the last accounts.'

Palmer stopped walking, as did Singh. His cold stare met her pair of innocent eyes. Palmer had pulled DS Singh out of the Yard's Cyber Crime and IT Unit after she had upgraded his office HOLMES programme in an hour after it had '*gone down*', a job that the outside contractors usually took two days to do and then probably only after waiting a week for a visit. Palmer had for some time realised the value of computers and their various programmes in the pursuit of criminals, and felt that having to use the overworked in-house unit at the Yard and the wait that entailed had to be overcome. What better way to overcome it than to prise one of their top programmers away and into his squad? Gheeta didn't need asking twice.

Palmer's immediate boss, AC Bateman was not keen on asking for her transfer, as he didn't want to upset the AC whose command the Cyber Unit came under; Bateman didn't want to upset anybody in his quest to reach the post of Commissioner and crept around everybody. Not to be beaten, Palmer had a quiet word with the chairman of the House of Commons Home Affairs Select Committee, an old school MP who, like Palmer, didn't hold much truck with PC and some human rights issues; he in turn had a word with the Commissioner, and Gheeta was transferred to Palmer's Serial Murder Squad within seven days. AC Bateman then did a quick about-turn and made a big thing of welcoming her, and made out that his input had clinched the transfer; but everybody knew that wasn't so.

The unwritten law between Gheeta and Palmer was that she had *carte blanche* to install whatever programmes she thought might be useful, but he didn't want to know about the ones she hacked from other law enforcement agencies worldwide, or any other below-the-line IT and cyber activities she downloaded from the dark web and used in the pursuit of criminals.

Palmer shook his head in recognition that he knew how Gheeta had come by the information on Bloom's accounts. 'Okay, but get Atkins to do it as well, legally – just in case we need to use it in evidence, got to be within the law.'

They wandered through the wide entrance into the first greenhouse. Gheeta picked up a steel basket from the pile. 'How much can I spend, guv?'

'You live in a fifth-floor apartment in the Barbican, Sergeant. You haven't got a garden.'

'I could do with some house plants to brighten the place up.'

'You're not there to water them, they'd die.'

'Seeing that we are out of uniform guv, does that mean that I'm off duty at the moment?'

'No, why?'

'Because if I was off duty at present I'd be classed as a civilian and I'd call you a mean old bastard.'

Palmer laughed. 'Water off a duck's back, Sergeant. Mrs P. calls me that all the time, and worse.'

'She'd have a ball in here wouldn't she, guv?'

'She would indeed. She's off to a local garden centre today with our neighbour – he's starting a rose garden and they're choosing the plants.'

Gheeta pointed to a sign board standing at the back of the greenhouse beside the exit into a courtyard. An arrow pointed through with ROSES under it. 'That might be interesting, guv.'

They walked through into the courtyard which was full of large pots of shrubs and fruit bushes. Halfway through Gheeta grabbed Palmer's arm and stopped him.

'Do you see what I see, guv?'

He had – it was a coiled hose for use in watering the plants, not the normal domestic garden hose but exactly like the one in the Hanley van that Frome had left them a photo of. Gheeta took out her mobile phone and made as though taking photos of the bushes, but zooming in on the hose – *click, click*.

'Can I help you?' a female voice asked. 'Having trouble making your mind up?'

They turned round as a young Bloom's worker approached them with a big smile on her face. 'There's so many fruit varieties it's difficult to choose. Which type are you after?'

Gheeta took the lead. 'Blackcurrants. My grandfather here is thinking of starting a fruit patch and he's keen on blackcurrants.'

The assistant gave Palmer a smile. 'Good choice sir, plenty of vitamin C in blackcurrants. What type of soil do you have?'

'Sort of dark grey,' said Palmer before he could stop himself.

The assistant laughed and Gheeta managed a false one too.

'Do you live locally, sir?'

'Yes.' Gheeta though it best if she took over the conversation. 'Just half a mile away.'

'Okay, then you'll have a good loam soil and we recommend the variety Ben Connan.' The assistant pointed to a bush dripping with blackcurrants ready to pick. 'It's a good large currant, as you can see, and very sweet – likes a loam soil and best kept a little damp, which is not hard with the English weather.'

'Ben Connan,' repeated Gheeta. 'Right, thank you for that. Now we are going to have a look at the roses.'

'You're welcome, just carry on through the next greenhouse and the rose house is on the right. Anything else we can help you with just ask one of the assistants.'

'We will, thank you.'

The assistant wandered off.

Palmer stood and looked Gheeta in the eyes, impassive.

'What?'

'Father I could take, but grandfather? You cheeky sod.'

Gheeta smiled and shrugged. They made their way to the rose house; it was enormous – at least fifty metres long and twenty wide – with paths running between benches packed with roses of all sizes, types and colours, as well as being packed with buyers.

They stood at the entrance taking it all in.

'Mr Palmer.' A voice shouted his name from behind them where Janet Bloom was hurrying through the greenhouse towards them. She was wearing a green trouser suit with Bloom's logo across the chest, green suede ankle boots and green cap hiding her blonde locks. Gheeta noted that the top of the suit was unbuttoned to reveal a certain amount of cleavage. She nudged Palmer.

'Down boy.'

Palmer smiled. 'No chance – not unless she makes a pretty mean steak and kidney pie.'

'I thought it must be you,' gushed Janet Bloom as she reached them, flapping her false eyelashes at Palmer so much Gheeta thought she felt a draft. 'We spoke to Jim Riley last night, and he said you'd been round and gave us a description. I'm Janet Bloom.'

Palmer took the outstretched hand and introduced Gheeta as DS Singh.

'What an awful state of affairs with Geoff and Linda. We never saw that coming at all, they seemed so happy – anyway, I'm forgetting my manners. Do come over to the office, Edward's over there.' She noticed the empty basket Gheeta was carrying. 'We won't get very rich with you two as customers, will we?' she laughed. 'Let me take that.'

She took the basket and slid it under a bench.

The office was through a keypad-protected door marked 'STAFF ONLY'. Inside was the opposite to Jim Riley's office: modern office furniture, two computer workstations, and two water coolers dispensing Malvern or Buxton spring water depending on your choice, both regularly filled with Stanmore tap water – Janet Bloom was very frugal with the company's money. Edward Bloom stood up from his chair behind the wide metal desk and was introduced.

'Edward, this is Detective Chief Superintendent Palmer and Detective Sergeant Singh. They are investigating Geoff and Linda's suicide.' She opened her hand towards Edward as he came round the desk. 'My husband, Edward.'

They shook hands coldly. Palmer was of course fully aware of Edward Bloom's criminal past, and Edward Bloom fully aware that Palmer would be.

'Do sit down.' He pointed them towards a pair of contemporary design Danish sofas that matched the desk; if nothing else Janet Bloom had some taste. She took a seat on a matching chair as Edward went back to his desk. 'Can I order you tea or coffee?'

Palmer removed his trilby and shook his head. 'Thank you, no. We've a lot to get through today so trying to keep toilet breaks to a minimum.'

They all laughed.

'I can't understand why this awful suicide is interesting the police so much,' said Janet. 'I know it's a terrible thing to happen but it's not a crime, is it?'

Funny way of putting it, thought Gheeta.

'And I doubt it will be the last, Mrs Bloom,' said Palmer, flashing her his killer smile. 'Trouble is it gets a bit involved when there's two of them in strange circumstances.'

'Strange circumstances?' Edward showed interest.

'Very strange circumstances, sir. For instance why would they drive to a motorway service station to do it? Easier to run the exhaust into the van in their own garage, or at their garden centre after work. Why go to a motorway service station? Very strange.'

Janet Bloom changed the subject. 'You do know that we have a financial interest in the Hanley Garden centre Mr Palmer, don't you?'

'I wasn't aware, no.' Palmer laid the trap.

'Yes, we put a considerable amount of money into it on a partnership basis. The Hanleys were old friends of ours and had hit a bad patch; basically we helped them out and they gratefully offered a partnership.'

'Really? How did you know they had, as you put it, '*hit a bad patch*'?'

The silence was deafening.

Edward broke it. 'Our bookkeeper told us. She does the Hanley books as well as ours and was quite worried.

'Not very professional of her was it, discussing one client's business with another client?'

Janet Bloom gave a false laugh. 'Well, she knew we were great friends and she was very worried for Geoff and Linda.'

'So that would be Alison Burnley then?'

'Yes, she's been with us from the start.'

'Before the start surely? She was bookkeeper to Angela Robinson, wasn't she?'

'Yes, yes I believe she was.' Edward Bloom shifted uncomfortably in his chair and was looking at his wife as he answered. Palmer's knowledge had surprised him.

'Funny that. We had a chat with Miss Burnley yesterday and she told us Hanley's problems stemmed from his gambling debts. Did she tell you that?'

'No, no, just that he was in financial trouble. Quite deep financial trouble.'

'Another funny thing is that Miss Burnley said she had no idea who had put the money in to clear the debt. That lady seems to have a very selective memory, doesn't she? I wonder why.'

Silence.

'Are you still breeding roses, Mr Bloom?'

Edward Bloom was getting visibly uncomfortable. 'No, no I don't do any breeding. Got enough on our plate without adding to it.' He gave a false laugh.

'BARB told us you used to, before you had a falling out with them. Geoff Hanley bred roses – very successfully too. He was apparently well on the way to the Holy Grail.'

Silence.

'Do you know what the Holy Grail of rose breeding is, Mr Bloom? I'm sure you do.'

'Yes of course, the black rose. Everybody knows that,' smirked Edward Bloom.

'Apparently Geoff Hanley was very near to breeding one. So if he was well on his way to fame and fortune with a black rose that would pay off his debt, why suddenly decide to drive to a service station, murder his wife and commit suicide?'

'Murder his wife?' Janet Bloom didn't understand.

'Well I don't suppose she leaped at the idea of a suicide pact with her husband, would you?' Palmer stood up. 'Well, we must be off – thank you for seeing us. Just one thing I think you might want to check out –

according to the Hanleys' solicitor and the HMRC files, the Hanley Garden Centre at the time of his death was a sole trader not a partnership – no changes to its constitution have been filed – so maybe you ought to chase that up, because there doesn't seem to be any other directors or living relatives who might register an interest; and in that situation the business will be put in the hands of solicitors to sell and any proceeds handed over to the Treasury. Well, nice to meet you both, but we must be going – things to do, people to see.'

Gheeta closed her laptop which had recorded the conversation and filmed it and followed him out. It wouldn't be acceptable in a court of law as she hadn't asked permission to record or film, and the Blooms hadn't been given an opportunity to have a lawyer present, but it worked as a good aide-memoire should they need it.

'Oh, one thing more,' she said as they all went back into the main glasshouse. 'Do you stock any aconites?'

Both Blooms answered together. 'No', 'It's poisonous', 'No never have.'

****

Back in Palmer's car he gave Gheeta a sly smile and raised his eyebrows. 'Well, how interesting was that?'

'Very interesting guv – very, very interesting.'

'I think we are on the right track, don't you?'

'Definitely, and I should think the phone line between the Blooms and Miss Burnley is red hot by now! I wonder why she didn't mention the Blooms were the providers of money to Hanley? She obviously knew.'

'Which beggars the question is Burnley straight or in cahoots with the Blooms? We need to keep an eye on her. Right, let's take a look at the Hanleys' house – I take it the local boys have taped it off?'

'They have – basic report was nothing out of place. They went in to see if they could find a record of any family relatives, but no joy.'

****

The Hanleys' Borehamwood home was a Victorian semi in a quiet leafy backstreet. The uniformed constable at the gate reported no activity except from nosy locals; Palmer couldn't see the point of keeping him there or of keeping the crime scene tape across the driveway, as it just increased the chance of a nosy local journalist starting to ask questions, and Palmer wasn't ready for any of that just yet. Reg Frome's forensics team had been in and no poison had been found, or indeed anything out of the ordinary at all.

They stood at the front door.

'We should have picked the keys up from the local station on the way here, guv. I didn't think, sorry.'

'Not a problem, Sergeant.' Palmer pulled out a set of lock picks from his coat pocket; years dealing with criminals of all kinds had taught Palmer a few skills that were not on the Hendon graduates' curriculum. DS Singh had seen him use the picks several times in the past and positioned herself behind him, cutting out any view from the street of what was going on.

It only took a few twists and the door was open.

'Well, if you ever fancy a change of career, guv?'

'Probably make more money,' Palmer smiled as they walked into the hall. It was well kept, tidy – a few letters on a half oval side table, nothing out of the ordinary. The dark frost of graphite on the surfaces and painted door jambs showed Frome's fingerprint team had been through.

Palmer checked the ground floor whilst Gheeta had a look through the two bedrooms, spare room and bathroom upstairs; everything was in place, no disturbance anywhere to indicate a fight or anything similar had taken place. The kitchen had a door out to the garden which they could see from the lounge was, as you would expect, immaculate. The flower beds threw out waves of colour along their borders and the lawn was fit for a bowls tournament.

'I hope somebody keeps on top of that, seems a shame if it's let off the lead,' Palmer commented.

'You could get Mrs P. and her Garden Club to come round and keep an eye on it guv,' Gheeta said.

'I'm not even going to mention it to her, or she would. Once all this caper is sorted out and put to bed somebody is going to be able to buy a very nice home here.'

A noise at the front door sent the pair of them into silent mode. Gheeta tiptoed to the lounge door and removing her peaked hat peeped round just as an envelope was dropped through the letterbox and a figure retreated from the door. She hurried into the front room just in time to see Janet Bloom get into a car alongside her husband and drive off.

'Now I wonder what we have here then?' Palmer was turning the envelope over in his hand as she joined him in the hall.

'Something from the Blooms, guv – that was Janet Bloom who popped it through the letterbox and Edward was waiting in the car at the end of the drive.'

'What are they playing at then? You'd hardly send a letter to somebody you know is deceased, would you?'

'I wouldn't guv, and you wouldn't, but the Blooms just have.'

'Let's have a look see then.' Palmer ripped open the envelope, took out a folded letter inside and opened it. He read it silently before passing it to Gheeta.

'Seems our earlier chat with the Blooms has got them worried about their partnership with Hanley.'

Gheeta finished reading. 'Or should we say their non-partnership with Hanley.'

The letter read;

My dear Geoff, It is now a few weeks since you agreed to put the Hanley's Garden Centre into a partnership with Bloom's. You have had the eighty thousand pounds we agreed on for that half share and I am a bit worried that my solicitor has not heard anything from your solicitor. Would you please move things along so we can complete our agreed deal asap. Yours, Edward Bloom.

'See the date.' Palmer pointed to the date at the top of the letter.

'A week ago today,' said Gheeta. 'What are the Blooms playing at?'

'They're trying to manufacture evidence that they were owners of half the Hanley's Garden Centre before the Hanleys died; if they legally were then in law they'd have first option to buy the other half once things settle down.'

'But legally they weren't half owners, guv – nothing had been altered or was in the process of being altered at Companies House. This stupid letter won't change that – and in any case, us witnessing it being delivered today could get them put on a charge of attempted fraud. I'd like that.'

'Yes it could, but I don't want them on attempted fraud – I want them on a murder charge, so this letter is going to disappear. It never existed, did it?'

'What never existed, guv?'

'The letter.'

'What letter?'

Palmer put the letter into his pocket and they left the house.

****

Janet Bloom broke the silence in their car.

'Where are we going now?'

'Burnley's, I want to have a good chat with her and put her right. Stupid woman, fancy saying she wasn't aware we were the people giving Hanley the money? Palmer knows now that she's our bookkeeper as well as Hanley's, because we told him that she told us Hanley had debts. If he asks her again she'll have to say she made a mistake and forgot – memory lapse brought on by shock at the Hanleys' deaths.'

'He suspects we did it as well, you know that don't you? He bloody well suspects us, you could tell from his attitude – and then that sergeant asking if we stock aconites, Jim said she asked him the same question. They know about the poison and they suspect us.'

'There's a big difference between suspecting and proving. They can't prove we had anything to do with it. Our story is strong – we were going into partnership with Hanley, so why would we murder him? Everything was ticking along nicely until the bastard changed his mind. Eighty grand Janet, he stole that eighty grand.'

'You're forgetting where that eighty grand came from.'

Edward Bloom laughed. 'Yes, that had slipped my mind. You have to admit, that was a peach of a plan.'

'Didn't work out though, did it?'

'No, and I don't know why. Do you think Hanley cottoned onto it?'

'No, I think he cottoned onto you and Riley stealing his black rose.'

'Yes, and I mean to keep it. That little treasure is worth a great deal more than eighty grand – you know that and I know that. Get it to market and I'll show those stuck up bastards at BARB. They'll lose thousands of pounds by not collecting on it; they'll be round on their hands and knees asking for the rights management, just you wait and see – and the garden centres and mail order boys will be falling over themselves to stock it in the thousands. I'm not sacrificing that. Burnley won't step out of line, she knows I've got enough on her to send her down for a long time.'

'So why are we going to hers?'

'I want her to have a word with Riley. I'll tell her what to say.'

'Don't forget it's Chelsea on Monday, royal visit and press preview – don't you upset the apple cart before then. I want that black rose as the centre of our display.'

****

Back in the Team Room Claire had some news for Palmer and Gheeta when they walked in.

'Two things of interest: first, the Hanleys' solicitor Mr Whitley rang. He's had a letter from the Blooms' solicitor saying he understands the Hanleys have been paid eighty thousand pounds by his clients in return for a partnership in the garden centre

372

business and when will the paperwork be ready; Whitley has replied that he knows nothing of any partnership deal and had no instruction to effect one before Mr Hanley passed away.'

'That's good.' Palmer was pleased. 'If Bloom's solicitors know their stuff they'll know that without signed papers by Hanley there just isn't any deal. Looks like the Blooms are trying every avenue they can to get Hanley's centre.'

'And the second thing is of more interest I think, sir.' She switched on the large plasma screen on the wall above the bank of Gheeta's computer servers. 'The motorway services CCTV has arrived at last.'

The screen burst into life, showing the lorry park with the numerical LED clock in the corner of the screen showing nine forty-three. The Hanleys' Transit drove into view and backed into a space between two lorries at the back of the area; the area was lit by basic streetlamps that didn't exactly flood the area with light. The picture was very grainy, but a figure could be seen exiting the driver's door and disappearing to the rear of the Transit.

'I think this is when whoever that figure is fixed up the exhaust pipe to the hose,' said Claire.

A time of three minutes elapsed and the corner LED showed nine forty-six as the figure emerged and made off towards the main cafe building and out of CCTV range.

'It's not a lot to go on,' Claire explained. 'But from the counter clock in the corner of the screen we can see the person went into the building at approximately nine forty-six. So, what he or she would need now is a means of leaving the services. They can either leave by this northbound side of the services onto the M25 and travel north or cross the motorway by the services bridge to the south side and travel south. Both sides have a National Express coach service that calls every hour; I checked the internal coach CCTV but nobody who got onto or left those coaches fits the Blooms' description.

'So that leaves the possibility that our Transit driver drove from the services or was driven from them. With the Blooms being suspects *numero uno*, I contacted the DVLA and asked for a list of all vehicles registered to them individually or Bloom's Garden Centres. There are four in total, so I thought going south from the services back towards the motorway exits for the Stanmore and Watford area would be the best bet, and had the Welcome Break CCTV of the south side exit to the motorway onscreen and looked for any of those four vehicles leaving after ten o'clock – that's giving whoever left the Transit about ten minutes to get over the bridge, find the getaway vehicle and drive off. I just prayed they didn't stop for a meal or I'd probably still be looking at number plates now.'

'Is that what you did?' Palmer was amazed at Claire's dexterity.

'Yep, I stopped the CCTV at every vehicle exiting the south side and pulled up the number plate on the enlarger. Fifth car out – bingo! Kia Creed Estate registered to Janet Bloom. We've only got the back view but there are definitely two people in it, driver and passenger.' She sat back. 'I put an ANPR check through on it and guess what?'

'What?' Palmer asked.

'Janet Bloom reported it stolen that afternoon. The police recovered it burnt out on an industrial estate in Watford the following morning.'

'Crafty pair aren't they, eh?' Palmer knew this was an old ploy, usually used by thieves who stole a car to use in a burglary and then torched it to remove all evidence that they were ever in it.

'Well not really, guv.' Gheeta had doubts. 'I mean we've got the car at the services, and the timeframe is right from all angles.'

'Yes it is, but it's all circumstantial – strong circumstantial, I'll give you that, and something we can use. Well done Claire, bloody good work – well done.'

Claire and Gheeta looked at each other in surprise. Praise from Palmer? Unheard of.

****

Palmer was in a good mood as he turned off the road into his short herringbone patterned brick drive at home. Things were coming along nicely in the case, the Blooms were in panic mode, and the evidence, although circumstantial so far, was mounting up. Yes, it had been a good day.

The good day came to a sudden halt as he hit the brakes to avoid running into a mini-digger lying on its side across his herringbone brick drive, part of which now resembled a builder's demolition tip. His eyes followed the deep scrape in the earth back through Mrs P.'s rose garden and through a large hole ripped in the laurel hedge between the Palmer's and Benji's front garden.

The porch door opened and Mrs P., Benji and Daisy emerged as he got out of the car.

'Before you start shouting it was an accident,' Mrs P. said as they approached.

'I should hope so,' said Palmer. 'I hate to think he did it on purpose.'

'I'm awfully sorry,' came Benji's trembling voice from behind Mrs P., where he had decided it might be safer than within Palmer's reach. 'I really am most terribly sorry, Justin – I'll have it all repaired, I'll pay for everything. I'm very sorry.'

'What happened?' asked Palmer – although he could see what had happened. But how?

'I lost control.'

Mrs P. thought she could explain it better. 'Benji didn't realise the digger was back wheel drive...'

'So when I turned the steering wheel to the right it went left, through the hedge,'

Benji blurted out, wringing his hands in front of him. 'And when I pressed the brake I hit the pedal that lowered the bucket instead and that's what tore up your drive and sent it over on its side. I really am so sorry, Justin.' He was almost in tears.

Mrs P. patted his arm. 'Never mind, Benji – it could have been worse, it could have landed on top of you and killed you!'

'Really?' Palmer nodded. 'Want to have another go?'

****

SATURDAY

'But it's not right guv, we ought to do something about it.' Gheeta was quite adamant.

They were in the Team Room and Gheeta had laid a series of photographs on the table that they had been looking at.

Palmer spread his hands. 'Okay, you're right – there's things that aren't right and should have been questioned at the time. But it's a closed case – it wasn't even classified as a 'crime' case. Those photos don't have Scene of Crime stickers on, do they?'

Claire had walked in and after exchanging 'good mornings' was taking off her coat. She had been to see DS Atkins in Forensic Accounts and collected the report on the turnover increases of the Blooms' business each time a new centre was added.

'What things aren't right?' She peered over Gheeta to the photos. 'Urgh, not nice.'

The photos showed a lady in check shirt and jeans on her back on a concrete floor with a chainsaw resting on her chest. The serious amount of blood around her head and shoulders showed she was very dead.

'Who's that?

'Angela Robinson, Edward Bloom's first wife.'

'Oh right, yes.' Claire remembered the file she had pulled on Edward Bloom's history. 'Chainsaw accident. Is that it?'

'It is,' said Palmer. 'Only the Sergeant doesn't think it was an accident.'

'Look.' Gheeta took a pose as though holding a chainsaw in front of her. 'She's right-handed, so her right hand has the trigger and her left hand would hold the front handle on top of the machine with her fingers on the brake guard in front of it. She's cutting wood and hits a solid metal snag and the chainsaw jumps and severs her jugular artery in the neck. She's dead before she hits the floor. The chain saw falls with her, right?'

Claire nodded. 'Yes.'

'So, it would land on her body and stay there – it wouldn't bounce 'cause it's heavy, one of those industrial ones, not a wood burner owner's type. So explain to me how the chainsaw in the photos has its blade and chain pointing to the right. It would fall pointing to the left, wouldn't it?'

'Yes, not likely to do a complete one hundred and eighty degree turn in the air – no way,' agreed Claire.

'I studied those photos for an hour last night. I knew something was wrong and then it hit me: that chainsaw is definitely pointing the wrong way. It's pointing the correct way if somebody else in front of her had taken it from her and swiped her neck and then thrown or put it down on the body to make it look like an accident. If she dropped it then it's pointing the wrong way'

Claire looked at Palmer. 'Sergeant's right, sir.'

Palmer gave in. 'Okay, write up a cold case review request and I'll pass it on.'

'Let's hope Janet Bloom doesn't decide to cut some wood with a chainsaw, at least not when her husband is around,' said Claire, taking her seat. 'By the way sir, how did Mrs P. get on with Benji yesterday on the rose garden trip?'

'Late cancellation.'

****

AC Bateman was forty-eight years old, slightly built and the epitome of a social

381

climber in society, but the ladder he was intent on climbing was in the police force; he sucked up to anybody in authority that he thought might assist in his career path towards his ultimate goal of being Commissioner. He was always immaculately turned out in a uniform with ironed creases so sharp they could cut bread.

His nemesis was his head, in that it was bald, totally bald. It didn't worry anybody except AC Bateman, who had tried every remedy advertised to re-thatch his dome: potions, creams, massages and all sorts of oils had failed to deliver on their promised results. It was hereditary; his father had been bald, his brother was bald, and he wasn't sure but he had a suspicion that his elder sister had started to weave false hair pieces into her receding locks at an early age. He had once tried wearing a wig, but the silence from everybody in the Yard on the day he wore it, and the number of staff who kept their hand in front of their faces to cover broad smiles as he walked past put paid to that idea.

There had always been a distrustful undercurrent to Palmer and Bateman's relationship; nothing you could pin down, but Palmer didn't like or agree with fast-tracking of university graduates to management positions in the force. He'd have them do two years on the beat first, see how they handled a seventeen-stone drug dealer waving a ten-inch knife who just did not want to be arrested. Bateman, on the other hand, would like to be surrounded with graduates with '*firsts*' in various '*ologies*', and was very pleased when the government brought in the minimum recruitment requirement of having to have a degree in order to even apply to join the force. He believed the old school coppers like Palmer were outdated dinosaurs, and that crime could be solved by elimination and computer programmes, which is why he had tried unsuccessfully to transfer DS Singh away from Palmer and back into the Cyber Crime Unit from where Palmer had originally poached her. Bateman had no time for an experienced detective's accumulated knowledge being an asset in the war against crime, and the sooner he could shut down the Serial Murder Squad and combine it with the Organised Crime Unit, CID and Cyber Crime the better. Cutting costs was paramount in Bateman's personal mission statement.

The trouble was that Palmer's team, the Organised Crime Unit, CID and Cyber

Crime were producing good case solved figures, which the political masters at the Home Office liked, and they therefore insisted the units carried on working as they were. But what really irked Bateman most of all was that they really liked Palmer too; the press also liked Palmer, and the rank and file loved him. So Bateman managed to keep the false smile on his face as he looked across his plush office on the fifth floor as Palmer took a seat opposite. He put down the daily reports on the case that Gheeta filed religiously, knowing Bateman's obsession with paperwork.

'Are you going to arrest the Blooms, Palmer? Everything seems to be piling up against them – couple of nasty pieces of work by the look of them.'

'I'd like to sir, but it's all circumstantial, nothing that actually pins the murders on them – no fingerprints or DNA in the van, no witnesses, and a story that a good brief would make sound very credible to a jury.'

'The Blooms' car leaving the M25 service area is pretty good circumstantial, Palmer?'

'It is, but the car was reported stolen and that service area is the nearest to where any joy riders who took it from the Blooms might reasonably be expected to head to for a break. No ANPR cameras there.'

'What about the aconite poison? I could issue a search warrant for the Blooms' house?'

'We thought of that sir, but surely they would have more sense than to keep it there. They've got three garden centres where it might justifiably be used and found.'

'Justifiably used?'

'Vermin poison – rats and mice, clears them in no time.'

Bateman pointed to the reports. 'And I see you think all this is tied into a black rose? You'd better enlighten me on that, I'm not a gardener.'

Palmer explained the financial significance of a black rose and the riches to be gained by being the first grower to breed one.

'I don't think it all started out that way,' continued Palmer. 'I think the acquisition of the centres was a way to launder more of the Manchester security van robbery money. As you can see from DS Atkins's remarks on the turnover increases, they are too high to be from organic growth of the business; but when Bloom got wind of Hanley's closeness to breeding a black rose and the money involved in that, he decided he wanted that for himself. The bookkeeper Burnley told Bloom about Hanley's debt and he moved in with an offer to clear it for half the business – the money went through but then something went wrong; maybe Hanley refused to share the rose breeding part of the business. We don't know, but something happened and Bloom killed the Hanleys – of that I'm sure.'

'All right. What I will do is pass the reports over to the CPS and ask them if they think they could prosecute with what we have and let's see what they say.'

Palmer knew the CPS's answer would be 'no way', but Bateman liked to keep his hand on things and make out he was using the right channels and not just pushing paperclips around his desk; even if the channels he used were already fed up with him wasting their time with similar requests in the past.

Palmer nodded and left. He made three cups of espresso coffee at the executive fifth floor Tassimo pod coffee machine before carefully taking the stairs to his second floor and the Team Room, passing the second floor basic 20p-a-time coffee vending machine that had a habit of sending down the cup after the coffee or no cup at all when Palmer used it.

****

'Do you fancy two cold cases, guv?' Gheeta asked him when he returned to the Team Room.

'Two?'

'Charlie Hilton, remember the name?'

'Yes, he was the chap who sold his garden centre in Barnet to the Blooms.'

'Correct.'

'Didn't the chap at the British Association of Rose Breeders think it was all legal?'

'He didn't know what we know about the Blooms, guv.'

Palmer sat down and paid full attention. 'Go on.'

'Well, whilst you were upstairs with Mr Bateman I thought I'd have a word with Mr Hilton's solicitor, so I checked with Companies House and he was listed on the change of owner documentation and luckily he's still in practice. Guess what?'

'Oh, come on – don't get all theatrical or I'll transfer you to Latin at the morgue and you can form a double act.'

Gheeta and Claire laughed.

'The short version of it is that the Blooms were going into a fifty-fifty partnership with Charlie Hilton. Sound familiar?

'Very familiar. Go on.'

'And then he died – heart attack. He had a history of heart problems and had two attacks in the previous year, which was the main reason why he wanted to retire. Anyway, straight away after his death the Blooms offered to buy the centre outright; the deal for the partnership had gone through, just as the chap from the BARB said, all thoroughly legal, and the Blooms were fifty percent owners, so when they offered to buy the lot it made sense for the Hilton family to accept as neither the wife nor Charlie's two grown-up children were interested in it and the deal went through without a hitch. Funny how he had a heart attack at that particular time; even his solicitor said it happened at the right time and the family were very grateful to the Blooms.'

'If I recall what Latin told us, aconite overpowers the heart and stops it.'

'Correct, guv.'

'Give him a call and see if the poison remains in the body and would show up on an exhumation.'

'On Charlie Hilton?'

'Yes.'

'Cremated – I checked.'

'Damn.'

'The other thing I checked was DS Atkins's report on the Blooms' accounts before and after their acquisitions of other centres. Charlie Hilton's garden centre's last accounts before his death showed a turnover of four hundred and seventy thousand that year; first year in the Blooms' hands their accounts showed an increase in turnover of just under two million, and the only addition to their business was Hilton's centre. Hardly likely for them to increase its turnover by nearly one and a half million in a year.'

'More of the Manchester security van proceeds being washed.'

'Seems likely, guv – and there is another interesting side to Hilton's business.'

'Oh, what's that?'

'Guess who was his bookkeeper?'

Palmer didn't need a second guess. 'She wasn't, was she?'

'According to the Hiltons' solicitor she was – and she was very, very helpful, his words, on getting the deal with the Blooms done and dusted.'

Palmer rubbed his chin in thought. 'Alison Burnley seems to be manoeuvring herself into a position of *accomplice to murder*.'

'Well, she's either part of the team or she's incredibly stupid. She's seen four people who got involved with Bloom in a business deal die, either during or a short time after the deal is done. It must have raised questions in her mind surely?'

'As bookkeeper to the Blooms she would have seen the increase in turnover each time – a big increase after Angela Robinson died and an increase far in excess of what the added Hilton garden centre would bring in organic growth. No, she's got to be part of it.'

'Or maybe Bloom has some sort of hold over her?'

Palmer looked at Claire. 'Burnley hasn't got a criminal record, has she?' He knew Claire would have checked.

'Clean as a new whistle, sir.'

****

Jim Riley sat in his bedsit pondering his position; still nothing in the local paper about the Hanleys' deaths. He really didn't know what to do, his mind was all over the place.

A knock at his door interrupted his thoughts.

'Who is it?

'Me, Alison.'

'You alone?'

'Yes.'

He slipped the chain and let Alison Burnley in. She took the nearest armchair and sat regaining her breath. 'Jesus, Jim... Your stairs are worse than the ones to my office...'

'What do you want?'

She waved away his request as she lit a cigarette and slouched back in the chair. 'Give me a minute to get my breath back,' she wheezed, taking a long drag.

'If Bloom sent you, you're wasting your time. Murderers, the pair of them.'

'You can't prove that Jim, nobody can – not even the police.'

'They told me. They poisoned the Hanleys.'

That had an effect on Burnley who sat bolt upright. 'Poisoned?'

'Aconite, fed it to them in a drink.'

'Christ, not another one.' She slumped back.

It was Jim's turn to sit bolt upright. 'Another one? What do you mean another one?'

'They killed Charlie Hilton that way.'

'What?!'

'He was quite happy doing a partnership with them, and then when it was done they poisoned him with aconite; nobody questioned it, he'd a history of heart attacks and the doc said that's what it was. Soon as the funeral was over the Blooms stepped in with an offer for the rest of the business which Charlie's family accepted.'

'If you knew this why didn't you tell the police?'

'I couldn't, I'd go to prison. Look at me Jim, do you think I'd last ten minutes inside?'

'Why would you go to prison? Are you working with Bloom? Are you part of it?'

'God no, no! I didn't know Edward Bloom until he came to work for Angela Robinson. I had a feeling he was no good and I was right – they said her death was accidental, but it bloody well wasn't. I can't prove anything, but no way would Angela have an accident with a chainsaw – for Christ's sake, the thing had an emergency stop on it! Police weren't interested and coroner gave an accidental death verdict.' She took a long drag. 'I couldn't say anything Jim, because I'd been milking Angela's bank account for years – not a big amount but a couple of thousand a month, putting through fake invoices and making cheques out to myself instead of the names on the invoices. She trusted me and I betrayed that trust. Bloom cottoned onto what I was doing and has held it over me ever since – I daren't go to the police.'

'Were you stealing from the Hanleys too?'

Burnley took a deep breath. 'Yes, and of course Bloom guessed that. If I was doing it to one, I would be doing it to all: Angela, Charlie Hilton and the Hanleys. I'd go down for a long time, Jim.'

'You deserve to, you thief.'

'Yes, I can imagine how you feel Jim – I really am very sorry, I wish to God I'd never started. But it was so easy and I could go abroad instead of Bournemouth, buy nice things – it just took hold of me. I knew it was wrong but I couldn't stop, and when Bloom told me he knew, I was scared; one word from him and I was sunk. So you can see that in my position I have to back the Blooms, otherwise my life's basically going to end in a prison. If you go to the police about the poison and the black rose and the Blooms get arrested, it will all come out – Edward said he'd see me inside with him. You can't do that to me Jim, you can't.'

Riley stood up. 'Get out.'

'What?'

'Get out – go on, get out! You deserve to go down, same as Bloom. I'll see the pair of you behind bars, and good riddance if you die inside.'

Burnley's mood changed to offensive. 'You'll go down too Jim, you're as much a thief as me – you're the one giving Bloom the black rose plants and cuttings you stole from Hanley. It's Chelsea Flower Show this coming Monday as you know, and they're unveiling the black rose on the Bloom stand during the royal visit – the mother plant is in bloom and it will be the sensation of the show. Bloom won't let you ruin that, no way.'

'Thieving a rose from Hanley is hardly the same as stealing thousands from his bank account, is it? I don't care anyway, I'll admit it and get a short sentence. It's not murder is it, and it's not knowing about a murder and keeping quiet either, is it? Get out.'

'Bloom will say you are part of the plan – he'll say you are in it up to your eyes. He'll take you down with him. Think about it, Jim.'

'Get out.'

He went to the door and held it open for Burnley to leave.

'And don't come back. I don't want to see you again, except in court.'

Burnley stubbed out her cigarette on a saucer and heaved herself out of the chair. 'You might regret it if you go to the police, Jim. Bloom's not the sort of man to cross; he's got a criminal record you know, so you may want to think carefully about what you do. Don't be rash, it's your future as well as mine.' She walked out onto the landing and the door slammed behind her without any further words between them.

Burnley made her way carefully down the stairs, out onto the street and across the road to where Edward Bloom was sat waiting for her in his car. She slumped into the passenger seat took her cigarette packet from her shoulder bag and pulled one out.

Bloom snatched it from her hand and threw it out of the window. 'No smoking in the car. What did he say?'

'He's going to the police in the morning.'

'Did you tell him what I said to tell him?'

'Yes, I told him he'd be in the frame as well, that you'd implicate him and you're not the sort of person to cross.'

'And?'

'Didn't make any difference. He's going to blow the whole thing apart in the morning.'

'Oh no he's not, he's not going to ruin our unveiling of the black rose at Chelsea – no way is he going to stop that. Get out.'

'What?'

'Get out – I said out! Get the bus home or grab a taxi. I'm going to sort out Jim Riley. Go on, out.'

'What do you mean *you're going to sort him out*?' asked Burnley as she struggled her large body back out of the car.

'Just that – I'm going to sort him out once and for all. Now go'

****

From his front window in the bedsit Jim watched as Burnley crossed the road and got into Bloom's car. A short time later she got out again and walked off. He was getting angry but his anger was tempered with guilt. His mobile rang.

'Hello.'

'It's Alison.' Her voice was shaking. 'Watch your back, Jim – Bloom's coming up and he said he was *going to sort you out once and for all*. I told you he's got previous – I'd get out the back way if there is one. What have we got ourselves into, Jim?'

He didn't answer. He finished the call and stood looking down at the Bloom car. The Hanleys had been good to him; he had a good job which he liked, they'd stood as security for him for the bedsit rent, and if he ever wanted time off he got it. He watched as Edward Bloom got out of the car. So he was going to *sort him out*, was he? He'd guessed Burnley had just been a messenger and he'd guessed right; she was backed into a corner by Bloom and his knowledge of her financial embezzlements and couldn't move. He watched as Bloom went to the car boot and took something out and slid it up his right jacket sleeve before crossing the road towards the bedsit entrance stairs – a knife? Riley's heart upped a pace; he was getting more and more angry. What had Bloom in mind? Stab him to death and hope the police thought it was a burglar he'd disturbed? Okay Edward Bloom, if that's the way you want to play it then that's the way I'll play it too.

He had to think fast. There was an old fire escape at the end of the short landing outside the bedsit but God only knows when that was last opened, or even if it did open – Jim's landlord wasn't exactly on top of the Health and Safety regulation demands. No, he had to take on Bloom, but he had an advantage knowing Bloom was on his way up; he needed to use that advantage, especially if Bloom had a weapon of some sort.

Jim thought quickly and opened the door a couple of inches and stood pressed against the wall behind it so that he wouldn't be seen by anybody opening it. He waited.

'Jim, are you there?' Bloom called his name from outside the door.

'Yes, who is it?' replied Jim.

The door opened slowly and when Bloom stepped alongside it Jim struck. He barged his shoulder against the door as hard as he could; it sideswiped Bloom and knocked him off balance sideways so he stumbled and fell against the armchair, a short steel rod falling out of his jacket sleeve. Jim was out and down the stairs like greased lightning; he ran up the street, dodging between the shoppers until he was a good hundred metres away from the bedsit entrance and only then turning to look back. Bloom wasn't in sight.

Jim slipped into a shop doorway and watched. It was a couple of minutes before he saw Bloom come out of the bedsit entrance and cross to his car. He was limping; good, that will slow him down a bit. To Jim's consternation Bloom didn't get in the car and drive off; he was just composing himself, rubbing his right knee and looking up and down the busy street. What would he do now? Jim waited. Shit! Bloom crossed back onto Jim's side of the street and started coming his way, looking into the shops as he came. Jim tried to blend with the shoppers and continued walking up the road. After another fifty metres he took a glance round; Bloom was still coming, and at that moment, a hundred metres apart, their eyes met. Bloom started to move faster, as fast as his limp would allow.

Jim ran; his car was parked in a side road the other way from the bedsit. He took the next left off the main street and then the next left again, and then again which brought him into the road where his car was. Panting like a dog in the hot sun he slumped into the driver's seat and took stock of things. He couldn't go back to the bedsit and the garden centre was out of the question; he needed time, time to calm down and gather his thoughts. He turned the ignition key and the engine started. He took a look in the rear view mirror – all clear, no Edward Bloom in sight.

Then the passenger window splintered into a million pieces of glass, showering him and the front seats; through the empty space where it had been he saw Bloom raising the steel rod ready to smash it through the windscreen. Jim grated into gear – any gear would do – and floored the accelerator. The car responded by leaping forward, its tyres screaming their protest and the gears shouting to be shifted up. In the mirror he could see Bloom stumbling after him, hampered by his limp; he threw the steel bar after the car in anger but it fell short as Jim's foot was still pressing the accelerator to the floor and had put some distance between them.

Jim prayed that the traffic in the main street would be moving and not at a halt. He was in luck, it was moving and he pulled out of the side street into it and away. Bloom would soon be back to his car and after him, so he took the next right and then zigzagged down roads he had never been to before; turn right, next left, next right, next left, straight on – he didn't know where he was and didn't care, as long as Bloom's car didn't show in his rear view mirror. After a while he hit the Edgware Road and knew where he was. He needed a place to stay that night, so he turned into Praed Street – plenty of B&Bs here. He turned into the side streets and soon found one with a small car park; he managed to park close against a wall so his missing window wouldn't draw attention. He tidied up the front seats and pushed the broken glass under them out of sight and then booked into a single room.

Flopping onto the bed his mind was whirring with a mixture of remorse and anger; a plan of revenge was already forming – a bloody good plan too. He laughed as he thought about how the plan would work. Burnley telling him that the Blooms were unveiling the black rose at Chelsea on Monday had stopped any thoughts of going to the police. If he had gone to the police it would take a few days for them to check his story and arrest Bloom. No, he had to act alone. The black rose was Geoff Hanley's and Bloom was not going to get it – Jim had worked out the ultimate twist. He laughed again as he thought about it – brilliant, bloody brilliant!

****

Palmer couldn't park on his drive as the workmen that Benji had hired to do the repairs had their tools and cement mixers on it. The deep gash had been filled and half the herringbone pattern bricks replaced; he was impressed with how much they'd managed in one day. The hole in the hedge through to Benji's garden had been tidied, but the jagged path the digger's wide tyres had made as it slewed through Mrs P.'s rose bed was still there.

He parked on the road at the end of his drive and walked up it as Mrs P. came out.

'Don't hang about, do they?' he said as she joined him.

'They haven't stopped all day, no lunch break. I think Benji must have put them on a time bonus.'

They both laughed.

Palmer pointed to the gap in the hedge. 'What about the hole in the hedge? You going to get something strong and sturdy to plant there?'

'Well, I was thinking about that. How about a gate?'

'A gate?'

'Yes, I mean Benji's always popping in with some problem or other – you know what he's like – and it would make it easier for me when I go round to help in his garden. I thought a nice steel gate, nothing elaborate. What do you think would go nicely there?'

'Razor wire.'

'That's not very neighbourly, Justin.'

'He's a walking disaster! So far this year he's burnt down part of the garden fence with his barbeque, flooded the front garden when his hot tub collapsed, and now this. I hate to think what's next.'

A sharp bang from the road caught their attention. Benji's brand new Kia Sorento was slewed across the front of Palmer's CRV where he had turned in towards his drive; Palmer's offside wing mirror and Benji's nearside wing mirror both hung limply from their fastenings. A somewhat distraught Benji was hurrying towards them.

'I'm sorry, I'm really sorry – I'm not used to having you parked there and I didn't leave enough room when I turned into my drive. It's only the wing mirror Justin, no damage to the car, I'll get it replaced. I'm so very sorry!'

****

Gheeta's current boy friend Jaz was waiting at foot of her Barbican apartment block waving a takeaway as she parked up.

'What have we got?'

'Thai.'

'Sounds good to me.'

In the apartment Gheeta took a quick shower and put on a bathrobe as Jaz set the table and put the food in the oven on a low gas to keep hot.

'Oh no,' Gheeta pointed to the computer, the Zoom indicator was flashing. 'I forgot it's Wednesday, family chat day.'

'It's okay, the food's in the oven it can wait.' He moved out of camera shot and sat down watching the activity on the Thames below as the tourist boats took their last trips of the day and the freight barges moved slowly down towards the docks.

Family chat day was the weekly evening internet get together of Gheeta, her mum from home in South London and her aunt Raani and cousin Bervinder in New York.

Gheeta clicked in. 'Hello mum, Aunty Raani, Bervinder, you all okay?'

They all were. 'Are you busy dear?' mum asked. 'We missed you last week?'

'Yes, always busy mum, crime never stops.'

'This is not a career for a young lady, no,' Aunt Raani was shaking her head. 'You should go and work with your family that is far better.'

Gheeta's family had a large computer parts supply company built by her father and both her elder brothers were in the business as well. Her father had made it clear that at any time she could join the firm in an executive position and quite often her IT expertise had been called on to test their products.

'I'm very happy doing what I am doing Aunt Raani, I love my job you know that.' She'd been down this path with Aunt Raani many times.

'You should be loving a husband and children at your age Gheeta, not loving a job your mother could find a suitable man.'

Gheeta's mum laughed, 'I could, I could probably find quite a few *suitable men,* but I won't.'

'What case are you working on Gheeta?' Bavinder asked changing the subject. She held her elder cousin in awe and had already at age 16 made up her mind she was joining the NYPD and from there moving into the FBI. But that couldn't happen until she reached the minimum seventeen and half year age requirement and if Aunt Raani had her way it would never happen, an arranged marriage would happen, both Gheeta and

Bavinder knew that wasn't ever going to happen.

'Murder in the greenhouse,' laughed Gheeta answering Bavinder's question.

'What!

'Well, it would take too long to explain but basically a Garden Center owner has bred a rare plant and others are prepared to kill to get it.'

'Kill for a plant?' Bavinder didn't understand.

'A plant worth a million pounds and maybe more.'

'Oh wow!!' Bavinder understood now. 'How many dead so far?'

Aunt Raani interrupted waving her hand, 'This is not a suitable conversation for a young lady, tell me Gheeta are you still going out with that nice young man Jaz?'

Jaz looked up and met Gheeta's eye with a surprised look.

'Yes, he's still around,' Gheeta said nonchalantly and smiled as Jaz's surprised expression faded.

'Has your mother and father met him?' Aunt Raani was on her favourite subject.

'Several times,' said Gheeta's mum. 'And we like him.'

Jaz wet his finger drew an invisible 1 in the air and gave Gheeta a large *'so there'* smile.

Aunt Raani wasn't impressed, 'But he is only a car salesman you can do better than that Gheeta, much better.'

Gheeta got her own back on Jaz, 'Yes, yes I suppose I could, I'll keep looking Aunt Raani.'

Gheeta's mum came to Jaz's rescue. 'He is not a car salesman Raani, his family own three Mercedes and two BMW dealerships, he's not standing on a second hand car lot in the Old Kent Road looking like Arthur Daly!'

'Who is Arthur Daly, do we know his family?' asked Raani.

'Never mind,' Gheeta's mum said through her laughter, she was fed up with her sister's old fashioned and outdated ideas about arranged marriages and family liaisons. 'Are you going to tell Bavinder who she should marry when the time comes?'

Aunt Raani nodded, 'I will make suggestions yes.'

'You can make as many suggestions as you like mum,' Bavinder said, 'But I won't be listening. When mister right comes along, *if* mister right comes along I'm grabbing him with or without your stamp of approval.'

'And when the one you grab isn't mister right and it all breaks down then you will wish you had asked your mother's opinion.' Aunt Raani sat back with a shake of her head.

'No I won't, I'll divorce him and grab another mister right!' Bavinder laughed. 'Anyway I'm not going to get married, I've told you a thousand times mum, I'm joining the NYPD in a year's time when I'm seventeen and a half and then I'll be working my way up and into the FBI.'

Aunt Raani shook her head, this was a battle she wouldn't win and she knew it. 'You'll both end up as spinsters you and Gheeta, sad and lonely in your old age.'

'No mum, I'll end up as boss of the FBI and Gheeta will end up as Commissioner of the Met.'

Gheeta laughed, 'I don't think that's very likely for me but I wouldn't be at all surprised if you got there Bavinder.'

Aunt Raani waved her hands negatively, 'No, no, no don't encourage her Gheeta, where am I going to get my grandchildren from?'

Gheeta's mum smiled, 'You should have had more children yourself if that's what you want.'

Aunt Raani looked to the Heavens in despair, 'You think the one child I have isn't enough trouble, you think I want more? You are very lucky sister, Gheeta has two brothers who have given you grandchildren all I have is Bavinder who gives me heart ache and worry.'

Gheeta was feeling hungry, 'I have to go I've got a meal in the oven and a load of reports to write.' A little white lie never hurt anybody.

They said their goodbyes and Gheeta switched off.

Jaz stood up and smiled, 'Your mum likes me.'

Gheeta smiled back, 'Don't get ahead of yourself Arthur.'

'Arthur?'

'Arthur Daly, I'm going to call you *Arfur* from now on.'

'Oh, so there is a *from now on then*?'

'Gheeta waved an admonishing finger, 'Don't get ahead of yourself *Arfur*, you know the rules, come when you're called and go when you're told to.'

'Yes ma'am.'

SUNDAY

Jim Riley watched the local early morning news on the TV in his room at the B&B; nothing about the Hanleys but lots about tomorrow's Chelsea Flower Show and the royal opening, with Monty Don talking to excited exhibitors as they put the final touches to their displays and show gardens. The Blooms weren't included.

After a good full English breakfast Jim paid his bill and drove to the Hanley Garden Centre. The staff were waiting outside as he pulled into the car park; Edward Bloom was nowhere to be seen. Jim let them in and shut the main door; there was half an hour until opening time so he called the staff together and explained that Mr Hanley was ill and staying at home, and that he, Jim, had a family problem he had to take care of and wouldn't be in for the weekend. He gave the cashier the keys and left the centre in her capable hands. He had one thing to do today ready for his plan to work tomorrow.

He left his car at the centre; if Bloom came there looking for him and the car was there, Bloom might think he'd be coming back for it. He wouldn't be.

He walked a fair distance away from the centre, keeping a wary eye out for Bloom, and then made his way to an internet cafe where he booked the minimum fifteen minutes with use of a printer and completed the final part of his plan. He checked the page he had typed as it came out of the printer; it looked good, very good. He smiled to himself, thinking of Janet Bloom's face when she saw it; the smile broke into a laugh.

He bought a strong card folder and Sellotape from the local WHSmiths and sat in a cafe with a coffee and carefully stuck the paper to the card. Now he had the rest of the day to himself; he couldn't go back to the bedsit – too dangerous and an obvious place that Bloom would check – so he jumped on a bus to the West End and spent the afternoon wandering around the shops, until he took a black cab across the river to Waterloo and booked into another bedsit. He thought that was far enough away from the centres and Bloom wouldn't find him if he was looking. He was happy that he'd covered his tracks.

****

Earlier that day Gheeta came into the Team Room where Palmer was going through the reports and Claire was digging away at the Blooms' pasts.

Palmer looked up and put the papers down. 'Well, what has he found out then?'

Gheeta had been over to Reg Frome's forensics unit where Peter Akins had brought her up-to-date on some new abnormalities that he had found as he dug deeper into the Hanley accounts.

'Well, it appears Miss Burnley has had her fingers in the till for a long time – in fact right from the start of her involvement with the Hanleys. And it wasn't just her fingers in the till, she had both hands in there. Atkins estimates she embezzled about twelve thousand a year.'

'Without Hanley realising?' Palmer was amazed.

'Oh she's a crafty one, guv. Geoff Hanley wasn't a money man at all – left it all to her. He used to sign all the cheques in a book and left her to get on with it, and that seems to have been the extent of his interest in the finances of the garden centre.'

'Preoccupied with his roses, I suppose.'

'Probably. What do you want me to do, get a warrant and bring her in?'

'Not yet – seems she isn't *clean as a whistle* after all. I get the feeling Miss Burnley might hold the key to open up this case and what the Bloom's have been up to. Let her run for a while longer.'

'Jim Riley might hold that key too, sir,' said Claire as she sat back in her chair and turned towards them. 'Guess who was on the same horticultural course and in the same year as him at Pershore College?'

'Alan Titchmarsh?' joked Palmer.

'Quite possibly sir, but of more interest to us, Janet Bloom was – or as she was then, Janet Jones.'

'Really? So they go back a few years then.'

'She passed out with Distinction and double A, and Jim with a B plus.'

'This is becoming a real can of worms, isn't it? Burnley wasn't the college bookkeeper, was she?'

'Not as far as I can see by the records, sir,' laughed Claire.

'Shame, that really would be a turn up for the books wouldn't it?'

'Hang on a minute guv, bells are ringing.' Gheeta sat at her keyboard and typed away for a couple of minutes and then scrolled down looking for something. 'Got it. I thought the name rang a bell.'

'Got what?'

'Well, according to the HMRC records for Angela Robinson's garden centre, a *Janet Jones* was on the payroll there for two years before Edward Bloom inherited it.'

Claire stood and looked over Gheeta's shoulder at the screen. 'That's the same year as she left college. So she went straight to work for Angela Robinson.'

'And there she met Mr Edward Bloom,' added Palmer. 'The final bits of the jigsaw are falling into place.'

Gheeta rose and went to the progress board at the end of the room and taking a felt tip drew arrowed lines from Angela Robinson's photo to Edward Bloom and to Janet Bloom writing *'née Jones'* below her, and then drawing a line between Janet and Edward Bloom and another from Janet Bloom to Jim Riley.

'Looking more like a proper crime road map now, guv.' She finished off by putting lines from Alison Burnley to Hanley, Robinson and Bloom.

MONDAY

Jim Riley was up bright and early; in fact he hadn't slept much that night. The plan was going round and round in his mind. He was first down to the breakfast room and scoured the national papers. No, still nothing about the Hanleys, and the news on the TV in the breakfast room didn't mention them either. So the police *must* think it was just suicide. Well, they wouldn't after today, oh no…

He collected the folder from his room, paid his bill and left. He hailed a black cab to take him to Watford and got out a few hundred yards up the road from Bloom's Garden Centre; being a Sunday the area wasn't that busy. He checked his mobile for the time: eight thirty. Good, no staff would be in the centre for at least half an hour, and that was all the time he needed. He let himself in through the staff door and made his way to the rose house, checking all the time to make sure he was alone. Mind you, when staff arrived they wouldn't be bothered about him; they all knew who he was and had seen him at the centre many times with Edward Bloom.

In the rose house he made his way to the far end corner benches where the black rose plants and cuttings were still in their neat lines where he had put them after bringing them from Hanley's after Bloom's threats in the bedsit. As he walked towards them he put down his folder and took a pair of shears from a bench. Standing still for a moment, he took a deep breath. 'This is for you Geoff,' he said softly, and worked his way along the bench cutting through the plants' stems and sweeping them and their pots off the bench clattering down onto the concrete floor. The pots of cuttings and bud wood followed. He was feeling good, almost elated by the act of destroying the plants. It felt right; the guilt about the Hanleys was evaporating.

The feeling was brought to a shuddering halt as a shout came from the door.

'Hey! What do you think you're doing?!'

Jim looked over his shoulder and saw the figure of Edward Bloom running between the benches towards him as fast as his limp would allow. Jim carried on cutting and slicing the stems as fast as he could.

'You little bastard, I'll kill you! Stop it!' came the shout getting nearer. Jim could hear the uneven steps of Bloom's limp were nearly on him. He turned to face him with the closed shears as protection.

Bloom was too near; the limping leg hadn't the strength to stop him. His eyes widened with horror as he realised that and impaled himself on the shears, his face jerking forwards to within an inch of Jim's, and then he sank to the floor where he lay on his back with the shears embedded deep into his chest and heart, the handles sticking up like masts on a ship. Jim stood speechless, watching the bubbling froth coming from Bloom's mouth turn red and the body settle limply onto the concrete as more red spread across it.

It was an accident, Jim told himself again and again; it was an accident, he didn't mean to kill him, it happened so quickly, an accident. The police wouldn't believe that – they'd think it was murder, of course they would. He had to go – he could run; he wouldn't get far, he knew that, but he had to get out of there. He had the plan – yes, the plan. He picked up the folder; he had to complete his plan then hand himself in – but the plan had to go ahead, had to. He left by the staff door, nodding to several staff members who were arriving. It wouldn't be long before Bloom's body was found, and they'd seen him there so the police would be after him. He checked his clothes – they were clean, no blood. That's good. He walked quickly away from the centre and called for an Uber on his mobile.

****

Palmer checked his watch: ten o'clock. The call from the Control Room had come through to him at home at nine; he had just returned with Daisy from a walk to the newsagent to pick up the paper. Benji's workmen were already on the drive setting the bricks in place with Benji fussing round like a mother hen, worried that a brick might be half a bubble out. In the end Mrs P., who could see the workmen were getting rather cheesed off with him, had called him in for a coffee and advised him to let them get on with it.

She was rather glad when the Control Room phoned and Palmer was soon whisked away by a patrol car. Bad enough with Benji in a state of permanent panic without Palmer putting his oar in with non-helpful remarks.

421

'Toad in the hole tonight,' she shouted after him as he ran down the drive – well, half a drive anyway.

'Beef sausages, not veggie,' he shouted back.

Now he stood in the Bloom's Watford Centre rose house watching as the OIC had the area taped off and forensics moved in with cameras and tape measures.

Reg Frome stood beside him. 'You realise we are going to have to fingerprint all those broken pots – every damn bit of them.'

Palmer shook his head. 'No, no don't bother Reg – just the shears. Riley was seen by witnesses leaving the place, I think you'll find they're his prints on it. Sergeant Singh's taking their initial statements now. I've put out a call to pick him up if we can find him. There's a TSG Unit checking his bedsit but I don't think he'll go there, bit too obvious.'

Sergeant Singh joined them. 'Right, that's four witnesses who saw Riley leaving – none saw him arrive so I would guess he came in early, he must have a key to the staff door. What do you want to do about telling Janet Bloom what's happened? Apparently she's at the Chelsea Flower Show today as it's the royal visit and press preview day. I've told the staff not to contact her or talk about what happened to anybody as it's best left to a FLO to break the news gently, and I've sent them all home until they get a call from us. I've got the local uniforms putting up crime scene tape sealing off the centre.'

'Good, well done. The Path boys will be here soon to take the body to the morgue; it's obviously not an accidental death so Professor Latin will have to do a PM. Nothing else we can do here so we had better get over to Chelsea in case Riley goes for Janet Bloom, although he didn't strike me as the type to deliberately kill somebody.'

'Nor me guv, but…' She pointed at Bloom's body. 'Maybe we are both wrong?'

****

The Royal Hospital Road was busy with tourists and people who had made the journey to try and catch a glimpse of the Queen as she arrived at the show for the royal preview.

Riley blended in and left the crowd at the main gate, walking on and around the block to the back entrance where the garden builders, staff and the plants and trees went in.

He had timed it right; many workers were strolling out for lunch and others hurrying back to complete the last minute tasks, hoping to impress the judges and the royal party. Security at the wide gates was lax, too many ins and outs to check tags and passes. Jim held his folder like a management trainee trying to impress and slipped in amongst a returning group of builders as they walked through the gates exchanging banter with the two guards. Once in the complex and a good distance from the gates, Jim left the group and made his way along the main concourse. He blended well with the folder held purposefully in his hand as he passed the gardeners and their sponsors, all exhibiting the last-minute irrational behaviour of people sure that they have forgotten something but can't think what.

At the top of the main concourse was the huge main marquee housing the trade stands, and somewhere inside was the Bloom stand. Jim walked in; it was busy inside, the same underlying atmosphere of mild panic as apparent as it was outside. The royal party had arrived, the deferential meet and greets, curtseys and bows had been made, and now HRH was on her way slowly up the concourse. The news of her arrival had spread and most of the people in the marquee crowded in the doorway hoping for a glimpse.

Jim walked along the outside row of display stands. He took a discarded cap off a wheelbarrow parked between two stands and put it on, pulling it down at the front in case CCTV was operational. A narrow access walkway ran between the back of the stands and the side of the marquee; Jim turned quickly between two unattended stands and entered the walkway. Avoiding the discarded plant pots, pallets and half empty bags of display grit and composts he moved along it, checking through the stands' back sheets looking for Bloom's stand. His heart nearly stopped a couple of times as he passed employees coming the other way or still arranging displays for their companies, but the firmly held folder in his hand worked a treat and gave him a degree of 'management status' as he passed them with a curt nod of the head.

And then he was there: the back of the Bloom's stand. He knew it was theirs by the rubbish and empty pots in the walkway behind it, pots with Hanley's stickers still in place. Jim felt a twist of anger in his body at seeing them.

'Her Majesty's halfway along now.'

He heard a female voice and very slightly moving the side of the black back drape to the stand he peeped through. Janet Bloom and two of her staff were giving the front shelves of the stand a last-minute soft brush.

Janet Bloom put her brush down. 'Okay, nothing else we can do now ladies. Let's go and have a quick look at the royal party and then get changed – I need to freshen up a bit anyway, come on. Give me your brushes, I'll get rid of them round the back.'

He'd had it! She'd find him there. Jim frantically looked around, but there was nothing big enough to hide behind. If she saw him, he would just have to run. He watched the end of the stand, waiting for Janet Bloom to come round the corner. She didn't; her hand did and threw the brushes towards the rest of the rubbish. Jim sat down and breathed deeply as he regained his composure. He gave Janet and her helpers a minute to get far enough away from the stand and then stood up again, peeping through the back sheet. He saw what he was looking for: slap bang in the middle of the stand, on top of a jet black plinth, stood a large plant in its pot covered by a light jet black fleece. Jim didn't need to look to know what plant was under that fleece waiting for the big royal reveal! He couldn't go to the front of the stand for fear of being seen; he had to put the final part of his plan into operation from the back.

He bent and slipped under the back sheet and slowly stood up and reached forward to the black fleece, and raising it a little way he pulled the Bloom's sign away from the front of it. He read it: *'**The Queen**, the first black rose, bred by Edward and Janet Bloom and dedicated to Her Majesty Queen Elizabeth II.'*

Jim put the sign in his folder and pulled out the one he had made at the internet cafe and replaced the Blooms' sign with it. Quickly he put the fleece back in position and then slipped back under the back sheet to the walkway. He ought to get out of the place now, get away as far as he could; the body of Edward must have been found and police would be looking for him after the staff at the Watford centre told them he had been there. He had one last part to the plan, but he couldn't resist seeing this part play out, he just couldn't.

He kept to the walkway and followed it round to the opposite end of the marquee. The noise was growing; he peeked into the main part and saw the royal party were walking slowly in. They moved along the row of stands, the stand owners hoping for a few words, but only one or two got a brief acknowledgement or nod of the head and a smile as she went by. Behind the royal party a row of security officers, plainclothes and uniformed police kept the following press horde at a respectable twenty metres distance. Jim tagged on behind them with the public. He spied Janet Bloom coming out of the staff only rest room into the main hall and hurrying to her stand. She had changed into a jet-black trouser suit with patent black high heels, and a wide black hair band tied back her blonde hair. Her two assistants had also changed into black skirts and jackets with the Bloom logo embroidered on them. The black wasn't in mourning for Edward that was for sure, so Janet couldn't know of his death? The body must have been found by now surely? Jim was confused.

He kept the cap pulled down and his heart lost a beat again as Janet Bloom gave her stand a last good look as Her Majesty moved to the adjacent one, and then at last to the Blooms' stand. She must have been primed that something was going to happen at this stand as the whole royal party stopped and the Queen said a few words to Janet after the perfunctory curtseys from her and her assistants. Then they all turned towards the display and an assistant went to the side and slowly pulled the nylon line that raised the fleece.

And there it was, the first mature black rose ever bred. A ripple of applause went through the crowd and very quickly died; but not as quick as Janet Bloom's wide smile died on her lips. Everybody could see the rose, and everybody could see Jim's sign in broad black font:

*'This rose is called '**Midnight Glory**' and was bred by Geoff Hanley and stolen by Edward and Janet Bloom who then murdered the Hanleys.*

Chaos, disorder and confusion hit the royal party, the press and the public as they read it. The press were the first to react, pushing through the royal security ring to get close-up pictures of the rose and the sign before battering a stunned Janet Bloom with pertinent questions.

'Did you steal it, Mrs Bloom?'

'Who's Geoff Hanley?'

'What's all that about a murder?'

'Have you murdered somebody for the rose?'

'Is it your rose, Mrs Bloom?'

The countless flashlights from the cameras trained on the rose and on Janet Bloom merged into one continual white glow lighting up the marquee. The Royal Protection Unit had the Queen away and into the staff area immediately and the show security staff helped Janet Bloom and her assistants fight through the throng to the same exit.

Jim Riley worked his way to the back of the crowd, out of the Marquee and along the concourse to the entrance and exit. He needed to get away, well away. There was a final part to his plan, and he needed to just book in somewhere for the night and compose himself. So far so good, but the final part was the part where it could all backfire.

****

'We are going to have to give them something, Justin. The phones are going mad.'

Lucy Price, the head of Media and Press at the Yard, was standing in the Team Room with Palmer and Gheeta. They had just got back from the Watford garden centre and the Chelsea Flower Show debacle had hit the news.

'I can't keep this under wraps for long, the journos know there's something big going on; they've checked the Blooms' Watford centre and the Hanley one and they're both closed with a uniform presence. This won't go away Justin, not with HRH being there at the time – tonight's new will have pictures and tomorrow's papers will probably all lead on it, it's a big story. I need a holding statement to see us through until tomorrow, and then I'll need a press briefing.'

Palmer knew they had to give out something. 'Okay, I understand. DS Singh will bring you up to speed and you can work out a statement to release. I have to get over to the morgue, Professor Latin wants to see me about Edward Bloom's body. He seems to have got to work on it pretty quickly, something's excited him. Keep the statement brief Lucy, no names – I don't want Riley doing a runner. Just something along the lines that after the Chelsea fiasco we have started an investigation into the Hanleys, who we understand are on holiday.'

'We can't lie, Justin. If that came back and bit us both you and I would be down the Job Centre.'

'Okay, then how about we are already looking into the mysterious deaths of the Hanleys and will hold a press conference tomorrow once we have more information? That should do it.'

'All right, we'll go with that one. Come on Gheeta, I'll get that out and then you can fill me in on what's really happening.'

Price and Singh left the room with Palmer; he had a car waiting to take him to the morgue and they went off to the Media Centre.

****

'It wasn't murder.' Professor Latin was adamant shaking his head. 'It wasn't murder, Justin.'

'Okay, explain.' Palmer prepared himself for another theatrical experience. He stood beside Latin in the morgue, wearing the required green plastic oversuit, overshoes, hat and mask. Edward Bloom's body lay stretched out on a steel bench in front of them; the shears were in an evidence bag beside it, Frome having taken the prints off them and sent them by police motorcyclist for running through the National Data programme for a match. Palmer had no doubt whose they would match.

'The shears were plunged into the body with both the person holding them and the victim standing in an upright position. In that scenario two things are apparent: one, they would have penetrated only a short way because the victim would have recoiled away from them and the attacker; and number two, they would have had a job even penetrating his clothes and body, as shear blades are sharp but not the ends of the blades – just quite blunt in fact. This man was not stabbed by the shears being used as a weapon.'

'So what do you think happened?'

'My professional opinion, and one I will prove in court if necessary...'

'It won't be.'

Latin looked disappointed at that. 'My professional opinion is that the victim impaled himself on the shears. I would suggest that the other person was using the shears and turned to face the victim, who was running towards him at the very moment the victim reached him whilst still holding the shears at chest level. The victim ran onto the shears, that's the only way enough force could have been exerted on the closed blades for them to penetrate the victims clothing, his rib cage and heart in one movement. He ran onto them, Justin – impaled himself. It was an accident; a rather nasty and fatal one, but an accident, not a deliberate murder.' Latin stood back a step from the body and crossed his arms like a lawyer in court having just given his closing statement and now defying anybody to doubt him.

'You seem sure of that?'

'I am, very sure.'

'Good. I'm quite glad, because both my Sergeant and I are of the opinion that the suspect for the person holding the shears isn't the type to deliberately use them as a weapon.'

****

Palmer returned to the Team Room. Gheeta gave him the news that the prints on the shears were indeed Riley's.

'He's not stupid is he, guv? Let's face it, if he went looking for Bloom with the shears as a weapon he would have had the sense to put gloves on – there's enough pairs laying around in a garden centre.'

'Latin thinks it was an accident.'

He explained Latin's premise to Gheeta and Claire.

'Sounds a reasonable explanation,' said Gheeta.

'Right then, let's recap what's happening.' Palmer counted off on his fingers. 'We've an arrest warrant out on Riley, FLOs are either with or on their way to Janet Bloom with the news and will stay with her for the night at least, forensics have the Watford scene tied up, and we have closed that garden centre and the Hanley's Garden Centre.'

'Short press release going out now,' added Gheeta.

'Good, and have we a uniform at Riley's bedsit?'

'Yes, all secured guv, and the local force are sealing off the Blooms' house, the Bloom stand at Chelsea has been isolated and screened off and forensics are there. I asked them to brush the sign on the Midnight Glory rose ASAP.'

'Any prizes for guessing whose prints are going to show up on that?'

'No.'

Claire added, 'I've asked for the CCTV from all the cameras at the showground for today to be sent to us.'

Palmer thought for a moment. 'Claire, check if there are any cameras focused on the road outside the showground; if there are we might get a shot of Riley arriving there. With a bit of luck he got there by cab and we can ANPR it backwards and see where he's coming from – maybe even an address he's using. And that's about it, unless you two can think of anything we've missed?'

'I think you should pop along to the Palace guv and get a statement from HRH.'

Palmer laughed. 'Probably the most exciting time she's ever had.'

'No, that would have been the time when she woke up and found that chap sitting on her bed,' said Claire.

'Chap?' said Palmer smiling. 'That wasn't a chap, it was Bateman hassling her for an MBE in the Honours list.'

They all laughed.

'Right then ladies, I think that will do for today. Home sweet home.'

'Steak and kidney pie, guv?'

Palmer smiled. 'Oh you know me so well, Sergeant. In fact it's toad in the hole with brown sauce tonight.'

****

Two things pleased Palmer when his squad car dropped him off at home: the drive was finished and looked good, and his car was parked on it complete with new wing mirror.

One thing that didn't please that much was the new wooden gate filling Benji's hole in the hedge. Oh well, can't win them all.

'Are you working on that Chelsea Flower Show shambles?' Mrs P. shouted from the kitchen as he hung up his coat and trilby and slipped on his slippers, after chasing Daisy round the hall five times before he managed to catch her and release them from her jaws.

'Yes, three murders and counting,' he replied as he went into the kitchen.

'Murders? Nothing about murders on the news, just that a black rose had been exhibited and somebody else has claimed it?'

'That somebody else who is claiming it is claiming it for a deceased rose breeder, and it seems the claim is right. That black rose might well be stolen property.'

'The Queen must have had a bit of a shock, by all accounts she was right in the middle of it.'

'She's all right, I popped in on my way home. She's had a couple of brandies and a fag to steady the nerves, she's fine – sends her regards and says can Daisy go and play with the corgis next week?'

Mrs P. ignored him and loudly put down a plate of toad in the hole in front of him before sitting opposite with her own plate. 'The drive's done, did you notice? And your car is back from the garage – didn't take long, did it?'

'They don't do repairs these days, just replacements. I bet that cost Benji a few quid.'

'You could offer to pay half.'

'What? Why?'

'You parked halfway across the entrance to his drive.'

'It's a double car drive, he still had a car and a half's width to drive through; and in any case if he hadn't ripped up our drive I wouldn't have had to park there in the first place.'

'Did you see the new gate?'

'Mmm,' Palmer mumbled through a mouthful of sausage.

'Looks nice, doesn't it.'

'I'll get a padlock.'

'You'll do no such thing, Justin Palmer. Anyway, I had a word with the chaps doing the drive and they're going to lay a similar herringbone brick path from the gate through the rose bed to the drive – look nice, won't it? Seven hundred.'

'Pounds?'

'Yes.'

Palmer laughed. 'Poor old Benji, does he know?'

'He's not paying for that, we are.'

'What?'

'He's paying for the gate.'

'I should hope so, he made the hole.'

'And one more surprise for you.'

'Go on.'

'You've just eaten two veggie sausages.'

TUESDAY

It was a plan that could go badly wrong. Riley showered, ate a good full English breakfast, paid his B & B bill and made his way by bus to Watford. He noted the police presence outside Bloom's Garden Centre and avoided walking past it by taking a detour round the back streets until he reached a leafy avenue where he could see the press and nosy members of the public outside the Blooms' detached Victorian house, being kept back behind crime scene tape stretched across the end of the drive manned by three uniformed officers. He knew the house well, especially the large en-suite bedroom where he had spent time with Janet when Edward was abroad buying and ordering stock for the centres. He walked past on the opposite side of the road and noted both Blooms' cars were in the drive; Janet must be home.

He walked on to the end of the street and turned right; sixty metres along that street an alleyway led off between the back gardens of the houses and a golf course – he knew it well as that alleyway had been his access and exit on his evenings with Janet. He peered along it; he couldn't see any people – the press obviously weren't aware of it or they'd have been all over it.

The large shrubs and trees that the residents had planted to stop stray golf balls from smashing their greenhouse windows gave him plenty of cover as he stealthily made his way to the back gate of the Blooms' garden. It was a steel bar gate so he could see through into the garden. All was quiet, a short path led from the gate through a shrubbery onto a lawn bordered on both sides by large shrubs planted for privacy from neighbours. From the far end of the lawn four wide flag stone steps led up onto a patio furnished with a large all-weather outside table and chairs. At the back of the patio the double French doors led off it into the back lounge; they were shut.

Riley let himself into the garden, releasing the padlock on the gate with the key that Janet had given him that he hadn't returned. He stooped down out of sight behind the plants and waited; there wasn't an officer posted at the patio, but maybe they made patrols every so often. He gave it ten minutes – no sign of anybody. Quickly he made his way to the patio, hugging the border for some cover. On the patio he stopped abruptly and ducked behind one of the chairs as one side of the French doors opened outwards. He held his breath.

'I wondered how long it would be before you came.' Janet Bloom smiled as he rose slowly from behind the chair, waiting for a police officer to join her. None did. 'Lost your tongue, Jim? You'd better come in, unless you intend to murder me and run like you did Edward?' She held the door open invitingly and went inside. Jim followed.

****

Palmer didn't really like working weekends, especially not Sundays. On Sundays he liked to relax and watch the football on Sky. Barcelona were his favourite team, but they seemed to have lost their way this season and had management issues – as well as Sky losing the Serie A contract. So he had to make do with his boyhood favourites Arsenal, and they were on that afternoon, a London derby against Tottenham. He was going to miss it.

In the Team Room he checked with Gheeta on the state of play.

'Janet Bloom is at home. She was sedated overnight; didn't want any relatives to be called in to be with her and sent the FLO away this morning. I had a word with the FLO and she says Janet is not showing much grief and seems in complete control of her emotions. The local uniform branch are at the house, as are the press and media. Did you see the papers this morning?'

'No, I don't bother – it's yesterday's news usually. I bet they had a feast with the Chelsea thing.'

'They did – depending on which paper you read that black rose is worth anything from a hundred grand to ten million.'

Palmer laughed. 'Anything on Riley?'

'No guv, no sign. Shall I put a mugshot out to the media?'

'No, not yet. Get a plainclothes officer to keep Alison Burnley company at home, nice and quietly, then all the places he might go are covered.'

****

'Sit down.' Janet Bloom pointed to an armchair in her lounge as she sat in one herself; between them an occasional table made a barrier. She showed Jim a key fob in her hand. 'See this, Jim? It's a panic alarm. Try anything and I press it and the house alarm goes off like an air-raid warning. I take it you've seen the police at the front?'

Jim nodded.

'Was it worth it Jim, was it really worth it? You're going to prison for most of the rest of your life. For what – for that?' She pointed to a sideboard behind Jim alongside the French doors that he hadn't noticed on the way in. On top of the sideboard the black rose mother plant stood, complete and in bloom. 'Lovely isn't it, Jim? And it's mine now, so you failed – killed Edward for nothing.'

'I didn't kill Edward, it was an accident.'

She laughed. 'Must have been some amazing accident for a pair of shears to plunge into his body up to the hilt. The police are after you for murder, Jim.'

'They know about Angela Robinson and Charlie Hilton – they know you killed them,' he bluffed, putting pressure on her hoping to make her act out the final part of his plan. 'Burnley told them.'

'Me? Not me, Jim. I didn't kill them, I'm in the clear. If they do get proof on any murders it will be against Edward – I knew nothing about it.'

'Alison Burnley is talking.'

Janet laughed. 'Poor Alison, who do you think the police will believe: me, or a bent bookkeeper who embezzled thousands from her employers?'

'I should have realised what sort of person you were at college. What did you do with the Vice Principal after you got your Degree? Dropped him like a stone I bet.'

'You'd win the bet, Jim. Men are so stupid and vain, especially the older ones. You think I married Edward for love? Don't be stupid, I married for money and all the trappings that brings. Love doesn't make the world go round, Jim – money does, and now I've got lots of it, and with the black rose much more than I ever imagined. So in a way I suppose I should be thanking you.' She paused for a moment. 'But I'm not. I'm going to press this button when we've finished.'

'Press it now, we've finished.' Jim was getting worried his plan might falter. Had he misjudged her after all?

'No we haven't, Jim. I intend to savour this moment – in fact I was going to open a bottle of champagne for us to toast my future with you, but then I remembered you don't drink – no fun toasting something on your own, so when I saw you hiding in the garden I put the kettle on for a cup of tea. Care to join me in a toast with tea? The water's boiled, probably be the last decent cup you'll ever have. I don't think prison tea can be much good.' She stood and made her way to the door, holding the fob between her fingers threateningly. 'Don't move. One move and I press this.'

Jim didn't intend to move; a slight smile turned the corners of his lips. It now looked like the plan was working – he hadn't misjudged her. Janet was back in no time with two cups of tea and a plate of biscuits. She put them down on the table in between them. 'Enjoy it, Jim.' She took a sip from her cup as Jim pretended to do the same and screwed his face up.

'Urgh, no sugar.'

'You don't take sugar, I remembered that from college. You don't take sugar.'

'I do now, I have type 2 diabetes. I can't drink that without sugar.'

'Okay, I'll get some.'

Janet left the room and Jim swapped the cups quickly. She returned with a sugar bowl and spoon.

'Here.'

He scooped a spoon into the cup and took a gulp. 'That's better. Bit of a funny taste – your milk off?' He drank more. Then he sat still and started to cough; the cough turned into a rasping and a struggle for breath. He slumped forward, trying to speak.

Janet Bloom laughed. 'Did you really think I'd let you go to the police, Jim? Did you really think I'd take the chance that they might believe just one little piece of your story and start to investigate – turn up our bank statements, take another look at Robinson and Hilton's deaths? Don't be silly Jim, no way was that going to happen. You've drunk tea with aconite, just like the Hanleys and poor old Mr Hilton. You've got about two minutes, Jim. Take a good look at the rose, Jim. Was it worth dying for?' She raised her cup in a toast. 'To the black rose, and the owner of it: me.' She drank some of the tea and offered another toast. 'To Jim Riley, the nearly man.' She emptied her cup. Jim stopped the rasping and sat up straight, looking Janet straight in the eye across the low table and his face broke into a smile. She showed surprise at first before looking at her cup and dropping it from her hand.

'You bastard, you guessed.' Her voice rasped the words out.

'Oh yes, I guessed. The only reason I came here today was to tempt you into poisoning me and you fell for it. Not all men are as stupid as you think.'

Janet Bloom was struggling for breath. The fob fell from her hand as she lurched forward onto the low table, her head sideways, eyes wide open. She tried but couldn't speak.

'Look at the rose, Janet – it's the last thing you'll see. Now you tell me, was it worth it?'

Her body slumped lifeless onto the table and the weight pulled it over as she slid off it onto the carpet.

Jim picked up his teacup. He checked the hall: empty. He could see the shadow of a policeman outside the front door; he made his way stealthily to it and slipped the catch on and quietly slid a bolt across that was beneath the lock – obviously the Blooms had been very protective of their property. He quickly made his way back down the hall and into the kitchen, washed and dried the cup and saucer and put it away in the cupboard with the rest of the set. He took a tea towel off the side and back in the lounge wiped down the table and the French door handles just in case he'd touched them. Picking up the key fob from where it had fallen on the floor he put it in his pocket, and then gathering the rose from the sideboard and draping the towel over it he went out to the patio, closing the door with his elbow, careful not to touch anything. He made his way to the rear garden gate and slipped through, closing the padlock on it. He stood still and silent for a few moments before taking out the fob and pressing the button.

Janet had been right – all hell broke loose. The decibel wailing of the alarm must have created havoc at the front of the house. Jim hurried along the alleyway to the street, throwing the fob and back gate key into an overgrown patch of nettles and weeds on the back of the golf course. He turned into the street at the end of the alley and at the Blooms' avenue he stopped and looked along to their house, where press, media and public were trying to work out what was happening; as the alarm screamed in the background, more neighbours were coming quickly from their houses and joining the clamour. He took the other way and quickened his pace.

Jim walked, and kept walking. He hadn't any more plan, it was over. He laughed as the tension left him – it was over, it had worked. He had taken a chance that Janet would try to kill him to keep her story running and it had worked; he guessed that if he had taken the poison she would probably have said he had the poison and tried to poison her but she saw it and swapped the cups. She would have said it must have been Jim who poisoned the others. She would have said... well, it didn't matter now what she would have said, because she isn't going to say anything now, is she?

After a while he collected his thoughts. What about the rose? He didn't want it, he wished he'd never seen it – he wished Hanley had never bred it. It needed to go and go for good. He looked around and spied a row of black wheelie bins lined up against a wall at the back of the pavement waiting for the refuse lorry; some were overfull and their lids propped open by too many bin bags of rubbish squashed inside, so the collection was due. He went to the ones that had lids shut and looked inside; the first two were full to the brim, the third was three quarters full only. He dropped the rose and the towel inside and shut the lid. Job done.

****

Palmer's squad car arrived at the front of the Blooms' house and drew up on the other side of the road behind an ambulance, three other police cars and a forensic Transit.

Gheeta pointed to it. 'Reg Frome's here already, guv.'

The crowd had quadrupled, mostly media, press and paparazzi. They recognised Palmer as soon as he got out of the car; he'd been hoping to surprise them and duck under the crime scene tape and inside before that happened. No chance; he was surrounded.

'What's going on, Mr Palmer?'

'Is Janet Bloom inside?

'Is Janet Bloom dead?'

'Has there been a murder, Mr Palmer?'

'Is the black rose inside?'

'Has it been stolen?

He caught sight of DS Singh slipping under the tape unchallenged as two officers pushed a way for him through the throng and under the tape.

'What it is to be a celebrity, eh guv?' she said when he joined her on the drive. 'How many autographs did you sign?'

Palmer dismissed the comment with a cold look and they crunched their way to the front door, which was splintered in two with one half on the ground and the other hanging from a brass hinge.

'What happened there?' he asked the officer standing guard.

'We couldn't get in, sir. The lady's panic alarm went off and she'd locked and bolted the door from the inside. We had to break it down.'

'No door round the back? asked Gheeta.

'There is a double French door.'

'Did you try those?'

'No.'

Gheeta raised her eyebrows at the officer in disbelief.

Palmer didn't want to get involved in an inquest as to what, why and who over the doors. 'Come on, let's take a look.'

A box of overshoes lay open by the door; forensics were making sure that anybody entering wouldn't contaminate the crime scene. They both put a pair on, Gheeta turned her laptop on and recorded the scene as they entered.

'Mind where you put your clumsy feet.' Reg Frome in a full white paper forensic suit, overshoes, gloves, mask and hat beckoned them from the lounge door.

'You got here quickly, Reg?' Palmer was surprised.

'Not really. Having done the forensics on Edward Bloom at Watford and at the Chelsea showground yesterday we are listed in comms as the forensic team handling the Bloom case so I got the call. She's dead, did comms tell you?'

'No.' Palmer was a bit taken aback. 'Just that there had been a serious incident at the Blooms' house, no details.'

Frome beckoned them both into the lounge where forensic plates were in place around a black body bag and a snapper was photographing the scene from all angles.

Palmer nodded toward it. 'Janet Bloom?'

'Yes, let me fill you in. When we arrived Janet Bloom was on her back on the carpet with the ambulance crew trying to revive her; they had taken over from the first responders who had tried for twenty minutes until the ambulance arrived and took over with all their paraphernalia, but no good – she was dead. Nobody else in the house, no sign of a break in and no weapon; no wounds are visible but pathology will have to make sure about that – not our department – but bearing in mind cause of death to the Hanleys, I wouldn't be surprised if it was poison. In fact it probably was, as we've found a small bottle of white powder in the kitchen cabinet that I'll get analysed as soon as we get back to the lab.'

'It's going to be aconite,' Palmer stated.

'Could be.'

'Suicide then?'

'Well, only one empty cup and saucer here on the floor where they had fallen when she fell and upset the table, plus biscuits and a plate. One cup does indicate it may be suicide.'

'That's hard to believe of Janet Bloom, guv,' said Gheeta.

454

'Yes, it is.'

'If she has been poisoned somebody else could have put the poison into her cup before she drank it.'

Frome shrugged. 'No forensic signs so far of anybody else being here.'

'I thought she had an FLO with her?' said Gheeta.

'Apparently Mrs Bloom sent her away. Her personal doctor came in at eight thirty and checked her over; she seemed fine, good state of mind, so he prescribed some antidepressants to be taken if she felt she needed them and she sent the FLO away at nine o'clock.'

'Okay.' Palmer left the lounge and peered into the kitchen. Something caught his eye, but he was interrupted by a uniformed DI coming up the hall.

'Detective Superintendent Palmer?' said the uniform.

'Detective *Chief* Superintendent Palmer actually,' replied Palmer. It had taken forty odd years in the force to get that title and he was justly proud of it.

'Apologies sir,' said the uniform. 'I'm DI Salcombe, local station – I've been allocated OIC on this crime scene. Day off and being short of officers I was called from home so not up to speed yet.'

'Day off? How do you get a day off if you're short of officers?' He waved his own question away. 'Never mind. This is my sergeant DS Singh, she will bring you up to speed and then I'll have a word, okay?'

'Yes, sir.'

Gheeta moved out to the patio and took Salcombe through the events. Palmer went back into the kitchen where the snapper had started to work.

'Make sure I get a full set of photos won't you.'

'Yes sir, will do. I'll have them ready for the morning.'

'Quicker than Boots then,' Palmer joked.

The snapper gave a false smile; he must have heard that remark a thousand times.

Palmer wandered through the lounge and checked the evidence bags forensics were accumulating: fibres and hairs from the carpet and chairs, fingertip strips and DNA scrapes from anywhere a human might rest their hands or head. What he was looking for was missing. He stepped out to the patio where

Gheeta had just finished with Salcombe who had made numerous notes.

'There's a golf course at the end of the garden, sir,' said Gheeta.

'Handy if you play golf. You play, Salcombe?'

'No, sir.'

'Me neither.'

'And there's an alleyway between it and the houses,' Gheeta finished her sentence.

Palmer took notice. 'With a back gate?' he asked Salcombe.

'Yes sir, they all have back gates.'

Palmer didn't need telling twice. 'Right, get that alleyway sealed off from any entrances to it. Tell DCS Frome about the gate – don't let anybody near it until he says so, and then I want a fingertip search along the whole length of that alley and its edges. If there was somebody other than Mrs Bloom in the house they certainly didn't leave by the front, and I'm pretty sure that there was another person.'

Gheeta raised her eyebrows. 'You are?'

'Yes, the officer on the door said the alarm was activated by, and I quote *'the lady's personal alarm'* – that's a fob, and there's no fob in the evidence bags.'

Gheeta could see the reasoning. 'So if Janet Bloom didn't press it who did, and why?'

'I don't think she pressed it, I think there was another person and it's beginning to look more and more likely. I think he or she poisoned Janet Bloom and went out the back way, setting off the alarm to cause panic once he or she was down that alley and away.'

'If there was another person.'

'Yes, but if there wasn't where's the fob? It can't disappear into thin air.'

Salcombe looked worried. 'My chief isn't going to be too happy to lose men on a fingertip search. We're short as it is and he's always moaning.'

Palmer bristled; he hated negative observations. If things had to be done you got on and did them.

'In that case I'll have Assistant Commissioner Bateman give him a call first thing and kick his arse, DI Salcombe.'

Salcombe smile. 'I'd appreciate that, sir.'

'Consider it done.'

****

Palmer walked slowly round Dulwich Park in the evening sunlight, which was growing stronger as each day of May passed. Daisy wandered in and out of the bushes in the vain hope of a squirrel to chase or a dropped dog biscuit to eat; no luck on either so far. He was so engrossed in his thoughts about the case that several *hellos* and *evening Justin* from neighbours passing with their dogs went unanswered.

It was a strange set of affairs. The Blooms were nasty people, or had been nasty people when alive; the whole case was centred on them murdering for gain, but the two people who were probably going to jail were basically innocent workers who had been dragged into it by the Blooms' avarice, their promises and their threats. Sometimes the law doesn't take enough account of mitigating circumstances. All right, both Riley and Burnley were guilty of misdemeanours and their futures would be blighted by them; but the real culprits had paid the price, and Burnley and Riley were collateral damage. He'd seen it many times before in his career, otherwise decent people being forced by intimidation, threats and fear into criminal acts they wouldn't dream of doing under usual circumstances. Weak people were the bread and butter of the criminal classes – always have been, probably always will be. If Riley and Burnley went to prison Burnley would probably be bullied to death, and Riley most likely come out a paid-up member of the criminal class. Palmer really didn't want to see them go down that road.

He sighed loudly.

'Come on Daisy, home time.'

WEDNESDAY

AC Bateman was only too glad to pull rank on the local officers at Watford and insist on an immediate fingertip search of the back alley, as he was already taking flack from the Home Office about the case; they in turn were taking flack from the Home Secretary, whose government had been elected on a 'tough on crime' agenda. But then all political parties shout that before elections, but truth be known they can't do anything about crime without tackling the basic reasons why people commit crimes, which is the widening gap between those who have and those who have not, with those who have not wanting to join those who have.

'What time is Alison Burnley coming in?' Palmer asked Gheeta as he returned to the Team Room to find DS Atkins there with Gheeta and Claire.

'DS Atkins has found a rather nice little scam in the Hanley accounts, guv. You'll love it,' said Gheeta.

Palmer sat down. 'Go on Atkins, what is it now?'

'Well sir…' Atkins sat and referred to his notes. 'There were a series of cheques for substantial amounts going out of the Hanley account in the six weeks prior to the eighty thousand pounds being paid in to it, and these cheques were all paid into the Bloom's Garden Centre account; although looking at the actual cheques returned to the bank they were actually made out to Bloom's, although in the accounts book the bookkeeper has listed them as being to various different suppliers.'

Palmer leant forward. 'Go on.'

'These cheques totalled eighty thousand pounds, and they sent Hanley into overdrawn status on his account to that amount.'

Palmer sat up and thought for a moment. 'Brilliant, bloody brilliant – what a scam… Bloom and Burnley working together send Hanley eighty grand into the red, and then step in and help him out, using his own money.'

Atkins nodded. 'Yes.'

'Bloody brilliant. What time is Burnley coming in?' he asked Gheeta.

'Ten o'clock, guv.'

'Right, take her through the results of her embezzlements that DS Atkins has listed. Over the years he reckons she's had about forty thousand pounds for herself off Robinson, Hilton and Hanley. It didn't go into her normal bank account either, it went into an Isle of Man account and the majority is still there. Atkins, you make a call and get a freeze on that account and then when we interview Burnley we can remind her of the Proceeds of Crime Act, which means she could lose that money and her house if the court insist on her paying it back in total plus interest. And this is important, Sergeant,' he said to Gheeta. 'Don't charge her. Tell her that we are still making enquiries and further charges relating to her being an accomplice to murder may follow. Frighten the silly woman and put her into a remand cell to think about it, and then get the duty solicitor in and have her write a signed statement. I'll want to talk to her maybe later today or tomorrow.'

'You think she'll cough up the money in return for a lenient sentence?'

'I think she will, she would be stupid not to. Forty grand or whatever is left of it won't be worth much when she comes out in twenty years' time – remind her of that. Any news on Jim Riley?'

'No, none. He's disappeared.'

The internal wall phone rang and Claire answered it. She listened and told the caller to hold on.

'He hasn't disappeared, sir. Jim Riley is in reception asking for you.'

Palmer and Gheeta looked at each other, wondering what Riley was playing at. Palmer broke the silence. 'Sergeant, go and take him to the custody suite – charge him with the theft of valuable plants from Hanley's Garden Centre, just a basic charge, and put him in a remand cell too. Not the same one as Burnley. Then when you finish putting the frighteners on Burnley do the same to Riley, tell him accomplice to murder charges may follow. Get a signed statement. Well, that's a turn up for the books.'

Gheeta smiled. 'We could have this case done and dusted today, guv. Do you want me to have a word with the CPS later and see if they'd be prepared to charge the pair with the evidence we've got?'

'That's being a bit optimistic, Sergeant – no, not yet. Right, you take care of

Burnley and Riley, I've got a couple of people to go and see.'

Both Claire and Gheeta looked at him quizzically.

'Who?' asked Gheeta.

'Never you mind, I have a plan.' He gave them a smile with raised eyebrows.

'I hope it's a good plan guv, not a Baldrick type plan?'

'Wait and see.'

****

'It could work.' Michael Whitley of Whitley Solicitors rubbed his chin thoughtfully. 'It would certainly seem an ideal way of getting closure to the case. I was talking to my father after your last visit, Chief Superintendent, and he knows Riley quite well; he was shocked at the Hanleys' deaths and equally shocked at the thought that Riley was involved. But now we know the full story and how the Blooms manipulated him, I'm sure what you suggest is a good move; no creditors have come forward with any claim on the estate so we can go forward with your suggestion. I'll draw up the necessary paperwork and clear it with HMRC once you get the Hanleys' bank to agree and get our insolvency chaps to start the ball rolling.'

Palmer stood up from the very comfortable chair in Whitley's office and they shook hands.

'I'll give you a call once I've seen the bank.' Palmer stood to leave. 'Oh, one more thing – have you a card?'

'Yes, yes of course.' Whitley took one from a desk drawer and passed it over. 'Have you ever thought of swapping your side of the law to our side, Chief Superintendent? I think you might be very good at it.'

They both laughed.

****

'I thought the lady in reception was pulling my leg, but obviously she wasn't.'

Palmer was in the HSBC bank at Watford with the Hanleys' business banker. The sign on his desk gave his name as Lloyd Barclay.

Lloyd Barclay smiled; he'd lost count of the times in his career that customers had questioned his name. He was really fed up with explaining it too, but always had to.

'My dad was a banker and so were my three uncles and my grandfather. I think they took a lot of stick in the banking world for having the surname Barclay and decided to take out their irritation on me. But to be honest, Chief Inspector, I don't think it's done me any harm – not likely to forget me, are you?'

Palmer laughed. 'That's true.'

'Would you like a tea or coffee before you bring me up to date with the Hanleys' affairs? Obviously we have everything on stop at present until the situation becomes clear.'

Palmer declined. 'Well, it is all fairly clear now. I think the best thing is for me to take you through the case from the beginning and then get your reaction to a suggestion to save the business and the staff's jobs. I've already spoken to the company solicitor and he's quite happy to give it a try.'

'Sounds good. Hanley had a good business overall – a few blips now and again but only one that gave us concern, and then that seemed to be settled pretty quickly. Go on Chief Superintendent, I'm all ears.'

After a long explanation of the case, the Blooms, Riley and Burnley's involvement and a way Palmer could see an outcome that satisfied all involved, Lloyd Barclay smiled.

'Ever thought of swapping the law for banking, Chief Superintendent? I think you'd be rather good at it. Yes, I can't see any objection to your idea. I'll get some paperwork sorted out to start the ball rolling.'

'Do you have a card I might have?'

'Of course.' Lloyd Barclay took one from a desk drawer and passed it over.

THURSDAY

'I think you've gone soft in the head, guv.' Gheeta was looking very surprised. 'I hope it works, but if it all goes belly up they'll blame you.'

'I think it's a great idea sir,' countered Claire. 'With the checks and balances you've put in place it can't go wrong.'

Palmer had spent the morning dotting the i's and crossing the t's of his plan in the peace and solitude of his cramped office across the corridor from the Team Room, and when he was satisfied all was in order and got the okay on the phone from Michael Whitley he told Gheeta and Claire what he had in mind.

Gheeta passed him a small evidence bag. 'By the way, Reg Frome sent this over earlier. It's what you expected, Riley's print as well.'

Palmer put it on the bench in front of him next to a set of the photos from Janet Bloom's house the snapper had sent over.

There was a knock on the door and the custody officer walked in followed by Riley, Burnley and two officers.

'The two prisoners you asked to be brought up sir,' the officer spoke.

'Ah, good, thank you George. Leave them with us, they'll be fine.'

'You sure, sir? I can leave one of my chaps if you like?'

'No, no, we'll be fine.'

'All right sir, sign here please.'

Palmer signed the prisoner transfer form and the custody officers left.

Riley and Burnley stood like two miscreant children called to the headmaster's office.

Palmer smiled at them. 'Sit down, you two. We are going to have a chat.'

He indicated two chairs the other side of the bench and waited whilst they sat down. 'Right, I am aware that neither of you are actual murderers, but a very good case can be put in court to have you charged with being accomplices to murder. My own view is that you were both a bit stupid and saw a way to riches without much work involved. What neither of you knew was who the people you were dealing with were, the people who held out the chance of money and status – in other words, the Blooms. Edward Bloom, a career criminal who probably murdered Angela

Robinson, and together with his wife Janet Bloom probably poisoned Charlie Hilton, and definitely poisoned the Hanleys. I think you, Alison , suspected them of having a hand in four deaths.' He stopped and looked at Burnley, who remained stock still.

'Yes.' Her voice was very faint. 'I had my suspicions.'

'But you couldn't voice them, could you Alison? Because you'd had your fingers in the till and Bloom knew it. A word from him and you'd be in court – career finished and a criminal record.'

Burnley hung her head a little as Palmer nodded and carried on. 'And you, Jim. You knew they killed the Hanleys, they would have told you and told you that they would implicate you in the killings if you told anybody, by virtue of you having stolen the black rose for them.'

Riley didn't move or speak.

'So you both came to be in the same situation; a relatively minor theft had led you both into a position where the Blooms had you over a barrel. If they were arrested and charged with murder, they could implicate you two and you would be charged with murder or as accomplices in murder.' He sat back and let that sink in. 'I don't believe either of you were involved directly in any murders or implicated in them. As bookkeeper, Alison, you had the open opportunity to embezzle because your employers trusted you too much, and you took that opportunity. As general manager, Jim, you could take roses out of the Hanley Garden Centre without anybody being suspicious; you kept Bloom up to date on the progress of the black rose as Janet lavished her attention on you, rekindling the old urges from your college days. You fell for it Jim – *femme fatale*.

'And when the black rose was just about ready for commercial exploitation, Edward Bloom came to you Alison, didn't he?' Burnley froze. 'He came to you and reminded you that he knew all about the money you were stealing; it wasn't great amounts, a couple of hundred a month, but it would get you sacked and your career ended if he told Geoff Hanley. But he offered a way out for you: steal a larger amount over a couple of months with the fake invoice system you used, an amount of eighty thousand pounds, and he would remain silent. You did it, didn't you Alison?' Palmer waited for an answer; there wasn't one, but an affirmative nod of Burnley's head. Palmer continued.

'And the money didn't go into your Isle of Man account, did it?' Burnley's head rose sharply. 'Oh yes Alison, we know all about that account. No, it didn't go there, it went into the Bloom's account, and on Bloom's instructions you told Geoff Hanley that he had spent too much and was overdrawn past his limit, and no doubt he had a great shock when you told him just how much past his limit. But help was at hand; you told him you worked for another garden centre who was looking to expand, Bloom's, maybe they would help? And help they did – they gave Geoff Hanley eighty thousand pounds of his own stolen money for a half share in the business and a way out of debt; debt that you told people was due to his gambling. You told me that too, but Geoff Hanley never gambled in his life.'

Burnley broke down and slumped sobbing with her head in her hands. Palmer ignored it. 'But the partnership never materialised. The money went through, but no book work or legal documents were ever drawn up by Mr Hanley's solicitor, because

Mr Hanley never instructed him to do so. I wonder why? You'd think Mr Hanley would be so grateful for being helped out of a financial hole by Bloom that it would all go ahead. But it didn't. Why? Was Geoff Hanley a bit suspicious? Maybe he cottoned onto what had happened? Bloom's character was well known in the British Association of Rose Breeders – they even banned him, so word might have got round and Hanley smelt a rat? Perhaps he checked your account book and saw that the money from the cheques that were made out to various suppliers all ended up in one account, the Blooms'; perhaps he played the Blooms, perhaps he let them give him his own money back, knowing all the time it was his, and never intended to take Bloom on as a partner? We will never know, but whatever happened the partnership didn't go through and that drew the anger of the Blooms and the murder of the Hanleys. All over a rose – a very special rose.'

Palmer turned to Riley. 'And all this time, Jim, you were unaware that your actions with the black rose had brought about two murders. You didn't know what was happening until my Sergeant and I paid our first visit to you; I can tell when people are

474

genuinely shocked by news, and you were genuinely shock by the news of the Hanleys' deaths. I'm thinking that you are an intelligent man, Jim, and it wouldn't have taken you long to piece things together; you knew the partnership was agreed, you probably didn't know about the eighty thousand pound scam but it didn't matter; as far as you knew everything was going to plan, the partnership was going through and that would negate your theft of the black rose as Bloom would then own half of it.

'But now with Hanley's death there was a problem. You knew something had gone wrong and Bloom had killed them; I bet that first meeting you had with the Blooms after we told you about the Hanleys' deaths was pretty explosive. No doubt they told you the partnership had not gone through, or maybe they said it had before the Hanley's deaths, so they were outright owners of the black rose now. You realised Janet Bloom had played you, they both had, and they had backed you into a corner like they had backed Alison into a corner. You had stolen a very expensive plant and double crossed your employer. Was it then that you decided to take revenge? Probably, but what kind of revenge? You couldn't kill the Blooms, that would be stupid – but you could stop them getting their hands on Geoff Hanley's black rose. You could tell the world about their scheme and out them for theft and murder. But how? Well, first you had to destroy the stock, and that's when Edward Bloom was killed...'

Riley interrupted. 'I didn't murder him, it was an accident.'

Palmer smiled. 'I didn't say you murdered him, Jim. I said he was killed. I know you didn't murder him – the pathologist will testify to that if need be. You couldn't possibly stab a pair of shears through his clothes and up to the handles into his body, not unless you're Superman, and you're not. The pathologist thinks he ran onto the shears whilst you held them. I think you were in the greenhouse destroying the black rose cuttings as part of your revenge and Bloom found you there and ran at you; you turned with the shears in your hand and he impaled himself on them, am I right?'

Riley nodded.

'I thought so. And then there was the Chelsea Show and the big reveal of the black rose on the Bloom stand – what an ideal place and time to let the world know the Blooms murdered the Hanleys. I have to say Jim, it was a brilliant idea, and it worked; I'd been trying to keep a low profile on the case until I had concrete evidence to arrest the Blooms with, and with one piece of paper you blew that away and had the press up in arms, and the black rose was the only story in town. That only left Janet Bloom – how could you get rid of her? You knew she would want to kill you; after all she would be thinking you had killed Edward. She knew we were looking for you and if you talked and told us about the poisoning of the Hanleys, her world would tumble down. We already knew about the poison Jim – we knew from the beginning, but we needed the proof. She guessed you'd pay her a visit and you intended to. You intended to let her have a go at poisoning you, but you would be prepared for that move, and you saw it as a way to complete your revenge. So you did pay her a visit.'

Jim Riley opened his mouth to speak but Palmer waved a silencing hand.

'Don't deny it Jim, you were there. You knew the house and you knew the back entrance; after all, you'd used it to visit Janet Bloom when Edward was away after she had rekindled your relationship. Oh yes, you were there; you went in the back way along the alley and sat with her in the lounge, knowing she'd try to kill you. How would she do it? You had taken a chance on poison, a chance that paid off – she did indeed try to poison you with a cup of tea. What did you do Jim, somehow swap the cups so she drank the poison she'd prepared for you? You did a good job tidying up afterwards, just leaving the one cup, the one with poison residue in it; you thought it would look like Janet Bloom was shattered with grief after the death of Edward and had taken her own life, taken her own life with the poison they had killed the Hanleys with, thus pointing the finger firmly at the Blooms as the killers. Very clever Jim, but not clever enough.'

Palmer pushed a photo of the kitchen across to Riley. 'Take a close look, Jim. Se the side of the sink? Two used tea bags – two, Jim, not one, Janet Bloom made two cups of tea, so who was there with her? Only one person it could be: you. You knew the back way, and nobody had come in the front as the local uniform boys had been there all night and day. One other thing, Jim, you didn't think it through. You set the alarm off on purpose as you left – the panel indicated it had been activated by a personal fob – but there was no fob near Janet's body or anywhere in the house. You didn't think of that, did you Jim? Everything had gone to plan, the poison, the cup swap, the clean-up and the escape through the back gate – but two tea bags and no fob were mistakes.' Palmer took the small evidence bag sent from Reg Frome and tipped out the key fob and back gate key. 'We found them, Jim, fingertip search of the alleyway – and guess whose print is on the fob button.'

Palmer sat back and took a deep breath. 'So, there we have it – two silly people getting involved in things they can't control and becoming sucked into a world of murder beyond their control.' He lightened up and smiled. 'But let's face it, neither of you are bad people at heart and I'm sure that the charges of theft, which are the charges that will be put to you by the Crown Prosecution Service in the County Court, will carry suspended sentences if my office were to have a chat with the judge at a pre-trial hearing.'

Both Burnley and Riley looked up with hope flashing across their faces. Gheeta and Claire exchanged mystified glances. What was Palmer up to?

Palmer held up a hand to diminish their raised hopes. 'I said *if my office were to have a chat with the Judge – if,* and that *if* depends on you two agreeing to a deal. And this is the deal. Have you heard of a pre-pack administration?'

Both Burnley and Riley hadn't.

'Okay, let me explain. A pre-packaged administration is when a company goes into administration and the solicitors handling that administration have already sorted out who the new owners will be and what they will pay; it's a way a company can continuing trading without a break in receipts and also loses its debts. Hanley's Garden Centre has been put into one such deal and will be bought out of it by you two.'

A shocked silence was broken by Riley. 'How? It can't be, I haven't any money to buy it with.'

'No, but Alison has, haven't you Alison? Alison has a quantity of cash that actually belongs to Mr Hanley, Angela Robinson and Charlie Hilton – thirty thousand pounds to be precise, all now frozen in an Isle of Man account. Ten thousand of that will buy the Hanley's Garden Centre out of administration and twenty thousand will go into a company trading bank account with two thousand in the safe for current use as things are set up. Bearing in mind Alison's past financial actions with company accounts, the bank will be monitoring the account closely and quarterly meetings will be arranged with the business banker allocated to the account.' He addressed Burnley. 'If that money doesn't go into the company account then a Proceeds of Crime order will whisk it away into the coffers of HMRC. I know which option I'd take.' He turned to Riley. 'You, Jim, will be general manager and all company cheques will need to be signed by both of you, who will be equal partners in the company. I have one proviso for you, Jim – you don't do any rose breeding. Agreed?'

Riley nodded. 'Agreed.'

Palmer looked from one to another of them. 'You will both go to court, but as I said before, whatever sentence you get will be suspended and you'll be free to get on and make something with your lives. Bear in mind that no agreement to this plan will undoubtedly result in you both going to prison, while an agreement will get you both suspended sentences and you keep your freedom as long as you behave yourselves. So, that's the deal. If you want a little time to consider it between yourselves you can use my office?' He sat back.

Riley looked at Burnley and they both stuttered into laughter brought on by relief.

Palmer laughed too. 'Okay, I think I've got your answer. Here.' He passed two business cards across the table. 'They are your company solicitors and bank. First thing tomorrow you go to the solicitor and sign the pre-pack agreement, then you go to the bank and have them organise a transfer of the Isle of Man money into your new business account and give specimen signatures. I'll have our forensic accountant unfreeze the Isle of Man account in the morning. Don't forget that ten thousand of that will be going to buy the business. Now, I really don't want to see you again until your County Court appearance; your solicitor will guide you through that as well. I suggest you compose yourselves and take a cab over to Hanley's and ring round the staff and tell them they still have their jobs, who the new owners are, and get them back to work. Then you'd better get selling lots plants and compost bags –

solicitors and bankers don't come cheap. I'll get the uniform officers and the crime tape removed by the morning. Off you go, and make it work.'

Palmer stood and indicated the door. Riley and Burnley were gushing in their thanks, and when Burnley gave Palmer a hug Gheeta stepped in before all the air was crushed out of him and ushered them out of the door, down the corridor and into the lift. She came back into the Team Room and gave Palmer a big smile and a quizzical look.

'So Chief Superintendent Palmer of the Yard has turned into Saint Justin of Yard then, has he?'

'If I can't persuade the judge to give suspended sentences I'll be Saint Cock-up of the Yard.'

****

Dorothy Randall was just about to take the first sip of her regular mid-morning cup of coffee sitting in the front room of her one-bed pensioner's sheltered accommodation bungalow on a small social housing complex off the Rickmansworth Road out of Watford when she saw the caretaker Harry Cribbs coming up the small path to her front door. She put her coffee down and opened it before he could knock.

'Hello Harry, what do you want?' she said as she opened it. Harry stood there holding what looked like a battered pot plant in his hands. 'Bought me a present, have you?'

'No.' Harry wasn't in a good mood; looking after twenty pensioners in their sheltered accommodation bungalows sometimes sent his stress levels through the roof. 'Mrs Randall, you know the rules about the wheelie bins – black for household rubbish and green for garden.'

'Yes, I know that.'

'So why did you put this in your black bin then? The bin men weren't very happy.'

'I didn't. What is it?'

'An old rose bush. Here.' He held it out to Dorothy. 'You can have it back and put it in your green bin.'

'It's not mine Harry, I didn't put it in the bin – must have been some passerby getting rid of it, not me. Quite pretty though, isn't it? Dark flowers, attractive.'

'You think so?'

'Yes. Leave it with me, I'll trim off the broken bits and put in my garden. Yes, I quite like it.'

'You're welcome,' said Harry, putting the pot down on front step. 'If you change your mind make sure it goes in the green bin, not the black one. Can I smell coffee?'

'Would you like a cup?' She knew she wouldn't have to ask twice.

****

THE AFTERMATH

The CPS went along with Palmer's request and asked for suspended sentences on Riley and Burnley, and bearing in mind their admission of guilt, lack of any previous convictions and Palmer's submission as to their characters, the judge agreed and gave four years suspended to each of them.

They kept the Hanley name for the Garden Centre out of respect and made it a success.

Bloom's Centres were bought by a national chain and took the chain's name.

DS Peter Atkins was so interested by the increase in Blooms accounts he got permission to put a small team of police forensic accountants together to dig deeper and has so far recovered three and a half million from the Manchester security van robbery that had been laundered through Bloom into various offshore accounts.

Benji's rose garden was completed with lots of help from Mrs P. and very little from Palmer, although he didn't buy a padlock for the gate!

Dorothy Randall had no idea that the rose bush she nurtured in her small back garden that was so envied by her neighbours could make her very, very rich indeed.

THE END

Printed in Great Britain
by Amazon

45607060R00274